WITHOUT CONDITION

BY SONORA TAYLOR

*To Evelyn, whose encouragement helps me to write,
and whose work helps me to write better.*

CHAPTER 1

January 2004

Darren saw his breath in the moonlight as he walked down the road. Branches sliced through the night sky, bare branches that wouldn't be visible save for the light of the moon. There were no street lamps, no homes with softly-lit porches. There were only trees, the moon, and a darkened road.

He cursed to himself as he walked. He should've asked that trucker to drop him off near Raleigh or Durham, somewhere closer to civilization. "I can take you as far as Leslie," the trucker had said with a drawl that Darren recognized as distinctly Carolinian, one that lingered on every vowel in every word. "That good by you?"

"Sure," Darren had said, grateful for any ride. He'd been stuck in Rocky Mount for hours. He'd gotten there from Richmond, which he'd gotten to from Spotsylvania, hitching the entire way. His truck wasn't working — it'd been a piece of shit even before the brake lines had been cut — and he was in too much of a hurry to wait for repairs. He had to get to wherever his girlfriend Polly had disappeared to.

It seemed, though, that Darren was doomed to disappear in Leslie, North Carolina. He regretted agreeing to the trucker's route the minute he'd driven away and left a dark, empty road behind him — one that Darren now had to walk along. Throughout his journey, he thought he heard more cars than actually appeared. The ghosts of rides he wouldn't take. The one sound that culminated into a car produced not a ride, but a slick speedster that drove right past his outstretched thumb. Darren dragged his feet, and wondered when the dark road would end.

Another phantom settled in his ears. Darren kept walking, knowing by now that no cars were coming.

The phantom honked. Darren turned and saw headlights coming near him. He jumped to the side, then gathered his senses as an honest-to-god pickup truck drove by him. "Wait!" he shouted, waving instead of sticking out his thumb. "Stop!"

The pickup slowed. Darren picked up speed. "Hold on!" he yelled, in case the driver decided to change his mind.

The pickup stopped. Darren skidded to a stop half a foot away, and pivoted so he wouldn't collide against the back. He ran to the passenger side and opened the door before the driver could leave. "You going to Raleigh?" he asked, his words coming out in gasps illumined by the cold moonlight.

"I could be," replied the woman in the driver's seat.

———

Darren gasped as he sat down in the truck. The seat felt like ice. He looked down and saw that it was covered in plastic.

"Sorry about the seats," the woman said as she started up the truck. "I make beer deliveries, and the plastic keeps the beer off of them."

"The bottles don't do that?"

"Not when they break."

"Gotcha." The seat began to warm beneath his body. He leaned back and sighed, enjoying the warmth of the truck and his view of the driver. He could tell she was pretty even in the dark, and could tell she was pretty beyond the bare minimum of being a woman in his vicinity. She wore a base-ball cap, and long blonde hair spilled from beneath of it, ending at her shoulders. It glowed white in the moonlight. Her breasts peeked out from behind her arms as she drove. They were small enough to fit in one's palm, but big enough to want to grasp them in the first place.

"So, you live in Raleigh?" the woman asked.

Darren tried not to sigh at his peace being disrupted. Women always had to end the magic by opening their mouths. "No," he said. "Just wanna stay there overnight."

"Why not drive?"

"Truck doesn't work."

"Did you leave it in Leslie?"

"No." Darren let slip a little impatience in the hopes she'd get the hint and stop speaking. Polly always talked too much. She talked so much that he could still hear her voice in his ears when he fell asleep.

The woman turned down a road that was somehow darker than the one Darren had been walking on. "This the way to Raleigh?" Darren asked.

"It's a shortcut," she replied.

"How do you get to the city through the woods?"

"Trust me. I've lived here my whole life."

"Well, I may not be from here, but I know the woods aren't where you go when you want to get to the city."

The woods cleared and Darren saw an illumined road, one with signs pointing to the highway.

"Well, with everything you know, maybe you should learn to trust your driver," the woman said.

Darren pressed his lips as she chuckled to herself. She was mouthy and she thought she was cute. Darren knew he could tell her otherwise, but he didn't want to be abandoned in the middle of the woods when he was so close to a city, close to a good motel and maybe a truck stop with a truck going all the way to South Carolina. He didn't know if Polly was there, but her parents were. It was a start.

"I'll trust you more when you get me to my destination," Darren would be damned if he let the driver get the upper hand.

"I'll get you where you need to go. I always do."

"Always do? You run a bus service or something?"

"You're not my first hitchhiker, and you won't be my last."

"You sure you should be picking up hitchhikers?"

"You sure you should be hitchhiking?"

"I can take care of myself. But you … well, all alone out here, I'd be worried about picking up strangers."

"Are you saying I should worry about you?"

"Of course not. I won't hurt you."

"Good to know."

Darren smiled at her, even though her eyes stayed forward. He wondered what color her eyes were. "You always this mouthy with hitchhikers?" he asked.

"You always ask drivers this many questions?"

"I do when they're beautiful women."

He saw her smile in the reflection of the windshield. While he stared at her reflection, her hand moved to his cock. Darren couldn't hide his gasp, even though he tried.

"You want me to pull over?" she asked.

———

Luck shined on Darren the way the moonlight shone through the tree branches. The branches threw shadowed fragments over the seat of the car, moving like fingers in an orgy that reached towards their bodies. Darren barely noticed them as the driver stopped the truck in the woods. He unbuckled his belt and moved towards her. She had a mouth on her, but she was too cute to turn down. Polly could live another day without him.

The woman placed her hand on his chest. Darren wondered why she wanted to stop what she'd been so willing to start before. She unbuckled her belt and moved towards him. The plastic seat covers had one nice effect: they allowed her to slide towards him, let her slink to his side of the truck and pour over him as she straddled his lap. She took off her hat, then grabbed his and put it on.

"What's your name?" she asked as she stroked his beard.

"Darren," he whispered. "What's yours?"

"Does it matter?"

"I mean, you asked mine —"

She kissed him hard and slid her tongue in his mouth. Darren closed his eyes and relished it. "What do you want?" she asked as she pulled away from him.

He grabbed her waist and pulled her closer. "I want to fuck you," he said.

"Tell me what you think of me," the driver whispered. She traced her lips across his neck as she spoke.

"I think you're hot," he croaked. Words became harder to say as his erection grew.

"You think I shouldn't have picked you up?"

"What do you mean?"

"You said I shouldn't be picking up strangers. You think I'm doing something stupid?"

Darren wasn't sure where this was going, but he wanted to make sure it didn't go to a place that left him with blue balls. "I don't think that anymore," he said as he ran his hands over her ass. It was firm and taut beneath his palms. He began to ache for her.

"You thought it before?"

"I never thought it. I was just looking out for you."

"Tell me what you thought before." She ran her tongue from his neck to his ear, and Darren groaned. "I want to hear it."

Darren wondered if this was some weird kink of hers. He'd play along if it meant getting laid. "I thought you didn't know where you were going," he said. "When we were in the woods and getting further from the road."

"You thought I was stupid?"

"I thought you didn't know where to go. I thought you'd get us lost."

"What'd you think when I grabbed your cock?"

"I liked it." He moved his hand to between her thighs. She gasped a little, but with pleasure. It was so uninhibited, so unbridled. It turned him on even more. "It made me want to fuck you."

She unzipped her purse, likely looking for a condom. Darren glanced over, but before he could see, she began to nibble his earlobe. He closed his eyes and groaned.

"You liked that I wanted to fuck you?" she whispered.

"Oh, yeah."

"You liked that your driver ended up being a whore?"

"Yes." She seemed to want to hear it, and Darren would say anything to get his first good lay in weeks.

"Tell me that. Whisper it in my ear."

Darren leaned close to her ear and made sure his lips were wet before he spoke. He thought of Polly, who'd thought she could just run away when she was done with him. He thought of Polly cutting his brakes and riding on some bus to wherever she'd gone, thinking she was safe. He thought of what Polly's face would look like when he finally caught up with her and showed her that she couldn't live without him — he'd make sure of it.

"You're a fucking whore," he breathed.

His whisper became a yelp as she yanked back his hair. "What —"

Searing pain spread across his neck. Darren tried to scream, but his voice curdled in his throat. He touched his neck, and knew before he saw the blood all over his fingers that it had been cut.

He looked in horror at the driver. She smiled as she held a bloodied knife in her hand. The last thing he saw in the moonlight was her eyes. They were blue.

CHAPTER 2

Cara smoked by the fire. All around her were black branches illumined in moonlight and the flickers of the flames. She breathed in cedar smoke and breathed out tobacco. She was used to fires — used to setting them, used to sitting by their warmth, and used to watching them die under a cold night sky. There wasn't much to keep her warm this far away from the city. Cara didn't mind living so far away. Her town was quiet, so quiet that the crack of the fire was sometimes indistinguishable from a gunshot. Cara preferred the woods at night, especially in the fall. The hunters preferred the morning. Cara preferred to avoid their fire.

Behind her fire, a small lake glistened in the moonglow. Its waters were still, the body rolled into it already a memory. Cara didn't pay it any mind. She knew no one fished there, or skipped rocks along its surface. It was a quiet lake, a cold grave that was easier to dig than mounds of earth. When she was little, Cara used to think the lake held monsters. She'd glance over the surface, looking for signs of the bottom. Now, at 22, she knew there were no monsters above or below the lake — only bones that wouldn't be found. Not if she had anything to do with it.

Cara sighed and flicked her cigarette into the fire. It was growing cold, and the smell of smoke couldn't stop the stench of Darren's blood from emanating off of her skin. She extinguished the fire with a bucket of water she pulled from the lake, then spread the muddied ashes into the dirt and grass. She adjusted his baseball cap on her head, then walked towards her truck. It was time to go home.

———

Cara lived on a former pumpkin farm, remote even by Leslie's standards. It sat at the end of a dirt road, her only neighbors trees, deer, and a slew of possums that she and her mother worked to keep off of their property. Cara and her mother had lived there her whole life, and both of them worked away from the land. Cara worked for a brewery, and her mother was a secretary at an office just outside of Garner.

Cara hoped her mother had had a long day, one that sent her to bed early, as she walked up their gravel driveway. She studied the windows. They seemed dark, but that didn't mean her mother wasn't home. Delores Vineyard wasn't one to waste electricity — if she wasn't in the room, that room would remain dark.

The stench and the stickiness of the blood were growing unbearable, and it was too cold to wash herself in the lake where she'd dumped the body. Cara decided to chance the dark, and walked inside. She'd walked the carpeted floors and wooden steps so many times that she knew that path even without turning on the lights. The house was quiet, and Cara smiled as she ascended the last step. She was alone. She could keep the workings of her evening a secret.

"Cara?"

Cara paused in the hallway. A small beam of light shone from under her mother's door. She was home. There was no avoiding her.

She could at least try, though. "I'm going to take a shower, Mom," Cara said as she sped towards the bathroom.

It was no use. "You're home awfully late," Delores said as she exited her bedroom. She wore a pink bathrobe, a tattered Harlequin novel in her hand. "Were you making more deliveries?"

"Yes, and I just got home, and need to —"

"Is that blood?"

Cara stopped outside her bathroom door. Delores moved towards her and turned on the hall light. Cara's evening was laid bare. She stood in the hall, her shoes clean and her jeans mostly clean, save for some dirt. She'd rinsed her hands in the water when she'd dumped the hitchhiker's body, but smears of blood still adorned her chest and neck. And there was the hat, which Delores knew had never been hers.

Delores stared at Cara, her mouth slightly agape. Cara looked at her feet.

"Is this … is this what I think it is?"

Cara looked up at her mother. She took a breath, and nodded.

Delores smiled. "I'm so proud of you."

———

"Mom …" Cara rolled her eyes as Delores moved towards her.

"You got another one!" Delores said.

"Can I please take a shower?"

"So what was this one like? Did he struggle?"

"No." Cara moved towards her room, keeping her eyes forward and away from her mother's excitement.

"He's your first in weeks! I thought you were dropping off."

"I have to. You want people to think there's a pattern?"

"All the good serial killers have one."

"And they all got caught." Cara had watched enough hours of *America's Most Wanted* and *Law and Order* with her mother to know exactly what not to do if she wanted her actions to stay hidden. She sighed as she unbuttoned her shirt. "Mom, really, I need to take a shower."

"Alright." Her mother shrugged. "You can tell me more afterward."

Cara rolled her eyes, then sighed with relief as her mother exited her room and shut the door. She peeled off her clothes and threw them all in the trash. They could be better disposed of later. For now, she needed to focus on cleaning her body. Cara closed her eyes as she stepped into the shower, the steam bringing the metallic scent of blood into her nostrils as the water turned red at her feet. He'd been her first this year, and while Cara was careful to not take too many, she couldn't deny that doing what she did best had felt good.

Cara stayed in the shower long after his blood had washed away. She felt soothed by the stream, and wished she could melt and flow as easily as the water. But she was flesh, and that flesh was beginning to wrinkle and turn pink. She turned off the shower, and patted her hair dry as she walked to her room.

She halted in front of her bed, staring at her dresser. The hat was gone.

————————

Cara knew exactly where the hat was. She walked downstairs and into their finished basement. The tan carpet and ugly wooden walls were a relic of the seventies, an effort on her great uncle's part to make every piece of the farmhouse he'd inherited feel a little like home. She glanced at his picture on the wall near a bookshelf filled with dusty, unread books, mostly tips on farming and a couple Joan Collins novels. Cara didn't remember much about Uncle Leo — he'd died when she was three — but his picture still brought a hint of warmth to her when she saw it, like she knew they were family even though she hadn't known him at all.

She ignored the pictures of her and her mother, or her mother and Uncle Leo's friend Terry holding Cara as a baby. Terry used to work on the farm. He'd taught her how to kill possums and had made her knife, which her mother gave to her for graduation. All of these meant something to her, but in a way that felt like breathing. Not in a way that touched her or made her stop in thought as she moved through her day.

On the other side of the basement was a large cork board. When Cara was little, Delores had converted it into a board for Cara's art projects and school accomplishments. There were drawings in crayon and watercolor, and a rare report which got an A+. Cara wasn't a bad student, but she also wasn't a remarkable one. In twelve years of school, she had one second place ribbon for a spelling bee, a few good tests, and a science fair project that was first runner-up — due largely to her partner, Tristan, who went on to major in biology at NC State.

Cara stayed in Leslie, and the cork board stayed the same. But between the papers and drawings were a slew of other items commemorating her accomplishments since school.

Delores grabbed a thumbtack from the box on the shelf next to the board and stabbed it into the cork, hanging up the hat she'd taken from Cara's room. It hung between a multitude of items Cara had kept: belts with garish buckles, an ugly key ring with some sort of blue creature Cara couldn't place, pocket knives, watches, other hats. Hats were easy. Men loved it when she took off her own hat and put on theirs while they fucked. Cara loved it because removing their hat made it easier to grab their hair and lift their necks.

"I would've brought it down for you," Cara said as her mother adjusted the hat so that it hung straight down.

"Figured I'd save you the trouble," Delores replied as she stepped back. She clucked her tongue as she looked at all of Cara's souvenirs. "I'm gonna have to get another cork board soon."

"Sorry to give you another errand."

Cara was teasing, but her mother still gave her a pointed look. "Don't be sorry. It makes me proud to look at this."

"Which is why it's in the basement, right?"

"You know why I moved it to the basement."

"I know — in case anyone comes inside. But you know that no one ever just shows up here."

Delores smiled as she patted Cara's shoulder. "No one except you."

Cara couldn't help but smile back. "Well, me and you, right?"

"Right. Uncle Leo showed me real kindness, taking me in. Lord knows Mama and Daddy were ready to throw me on the street if it meant not embarrassing them at church or around town with a pregnant belly."

"It was nice of him," Cara said, hoping to steer the conversation from Delores' bad memories of her hometown. Her trips down memory lane all led to bitterness and never to the only thing Cara ever wondered about: who her father was. Delores wouldn't tell her, and Cara had asked less with each passing year until she stopped asking altogether. But like her faded memory of Uncle Leo, she sometimes felt the question like a small beat in her heart, one that happened to catch her attention when she was alone or when her mother mentioned the past.

Delores didn't bring up the past very much, and when she did, it was usually a passing remark about wishing Terry was back on the farm to help them with vermin, or wishing Uncle Leo a posthumous happy birthday. Their life on the farm was with each other. Delores was content to spend her mornings and evenings with Cara, punctuated only by her job.

Cara was reasonably content, but she wasn't sure if she'd say her life in Leslie was what she wanted. It was a life that happened to her. She liked things well enough — her job, her home, her dates, and especially her kills — but that was all they were: enough.

Still, enough was better than nothing at all. She and her mother walked back upstairs, flicking off the basement lights and plunging their memories and accomplishments back into darkness.

CHAPTER 3

1987

Cara's earliest memories were quiet. She remembered looking out her window as a little girl and looking at the trees
beyond the remains of Uncle Leo's pumpkin patch. They
seemed to disappear into the mountains, while at the same
time swallowing the grass. Nature moved in and out of itself,
like the waves on the shore Cara saw in her mother's pictures
of the beach near the house she'd lived in as a little girl.

"Can we go sometime?" Cara asked once. "Maybe visit
your mommy and daddy?"

"No," Delores replied. She set the photo down, went out
on the porch, and smoked. Cara knew her mother only did
that when she was upset, and knew not to ask that again.

Fortunately, her Uncle Leo's friend Terry was there, and
he took her on a critter prowl around the farm. Terry fas-
cinated Cara. He was tall, with tanned leathery skin that
looked like it could withstand all the natural elements. He
had long black hair that Terry sometimes let her braid while

all three of them watched TV, and he always wore a black leather vest adorned with medals and patches. "My Girl Scout badges," he said with a grin when Cara once asked what they were.

He helped Uncle Leo, and then Cara's mother, with chores around the farm, even after they'd stopped selling pumpkins. His main chore was catching critters. Critters loved finding their way to Vineyard Farm, looking for the food they no longer grew and, in lieu of that, looking for shelter from rain and from developers buying up the forests all around them and building office parks. The critters showed up no matter how many traps Delores set out or how many marigolds she planted to keep the bugs away.

"Animals get used to traps," Terry told Cara as they hiked the perimeter the week before her first day of school. "One of them'll get surprised by a trap, but then the rest'll move around it and build new routines."

"What's a routine?" Cara asked as she looked under the bushes for any possums or squirrels that might've scurried underneath.

"Something you do over and over, like eating dinner at night — or starting next week for you, going to school." Terry smiled as he knelt down next to her. "Tell that to your teacher next week. Impress her with your smarts."

"What's impress mean?"

"To make her proud."

"You mean like Mommy says she is when I draw her something?"

"Yeah, like those drawings of yours she's got all over the fridge. She does that because she's impressed."

They were shushed by a rustling of leaves. Terry held up a finger, and Cara pressed her mouth shut in an extra effort to stay quiet.

"But animals love routines," Terry whispered as he looked through the bush. "They add anything new to their routine, and they adjust. Traps help, but the only way you can stop their routines —" Terry stopped, pulled out a switchblade, and swung it down into the brush all in a seeming second — "is to stop them."

Cara heard a squeal, one that disappeared as quickly as it came. Terry raised his arm, and Cara saw a small possum — bigger than a baby but smaller than a mama possum — lying still on Terry's blade.

"Cool!" Cara breathed. Terry laughed, but stopped when Cara reached towards his kill.

"Cool, but dangerous. Let Uncle Terry get the critters with blades, okay?"

"Then what can *I* get them with?" Cara asked with a pout as they started to walk back to the farm. Terry pulled the possum off the blade, and Cara paused from pouting to laugh at the way the possum flew through the air and back into the bushes.

"Worry about getting good grades. Your mom and I will worry about the critters."

Helping Terry catch critters and helping her mother around the farm was most of Cara's life until she started school. It was then that she began to understand why her mother preferred to keep limited company.

————

1987-1988

Critters were the last thing on Cara's mind as she and her mother waited for the school bus the next week. Cara watched as her mother paced, and wondered if she should be more nervous. She started to tap her feet, like she'd seen nervous people do on TV.

"Don't be scared, sweetie," her mother said with a smile. "You're going to have so much fun at school. Learn new things, maybe make some friends ..."

"Uncle Terry's my friend."

"Friends your own age. You'll have more fun with some little girls at school. Don't want child services wondering why your best friend is a 50-year-old biker who works in a knife shop," Delores added with a chuckle.

The bus rounded the corner. Delores stooped down and gave Cara a hug. Cara closed her eyes and held her mother close, comforted by the smell of rose shampoo and secondhand smoke that always accompanied her mother's embrace.

"Have fun, sweetheart."

"I will." Her mother seemed sad, and Cara didn't know why. "I'll bring you a drawing," Cara added.

Delores smiled, and Cara felt better. "That'd be nice. Bring me a real pretty one, and I'll put it up in the living room."

"I will." Cara beamed as she scampered towards the bus. Its doors opened with a hushed roar that reminded Cara of a friendly dragon. She hopped on and took a seat near the back, then looked out the window as they drove away. Cara saw her mother light a cigarette and look out over their empty fields.

———

Cara looked in awe at the classroom and all of the kids who were in it. She saw some kids she'd seen in the pews at church, but she knew almost none of their names and she'd never been this close to them before. She saw two girls talking to each other on the carpet.

Cara decided it was time to make friends. "Hi!" she said as she marched towards them.

They both looked up, startled.

"Hi!" she repeated.

"We heard you," one of them said, a girl whose hair and freckles reminded Cara of falling leaves in autumn.

"What're your names?" Cara asked, unfazed.

"I'm Jennifer," the other one, a girl with short black hair and bangs as straight as one of Terry's nicest knives, said with a small smile. "This is Amanda." The freckled girl nodded but didn't say anything.

"I'm Cara."

Jennifer and Amanda grinned, and Cara didn't feel the warmth she thought she was supposed to feel when someone smiled.

"We know who you are," Amanda said.

"You live on the old pumpkin farm," Jennifer added.

"Yeah," Cara said, relaxing a little.

"Your mommy's name is Delores, right?" Amanda said. Her voice dispelled any hope of Cara feeling comfortable.

"Yeah," Cara said. It was strange to hear her mother's first name coming from a girl her age.

"My mommy says Delores came to Leslie in secret and wants to see every guy here to try and find a daddy for you."

Cara flushed, but wasn't sure why. Nothing sounded wrong with what Amanda implied, except that it wasn't true — her mother almost never went out, and the only guy Cara ever saw her with was Terry. But she got the sense from Amanda's smile — a smile that didn't seem like it should be a smile at all — that she was saying something bad about her mother.

"Have you found a daddy?" Jennifer asked, more innocently than Amanda and yet somehow in a way that made Cara feel worse.

"I don't have one," Cara said. "I live with Mommy and sometimes Uncle Terry."

"The guy at the knife shop's your uncle?" Jennifer asked.

"No, he's Mommy's friend. I just call him that. My real uncle's dead."

"When did he die?"

Amanda cut in before Cara could answer. "My mom says that moms without husbands have a lot of uncles around the house," she sneered. "Is Terry Delores' *boyfriend*?"

"Don't call her Delores," Cara spat. Amanda and Jennifer looked momentarily startled, and Cara used her flash of satisfaction to add, "She's my mommy and you should call her Miss Vineyard."

"Mom says I only have to call ladies by their last names, and she says Delores isn't a lady."

"Of course she's a lady. She's my mommy."

A chime broke their talk, and Cara looked with gratitude towards their teacher playing a triangle in an effort to quiet everyone down. She scampered as far away from Jennifer and Amanda as she could, and some of the other kids just to be safe. She stayed away even when they were allowed to play, instead moving towards the paper and crayons so she could draw something for her mother.

————

Most of the other kids weren't like Jennifer and Amanda, but Cara still felt like she belonged on the back corner of the rug each day in class and in a seat by herself on the bus. Some kids let her join them to play with blocks or to be on their kickball team at recess, but they went back to their own clusters by the time they returned to class. Despite her mother's wishes, Cara could only cite Terry as her best friend by the time the school year ended.

Terry was her first friend, and Terry became her first memory of heartbreak. "I'm moving away," Terry said one summer morning as they prowled for critters.

"Far away?" Cara asked.

"Kind of far. Out near Apex — you know where that is?"

"No."

"Well, it's about an hour and a half from here. By the time you finish watching one of those cartoon movies that drive me crazy, you could drive to see me."

"Will you still help us catch critters?"

"Not as much. I'll be starting my own shop, and spending time with my new family."

"You found a family in Apex?"

Terry chuckled, and even at six, Cara could see he was minding his words. "More like it found me," he said. He stooped down and smiled at Cara — a real one, not like the kind Amanda wore. "But I know you'll help your mom keep the critters away from here, yeah?"

"Yeah," Cara said. "Until you come back."

Terry gave Cara a tighter squeeze than usual before he got in his car and left. "When will he be back?" Cara asked as he disappeared down the driveway.

"I don't know," Delores said as they walked inside. "He's moving far away, and he'll have a baby soon."

"A baby? How?"

Delores laughed a little. "I guess you're just about ready for that talk."

"He said he was going to Apex for his shop and his new family."

"That's right — he's starting his own knife shop and he's going to have a baby with a woman he met there."

"He said his new family found him. Did the woman and the baby come into the shop and find him there?"

"Jesus Christ, Terry," Delores said to herself as she laughed some more. "The woman's *having* a baby, but what Uncle Terry meant was that it was … well, it was a surprise for him. It was a surprise for them both. He met her a few months ago, and then she called him and said they were having a baby."

"Oh." Cara didn't know what was so funny about that, or why Terry acted so secretive when he told her.

"But he's going to be spending a lot of time opening his store and getting ready for the baby — not to mention getting used to living with a woman."

"He kind of lived with you, though."

"But I wasn't his girlfriend. It's different — he just helped around the farm and was a good friend to both of us."

"Was? Is he not our friend anymore?"

"He is, but he probably won't be back anytime soon, sweetheart. Not with everything he has going on."

It dawned on Cara that the hug Terry gave her was his last, that their prowl for critters would be something she'd do alone. Cara felt a lump rise in her throat.

"But we'll keep the farm going together," Delores said, giving Cara a squeeze. Cara leaned against her mother, taking comfort in her hold.

"And you'll be starting first grade in a couple months. You can get off the farm for awhile and make some new friends."

Cara stayed quiet.

———

1988-1990

First grade started. Desks replaced the carpet on the floor, and worksheets and journals replaced coloring and reciting the alphabet. What stayed the same were the other kids. Cara sat in the back, hoping to avoid the ones who were mean to her, like Amanda.

Even in the back, she still managed to draw attention — and now, it came from her teacher. Mr. Murphy told Cara to pay attention more, to only raise her hand if she actually knew the answers, to write more in her journal entries and to not just write about her mother or her farm.

Cara didn't know what would make Mr. Murphy happy, but she knew what made him mad. She found herself missing Terry, someone who never got mad. She drew a picture of Terry when Mr. Murphy asked them to draw their heroes. Mr. Murphy didn't like that either. He called her mother and had Cara show her the drawing herself.

"Is that Terry?" her mother asked. Cara smiled, happy that her mother knew who it was.

"Mrs. Vineyard," Mr. Murphy said.

"Just Miss," Delores replied curtly.

"Ms. Vineyard, this is someone Cara knows?"

"He used to help us around the farm. And as Cara drew here, he helped keep the critters out of our pumpkin patch."

Mr. Murphy frowned in the direction of Cara's picture, which showed Terry holding up a knife with a dead possum speared through the blade. He stood like the athletes Cara saw on TV. "He's my hero," Cara said. "And the possum's like his medal or his trophy."

Her mother gave her a small smile, almost like a secret between them; with a hint of sympathy in her eyes. "I know you miss him, honey," she said.

"This man speared animals in front of her?" Mr. Murphy asked.

Delores lost her smile and looked back up at Mr. Murphy. "Cara's taken some artistic license here, but I can assure you Terry was safe and far from sadistic when it came to dealing with vermin."

"I don't think Terry's the sadistic one here."

"What's a sadistic?" Cara asked, but her mother ignored her.

"Cara drew someone she admired, and doing something she remembered him doing. Why did you bring me in for this?"

"Six-year-olds shouldn't be drawing this."

"Who did some of Cara's classmates draw? Soldiers? Hunters?"

"It's just such a violent drawing. Look — she colored the blade red and drew dots coming down from it …"

"Artistic license, and one we'll talk about."

"Thank you." Mr. Murphy didn't look pleased despite his thanks; but Cara wondered if he'd ever look pleased.

Her time with her classmates wasn't much better. Cara saw the same things she saw in kindergarten. A few kids would put her on their team at recess, or look in awe at her new Barbie that she brought to school. Even that was short-lived. "That's an *old* Barbie," Amanda sneered. "I saw it at the Dollar Store."

A few kids laughed, and Cara looked down and skulked away. It was easier than saying anything out loud. "I'll play with you," she heard a voice say. She briefly turned and saw Jessica standing nearby.

Cara didn't want to see anyone. "I want to play alone," she mumbled. Jessica shrugged and scampered away to re-join the other kids.

Cara tried her hardest to ignore the other kids, but they seemed insistent on pulling her back in — especially Jennifer and Amanda. Cara often saw them look at her and speak in whispers. Cara couldn't ignore them when those whispers were accompanied by giggles.

One day, close to Christmas break, Cara couldn't take it anymore. "What are you saying about me?" she demanded when she saw Amanda whispering to Jennifer yet again at recess.

"Nothing," Amanda said. Her frown wrinkled her nose and made her stupid mouth almost disappear. "Why would we talk about you?"

"You're always whispering and looking at me."

"We're talking about how nosy you are," Jennifer said before sticking out her tongue.

"Stop talking about me, or I'm telling."

"Telling who?" Amanda asked with a mean smile. "Mr. Murphy? He doesn't like you. No one likes you."

"Go away," Jennifer said, which was unnecessary, for Cara had already turned away.

She regretted trying to confront them, and regretted it even more the next day. Cara walked past Jennifer and Amanda, not even looking at them. Their voices, though, landed in her ear — she heard the hushed noises of whispers, but not what they were saying. Cara closed her eyes and tried to ignore them.

Their whispers continued at an amplified volume whenever Cara walked by. She started to hear them, and all they were saying was "Psst psst psst," making a whisper noise in rapid succession. It still stabbed Cara's ears like any insult.

She had a brief reprieve over Christmas break, which she and her mother spent alone on the farm with hot chocolate, a few presents, and Christmas specials on TV. But the whispers — fake or real, Cara could never tell — started up as soon as she was back. Whenever Cara would try to confront them, they'd stop. A few other kids joined in as the weeks passed. Cara did her best to ignore it, but even when the other kids said actual insults to her, what bothered her the most were the whispers — especially when they continued even after first grade became second.

"Hey Cara!" Amanda called on the first day of second grade. Cara had hoped to spend recess alone, a day of solitude after a summer away from them, but Amanda wouldn't have it. She walked towards Cara. "We're talking about you! Psst psst psst!"

Cara kept walking. It was a new year, with a new teacher and new classmates. She wanted to try and ignore the old ones.

"Don't you want to hear what we're saying?" Amanda's voice was closer behind her.

"Go away," Cara mumbled.

"Psst psst psst!" Amanda circled in front of Cara and got in her face. "Psst psst psst!"

Amanda's scream was loud enough to quiet all the surrounding kids. Cara stood still with her clenched fist by her side, watching coldly as Amanda held her bleeding nose.

"I'm telling Ms. Corbett!" a boy cried. He ran towards the school while other kids swarmed around Amanda to make sure she was okay. Cara stood in the basketball court, simply watching. She didn't feel bad. She didn't feel bad when Ms. Corbett walked her to the principal's office, and felt nothing as Principal Jones talked on and on about not tolerating bullies and how she'd call her mother.

Cara only began to feel bad when her mother stormed into the principal's office, eyes on fire pointed directly at her. "Fighting?" Delores shouted as she sat down next to Cara. "Cara Grace, you're better than someone who fights other kids at recess."

"It wasn't my fault," Cara protested weakly.

"Ms. Vineyard," Principal Jones began, "I'd like to speak with both of —"

"I'll speak to my daughter, thank you," Delores spat. Principal Jones leaned back and folded her hands. Cara smiled a little at her mother scaring an adult, but the smile was short-lived.

"And what do you mean it wasn't your fault?" Delores continued. "Did the devil possess you and make you throw a punch?"

"Amanda kept making fun of me. She always makes fun of me."

"Then you tell a teacher —"

"She pretends to talk about me. She's been doing it since last year. She and the other kids would see me walking by and keep saying 'Psst psst psst' and laugh at me, and Amanda followed me today and said it right in my face."

"You still shouldn't have punched her, Cara," Principal Jones said.

Delores glared at Principal Jones, and Cara swore she saw her flinch. "And where's Amanda now?" Delores asked.

"The nurse's office," Principal Jones said, regaining some composure. "She needed ice —"

"Why isn't she here with an ice bag, then? Why's Cara the only one in trouble?"

"We don't tolerate fighting —"

"But you tolerate bullying?"

"We … Amanda's friend Thomas just said Cara punched her, and we didn't see Amanda teasing Cara —"

"I don't believe that for a second. Cara says they've been doing this for over a year. None of you noticed?"

"Kids play —"

"There's playing and there's teasing, and what Cara just told me was neither. I went to school with plenty of

Amandas. I know a bully when I hear one. I'll punish Cara for fighting —" Cara pouted, then stuck her lip back in when Delores shot her a look — "but I want to know what you and Cara's teacher are going to do about Amanda."

"Well, we can't do anything unless Cara tells us, and she hasn't told us anything until today."

Cara bowed her head in embarrassment, wishing she'd thought to say something to her teacher. Her mother's eyes flared. "She's a child!" she exclaimed. "She's seven years old and you expect her to tell all of you what these kids apparently do to her every day? Who's watching these kids? Surely you notice when one of them's being a bully?"

"Cara punched Amanda, Ms. Vineyard," Principal Jones said calmly. "That's what we're discussing right now. We can deal with Amanda and Cara not getting along later —"

"Not getting along. Right." Delores snorted, then stood up and hooked her purse over her arm. "I'll take care of this. What's her mother's name?"

"We'll handle it —"

"Amanda's last name is Fields," Cara offered, seeing a second chance to tell someone else and maybe get Amanda to stop.

"Fields?" Delores looked back at Principal Jones. She didn't glare, and yet her narrow eyes were sharper than any of the looks she'd given before. "Is her mother Sylvia Fields? The same Sylvia Fields that's the head of the PTA?"

Principal Jones looked down at her desk. "Ms. Vineyard, I can assure you that all the children here receive equal discipline —"

"I'm sure you can." Delores took Cara's hand, and Cara jumped up. "Goodbye, Ms. Jones."

"Is Amanda going to get in trouble?" Cara asked as they walked towards her mother's truck.

"I hope so," Delores said with a sigh.

Cara went to class the next day, but Amanda didn't act like someone who'd gotten in trouble. She did, however, act like someone who'd been hurt. "What happened to your nose?" Jennifer asked the next morning, for she'd been sick the day before.

"A basketball hit me," Amanda grumbled. Cara wondered why she'd lied, and thought with a small bit of pleasure that maybe, at last, she'd made Amanda feel shame.

Amanda was still mean to Cara, but she no longer pretended to whisper around her. Cara wondered if Principal Jones had spoken to Mrs. Fields. As Cara thought about it, she wondered if her own mother had even talked to Mrs. Fields. Her mother didn't bring it up, and Cara didn't remember hearing her mother on the phone.

Cara thought about asking her mother about it, but something inside of her told her to keep it a secret, to bury it and toss it away like a dead possum Terry caught with his knife. Cara buried it away, the only memory of that incident being the faint sound of a whisper she sometimes thought she heard.

1990-1993

Second grade became third. It didn't bother Cara much to not have friends. It seemed to bother her teachers more — namely her third grade teacher, Mrs. Vaughn. "Why don't you want to play kickball with your friends?" she asked Cara during the second week of school at recess.

"They're not my friends," Cara said as she played with a Barbie she brought from home.

"You can't make friends if you're over here by yourself."

"I like playing by myself." Cara could spend hours by herself on the farm — and there, her mother didn't mind if she played by herself. Her mother never bothered her about making friends. Her mother was fine with it being her and Cara on the farm, and Cara was fine with that too.

At school, though, her loneliness wasn't fine. "Try and make some friends though," Mrs. Vaughn replied. "You don't have to play kickball, but maybe find some other kids who are alone on the playground. They may want someone to play with."

Cara looked up and saw a kind smile on Mrs. Vaughn's face. She couldn't ignore its warmth, and her resolve softened a little. "Okay," she said with a shrug. Mrs. Vaughn walked away, and Cara looked around the playground. She saw one girl going across the monkey bars. The girl smiled in her direction.

Cara turned. She didn't like the monkey bars. She saw a boy sitting by himself against the wall, playing with a Ninja Turtle. She walked up to him. "Hi!"

He looked up at her. He didn't smile, but he also didn't sneer. "Hey."

"Want to play?"

"Sure. You like Ninja Turtles?"

"I only have Barbie."

"Barbies can have other names, right? She can be April."

"Okay." Cara sat down and they started to play. Cara liked that the boy — whose name was Aaron — didn't whisper and didn't seem to be waiting for an opportunity to tease her. He just played with her and stayed focused on their game. He didn't even mind when Cara turned April into Ninja April, and looked impressed when Cara caught a mouse walking by the brick wall of the school.

"How'd you catch that?" he asked.

"I catch them on the farm." Cara wasn't old enough to use a knife or set traps, but she still tried to catch critters when she could.

"Cool. He can be Splinter."

"What if it's a she?" Cara couldn't tell with mice. She flipped it over to check like she'd seen people on TV do with dogs and cats. The mouse wriggled in her palm and chewed at the sky. Cara was careful to keep her fingers away from its teeth, so she wouldn't catch the rabies her mother always warned her about.

"Then *she* can be Splinter."

"I thought Splinter was a rat."

"You want to catch a rat?" Aaron smiled deviously, and at the sight of it, Cara felt a rush from her heart to her stomach, one she'd never felt before and wasn't sure how to place. "You want rats to crawl through the school and scare everyone?" he asked.

Cara smiled back. "They'll take over the school and it'll be one big sewer."

"And Splinter the Mouse will be their king — or queen."

"Cara!" Aaron and Cara looked up and saw Mrs. Vaughn looking frightened. "Put that mouse down. Where did you find it?"

"It was running near the school," Cara said as she dropped it. The mouse landed with a thud, then flipped over and scampered away.

"Don't play with mice," Mrs. Vaughn said with a frown. Cara looked down as Mrs. Vaughn walked away. Even when she'd done what she was told, she still got in trouble.

"I'll bring Splinter tomorrow," Aaron said. Cara looked back up at him. He still smiled at her. "He's not as cool as a real mouse, but he's a toy and Mrs. Vaughn won't get mad."

Cara smiled back — just a little, but it was enough.

She played with Aaron at recess the next day, and for several days after that. Their friendship stayed on the playground and was rooted entirely in whatever toys he brought from home, but Cara still enjoyed it.

Cara found herself noticing more about him as they played together, like how his bangs hung over his face or how his red He-Man shirt looked the best on him. She sometimes imagined the two of them walking in the woods around their farm, or imagined him laughing quietly like he did sometimes in class. She once imagined kissing him, just to see what she thought of it. She didn't mind the thought.

Still, they stayed friends, which was fine with her. Some of their classmates saw it differently, and asked Aaron about his girlfriend or if he liked being Cara's boyfriend. He'd always flush and not reply, and Cara knew they wouldn't play together at recess on those days. But the teasing would ebb, and Aaron would walk up to her and ask if she wanted to play Ninja Turtles, and all would be right again.

Third grade became fourth. Aaron moved away over the summer. Cara missed him, but playing with him and having a friend for one year gave her some confidence. It also seemed to give her a boost, even with boys who'd teased Aaron about her the year before. "Want to play with us?"

Charlie asked her at recess on the first day of school, with Devin by his side.

Cara agreed. She found boys much easier to play with than girls. Some of the boys were mean — they picked on her in class, or called her a girl as if it were something to be ashamed of, but when they were mean, they were both blunt and brief. It wasn't drawn out the way it was with Amanda. It wasn't inconsistent the way it was with Jennifer. And they never whispered — Cara always knew what they had to say.

So while she mostly remained on the periphery of her classmates, the space that was the safest, she found it easier to intertwine with the boys. As fourth grade became fifth, their interactions stayed within the realm of friendship. She enjoyed playing with them and sometimes admired the way they looked. If they flirted with her, it was gentle and hidden — saying she was cool, calling her brave when she caught mice, patting her back after a good game of kickball as Cara adjusted the straps on the training bra she'd just begun to wear. But Cara and boys stayed on each other's periphery, never holding hands or sneaking behind school walls like Cara saw teenagers do on TV.

Then fifth grade became sixth.

———

1993-1994

Cara started sixth grade, and her eyes wandered around boys she'd known that grew over the summer, boys she hadn't known that came from other elementary schools, and especially the older boys in seventh and eighth grade who were so tall and looked so handsome as they walked to their lockers. Cara wandered home from the first day of school in a swirl of hormones. She felt a need to lie in bed. She trained her focus on Mr. Hampton, her English teacher. He had sandy blond hair and green eyes, and the way he talked about their syllabus made her want to read every book right then and there, read them while sitting on his desk as he kissed her legs and unzipped her jeans. Cara opened her legs and placed her fingers between her thighs. She imagined Mr. Hampton in their place, and had him the only way she could and the only way she knew she should.

Cara couldn't have Mr. Hampton outside of her dreams, but when her dreams ran dry, there were boys at school that were ready and willing to fill the well. She began to notice them noticing her. Sometimes they were lewd and loud, and Cara looked the other way as they laughed and called, "You'll want me later!" But most noticed her the way she noticed them — with locked eyes, a smile, and a quick look away as their lurid thoughts threatened to become actions.

Boys, however, didn't seem to mind acting. Cara's elbows were grazed by many fingers, the small of her back brushed many times, her body brought into a quick hug between friends from a boy Cara had only known for one day. She knew it wasn't just a friendly hug, knew that even on the rare occasion a hugging boy didn't give one extra squeeze that happened to push her breasts against his chest. She knew, and she didn't care. She liked to be near them, liked to see their arms and feel their chests as they pressed themselves against her.

Boys became as much a part of Cara's routine as school. She met boys in her new classes, they'd lock eyes and steal touches, and she'd ask the ones she liked to have lunch outside with her or wait for the bus around the corner from everyone else. Cara heard warnings from various adults to not get too close with boys, that they only wanted one thing and they'd do anything to get it. Cara didn't see what the problem was; she wanted it too.

She only caught a glimpse of the problem with Lucas. Lucas was a boy she really liked, one who sat next to her in English class and made her laugh with the voices he'd make for the characters while reading aloud. They had a test coming up, and Cara asked him if he wanted to come over to her house after school and study. His eyes lit up when she asked. He and Cara had studied before, but only outside at lunch, and only with their knees touching or with a couple stolen kisses quick enough to disappear before a teacher showed up. At home, there were no teachers — and much to Cara's delight when they walked inside, there was no mother either. *At the store*, a note from her mother read on the door. *Back before dinner.*

Cara barely read it before darting upstairs and leading Lucas by the hand. He pulled a book out of his backpack, but Cara took it and tossed it on her bedside table. "We can study when Mom gets home," Cara said as she took his hands. She kissed him on the lips, and when she pulled away, Lucas pulled her back. He kissed her, then kissed her again and again and again.

They sat on her bed, still kissing. Cara felt a little nervous. For all the time she spent with boys, she'd never had sex with any of them. They kissed at school, sometimes kissed over and over if they decided to cut class; and the older ones were bolder about touching her breasts through her shirt. But she'd never seen a boy naked and she'd never kissed them anywhere but their lips and neck. She liked having sex in her daydreams at home. But now that she was home with a boy, a real boy who touched her himself, she wasn't as certain.

She did, however, like kissing Lucas. She liked the way it felt to roll around with Lucas on her mattress, liked the way his teeth grazed hers as they kissed. His hands were soon under her shirt, and now that they were home, away from teachers and students and anyone else who could watch, Cara took off her shirt. Lucas' eyes widened, and Cara lifted his shirt so she could see him too. He took it off, then rolled back over her and began to kiss her neck, her stomach. He touched her breasts and moved to unhook her bra.

"Cara!"

Cara rolled off of Lucas, and felt a blanket of ice cover her entire body when she saw her mother in the doorway. "We weren't doing anything!" Lucas said.

Delores rolled her eyes. "You'd be doing something if I wasn't home," she said.

"I better go," Lucas said, getting to his feet.

"How? You gonna walk? Come on downstairs. I'm calling your parents."

Lucas and Cara didn't make eye contact as they pulled on their shirts and followed Delores. Lucas mumbled his number once they were in the kitchen. Delores called his parents, but all she said was, "Can you come pick up Lucas? They're done studying." Lucas and Cara did their homework and didn't look at each other. When Lucas' father reached the farm, Lucas left without a word.

"Why didn't you tell Lucas' dad what you saw?" Cara asked when Delores returned to the kitchen.

"I embarrassed both of you enough already. I'd say something if I caught him touching you without you wanting him to." Delores sat down and gave Cara a pointed look. "You wanted him to, right?"

"Yes. I invited him over."

"I thought so." Delores tapped her fingers on the table, then took a cigarette out of her purse. She rolled it over and over in her fingers in lieu of smoking it. Cara knew from years of watching her mother get agitated that the smoking would come later, on the porch and away from her.

"So," Delores said. "Let's talk about you inviting him over. He your boyfriend?"

Cara flushed. "No."

"You want him to be your boyfriend?"

"Mom …"

"You like touching and kissing him on more than just the lips?"

"Mom!"

"Cara, if you're too embarrassed to be honest with me about boys, then you're too young to do what I saw you guys doing earlier."

"I don't have to tell you everything though. That's weird."

"But you need to be honest with me about sex. I don't want to know everything you're doing. I don't need to. But I need to know you're being safe and I need to know if boys are treating you well. Are you having sex?"

"No. Just touching and kissing."

"You're probably thinking about sex though, right?"

Cara didn't reply.

"Do you want to have sex with Lucas?"

Cara wouldn't mind having sex, period. But despite the usual comfort she felt when talking to her mother, she wasn't sure she wanted to tell her that. It seemed like a secret she should save for herself, like the moment she was supposed to have with Lucas earlier that afternoon.

"I like Lucas," she said. "I like kissing and touching him."

"So just do that. Don't be in such a hurry to go further. It'll be better with someone you care more about — and also better when you're older. I think you're too young to be having sex."

Cara didn't know if she agreed, but she had a feeling that with something like her mother's thoughts on sex, her agreement didn't matter. Delores touched Cara's shoulder. "Now, please tell me: did Lucas make you do anything you didn't want to do?"

"No. None of them do."

"Them?" Cara looked away as Delores removed her hand, but she could still detect her mother's frown. "Lucas isn't your first boyfriend?"

"He's not my boyfriend."

"Who else have you seen?"

Cara shrugged, then sighed. She knew that if she tried not to talk, her mother wouldn't let her leave the room. She also knew her mother would see right through any lies she tried to tell. It was why she preferred to say nothing at all to her. But even secrets were only kept so long between her and her mother.

"I like to kiss boys sometimes at school," Cara said. "They're cute, and it's not a big deal." Delores sighed, and

Cara furrowed her brow. "You just said it's okay to kiss and touch boys."

"It's not that. Not only that. I mean …" Delores sighed again and set down her cigarette. "Your teachers have called me a couple times. They're concerned because they've heard your classmates saying things about you. They're concerned you're moving too fast and setting a bad example for the other students."

Cara looked at her mother in silent shock. Teachers had called her mother. Her classmates talked about her to them, talked about her doing things that she thought were private. Her thoughts immediately went to Amanda and the other girls who sneered at her when she ducked around the corner with another boy. They never liked her anyway. What did she care what they thought about her? But telling the teacher, who then told her mother …

"I told those teachers they should be more concerned with the example those boys are setting when they talk about you and spread rumors —"

Cara's eyes widened. "Boys?"

"Yes. Apparently your teachers overhear some colorful conversations between them in the locker room and the hallways."

"Boys don't talk about me. It's the girls that talk about me, and I don't give a shit what they think about me."

Delores laughed, but it matched the sadness that settled in her eyes. "I know you've had problems with the other girls, problems I wish your teachers would fix when I've talked to them about how you're excluded," she said.

Cara snorted. There was nothing any teacher could say to those girls to change their minds about her. Her role in their lives was decided, and Cara had no problems filling it.

"But while girls whisper, boys talk. And when boys talk, people listen." Delores gave Cara's hand another squeeze. "Just make sure those boys are listening to you — and make sure you're listening to what *you* want, not them. Okay?"

"Okay."

Boys talked, and Cara discovered that Lucas talked too. She began to catch wind of Lucas' side of the story, which had them going much further than they'd even approached before her mother walked in. She heard this through the whispers of other girls who looked in her direction and the actions of other boys who came onto her more strongly. Cara had no problems pushing them away, not as many problems as they had. They'd swear at her and try to keep going forward, at least until she slapped or shoved them away before storming off. Boys talked, and boys could talk all they wanted to. She'd still decide what she wanted to do with them, and when, and with who. Girls whispered, and girls only whispered more with each boy Cara saw despite the rumors about her growing in number.

"Why do you hang out with so many boys?" Amanda asked her point-blank outside of Spanish class. It was weeks since Lucas' story had ebbed, but the murmurings about Cara still fizzled like sea foam on the school's shore.

"They're my friends," Cara said.

Amanda sneered. "They only hang out with you because you're a slut."

Cara narrowed her eyes. "If that's all it takes, then why don't they hang out with you?"

Amanda gasped and sped back into the classroom. Mrs. Rodrigues took Cara to the principal's office. Principal Day called Delores to tell her what happened. Delores picked Cara up from school after she'd served her detention.

"What'd Amanda say to you?" Delores asked.

Cara smiled. She knew her mother would understand.

————

1996-1999

Sixth grade became seventh. Seventh became eighth. Cara still saw boys. She found it easier to ignore the whispers of girls when she was in their company, even as boys whispered in her ear with increased vulgarity. Cara didn't care. Anything was better than silence.

High school brought a wave of the mundane. Cara walked into the doors of Leslie High to discover even more new faces, so many faces that she walked through a hum of voices no matter where she went in the hall.

One face, though, was notably absent. Cara saw Jennifer in homeroom with an Asian girl that Cara hadn't seen in middle school, but didn't see Amanda. She didn't see Amanda in any of her classes. Cara wondered if she was sick.

By the third day of no Amanda, she wondered too much to keep her questions to herself. "Hi," she forced herself to say to Jennifer in homeroom. All she wanted was an answer, but she knew that pleasantries were the quickest way to get it.

Jennifer smiled at her with a hint of surprise. "Hey Cara. What's up?"

"Where's Amanda?" One pleasantry was enough.

"Oh. She and her family moved to Raleigh this summer."

She'd moved. Amanda was gone. The one who'd whispered the most, the one who'd made her life a living hell since kindergarten, was gone.

Cara felt nothing. She didn't understand why.

"Did you have a nice summer?" Jennifer asked. Cara barely noticed.

The Asian girl sitting next to Jennifer waved to Cara with a smile. "Hi! I'm Lisa," she said.

Cara noticed, but only gave a curt nod and said, "Cara." She didn't have time to make friends that were just being polite before they turned around and whispered about her once she'd walked away.

The bell rang, saving Cara from more false pleasantries. She took her seat with relief of being freed from Jennifer and Lisa. She could almost hear the looks they were exchanging in lieu of talking about her. They'd talk about her later, once the teacher was done speaking and they could gossip in peace. Cara could hear them as clear as day. She played their likely words about her over and over in her head, adding a few more and creating a loop that was only broken by the bell.

———

Cara's greatest wish in school had been for Amanda to disappear. Her absence did nothing for her, though. With each passing week, Cara found that the things she thought would cheer her up did nothing. Her classmates didn't tease her. They either left her to herself or, oddly, tried to talk to her.

Cara wasn't having it — she knew better — but she also couldn't deny that it was almost lonelier to move quietly on the periphery of her peers than it was to be mocked by them. It was loneliness she didn't mind, but she couldn't deny that the silence settled on her like a small weight that grew gradually each day, like a new pebble added to a mound one by one until the weight was suddenly crushing.

There were moments of relief. Boys, for instance, were still her constant supply. She met up with old ones she hadn't seen over the summer and met new ones that high school delivered to her. Cara took particular delight in older boys, juniors and seniors that actually seemed to know what they were doing. She lost her virginity to a senior named Dominic right before Christmas. They fucked over the entirety of Christmas break, taking advantage of their parents working during the day while they were home from school; and then he cooled things off when they returned to school in January.

Cara didn't mind, but Dominic seemed to want her to. "I just don't want to break your heart later," he explained at her locker one morning. "When I'm at college and all, and —"

"You won't break my heart," Cara said with a shrug. "It's fine."

Dominic only grew more agitated. "Look, it was fun, but —"

"It was, but now it's done, and that's fine."

"You don't want to see me anymore?"

"Not if you don't want to."

"I just figured you'd be … I don't know, more upset."

"I'm not." Cara wasn't, and also knew that boys didn't like it when girls got upset. She figured Dominic would be thrilled.

He seemed to be anything but. "You lost your virginity to me and you're not upset about this ending?"

"Do you want me to be?"

"No, but Jesus, I didn't think you'd feel nothing."

"I don't feel nothing. I'm just not upset or heartbroken. We fucked —"

"Keep your voice down," he said as he looked for teachers.

"You don't want to fuck anymore, and I won't make you if you don't want to. I'll move on. There're other guys."

Dominic glowered at her. "Slut," he spat, before he turned and left. Cara felt a small sting at hearing him call her what she'd heard so many others call her before — and yet, she felt a small comfort at hearing it out loud again.

———

Cara didn't see Dominic again, but all that week, she heard his last words to her as she walked through the halls. She heard it in her classmates' heads as they glanced at her and quickly looked away, heard it when other senior boys would walk up to her and casually ask if she wanted to have lunch off-campus in their cars, skip class, or hang out after school. She heard it when she saw other girls talking to each other, heads bent over notes they weren't taking as they chose instead to gossip in each other's ears.

Cara's ears were buzzing, just like they had ever since first grade and Amanda made it a point to buzz in her ears. Amanda wasn't there, and it wasn't until Cara felt the sting of Dominic's insult that she realized how much she'd missed the anger that Amanda made her feel. It was a horrible anger, one that churned in her stomach, seeped through her skin, and coated her brain until it felt like nothing else was there. But when Amanda wasn't there, then there truly was nothing — and that made Cara feel worse.

As freshman year stretched on, she found company in the imagined words. She'd hear them in her ears even when she was alone. When she heard nothing, then felt nothing, she made herself hear it. Made herself hear their insults and feel their judgment, cloaked herself in it as if she were hearing Amanda, hearing Dominic, hearing everyone around her say what they all knew about her. It made her angry, and Cara found comfort in that anger.

It became so comfortable that Cara soon forgot to turn it off — and sooner after that, forgot that they were words that she created. The words became a swarm, one that sometimes buzzed so loud that Cara would shout to herself to shut up.

But it wasn't to herself. It was to everyone that talked about her, everyone that whispered once she dared to leave the farm and make an appearance in the town she called home. It was only ever quiet on Vineyard Farm, where the only words she heard were kindness and pride from her mother.

Vineyard Farm was a comfort, but it wasn't enough. Summer at home meant more stifling loneliness, one that Cara's head couldn't help but fill with words no matter how many afternoons she spent by their lake nor how many critters she killed. She sometimes took her time with the possums and rabbits, plunging her uncle's rusty knife into their flesh and taking their squirming bodies to the lake before cutting long, jagged lines across their skin to quiet their screeches. Their blood on the grass seeped the way the words did in her veins. Cara imagined the words flowing into the lake along with the blood, drowned and forever quieted.

They were never quieted, though — not unless Cara did something about it. She eventually went back to school, eventually saw smiling faces she knew hid secrets and judgment. Back to girls who gave a passing wave or else looked away with sneers, back to boys who were willing to make out behind the school or fuck in their cars after hours, and in exchange had stories to tell about her to their friends.

In between the moments of being brought back into her classmates' fold, their words would fill in her bouts of loneliness, stings and whispers she took decreasing comfort in. It sometimes helped to add bodies back to the whispers, see the faces of people she knew were speaking or she knew had spoken, even if they weren't in class with her. When that wasn't enough, she allowed herself to react in her head. She'd smack a girl's cheek, punch a boy's stupid grin. It was okay to think those things. She wouldn't get in trouble inside her own mind. She wouldn't get in trouble even when the smacks became kicks, or when her hands held her uncle's rusted knife.

Cara couldn't stop the whispers. When she trapped them in her imagination, then set them free, they just came back; and usually brought more. They were a routine, and as Terry told her all those years ago, the only way to stop a routine was to disrupt it. Nothing disrupted a whisper faster than a slit throat.

She of course kept those actions in her thoughts. She knew her uncle's knife was just for vermin on the farm, knew that she'd be seeing more than a trip to the principal's office if she hurt anyone at school. She didn't actually want to hurt anyone at school. She'd just entertain the notion, think about it when the whispers became too much to bear and she wanted to feel like she could do something about it. Feeling like she could do something about it, something that stopped the whispers and talk that nothing else she did seemed able to stop, was better than feeling nothing at all.

————

1999-2000

Cara arrived early on the first day of her last year at school. She wanted to arrive before the other students, to see an empty campus in front of her. Her footsteps echoed in the empty halls, the only other people being the janitor and a few teachers. Cara remembered her first day of kindergarten, how she'd been so excited to meet more people than her mother and the critters that wandered around Vineyard Farm. Meeting others hadn't been what she'd hoped at all. It only made her feel more alone, made her know for certain she wasn't wanted anywhere except at the farm. Her suspicions had only been confirmed by her own thoughts, her own anger that people saw eventually if they made the mistake of getting too close to her.

Her senior year went by in a blur. Her classes didn't matter. She avoided other girls and only saw a couple boys. They were all the same. Cara saw them, did the things with them she liked to do and that they wanted her to do; but that was all. She knew better than to get close to any of them.

A pointless fall became a grey spring. Cara almost didn't register the last day of class until she hopped in her mother's truck, drove herself home, and realized she'd never drive to Leslie High or any school ever again. She'd be back on the farm, would stay there all summer and stay there again in the fall. She clenched the steering wheel as she drove.

"My little girl, a high school graduate." Delores smiled as she fussed with the sleeves of Cara's graduation gown. "Out in the world, ready to do amazing things."

Cara didn't agree. She also didn't disagree. She just stared in the mirror, her eyes looking into the nothing that lay ahead of her.

"I'm sorry we can't afford tuition for college," Delores said as she stroked her arm.

Cara shook her head. "It's fine, Mom," she said.

"I'm sure it's hard seeing your friends going to school, though —"

"It isn't." That would require having friends. "I told you, I don't want to go to college anyway."

"I know you'll find something to do. And in the meantime, I get to keep you here a little longer." Delores squeezed Cara's arm, and Cara didn't understand why she felt a little unsettled. She shook the feeling away.

"Well, just because you're not going to college doesn't mean we can't celebrate." Delores reached behind her bed and pulled out a gift bag. "Happy graduation, honey."

"Oh, thank you." Cara was truly touched, and her mother's kindness made her forget for a moment that she had nothing left for her at the end of the podium. She pulled something out from under mounds of pink tissue paper, and saw a blue leather pouch with a polished handle sticking out. "What is it?" she asked as she grasped the handle.

"Careful with that. Hold the sheath too."

"Sheath?" Cara still did as she was told. Her eyes widened as she grasped and pulled the handle to reveal a gleaming, silver blade beneath the pouch.

"It's from Terry," Delores said. "Remember him?"

"A little." It was a lie — Cara remembered him well, and still felt a little sad sometimes when she thought of traipsing their fields with him as a girl. In that moment, though, Cara was too entranced by the knife to get caught up in her memories.

"That's real leather," Delores explained, "and polished bone on the handle. Terry said it's one of a kind, one of the first ones he made."

"Why'd you get me this?" Cara looked at her mother and added quickly, "I mean, it's beautiful, but —"

"No, I understand." Delores laughed a little. "I wanted to get you something for graduation, but I didn't think you'd want a necklace. And even if I could afford to get you a car, you've pretty much claimed the truck for yourself. I was thinking about how much you've grown up, which of course made me think of when you were little. I remembered how much you liked getting critters and keeping them out of the yard. But even if it never touches an animal, it just seemed like something you would like. Something nice, something pretty, and something a little bit dangerous." Delores gave her a bemused grin. "Something kind of like you."

Cara gave a bemused smile back. "I do like it. I like it a lot. Thanks Mom."

———

June-December 2000

Summer had once been a time of reprieve. It was three months away from school, three months away from her peers and their whispers. Summers were quiet, and it was a quiet Cara missed whenever she arrived back at school for another year.

For the first time in her life, Cara felt stifled by that quiet. School was a field of landmines — it was mostly mundane, mostly kind of lonely, and disrupted by insults from people like Amanda or jolts from boys like Aaron, Lucas, or Dominic. But jolts were better than nothing. Jolts disrupted her routine, and Cara realized over that lonely summer on the farm that there was a certain pleasure to that disruption.

She sometimes jolted herself with the memories of landmines. She'd hear their whispers and clench her teeth as she walked in the woods, hear their laughter mingled in with the cries of a raccoon as she stabbed one on an evening prowl. Even that began to fade. As she dragged the animals to the woods and left them for the flies to devour, she'd feel as cold and empty as their bloody corpses. The heat that left their bodies and entered her hands only lasted so long — and there were only so many animals.

There was only so much on Vineyard Farm, and when she'd come home from working an odd job, or stay home while looking for another, she increasingly felt that it wasn't enough.

Her mother thought it was enough, and their disagreement on the matter grew into a budding wedge, like a crack along a windshield that didn't shatter, but threatened to with every rock that smacked against it. Their dinners became more and more quiet, the television a third party that both would rather pay attention to than the other. Delores' words of encouragement throughout school faded, to where Cara's accomplishments around the farm were acknowledged with a nod or a grunt. Cara often found herself looking at the cork board in the living room with her limited school prizes. A ribbon, a certificate, some tests, a few drawings. They were small in number, but they'd made her mother proud; and Cara thus felt comforted to see them on display.

Summer cooled into fall. Halloween passed into Thanksgiving. It was dark early, and animals were scarce. Cara had a part-time job at a garden supply store making deliveries, but she didn't know how long the manager would tolerate her lack of desire to actually be in the store. She was much happier hauling bags of dirt and other supplies in her truck, even if it meant laying down ugly plastic covers on the seats to keep the mud from staining them.

Cara dropped off the dirt early in the evening one day in December. "Go on home," the manager said with a nod. It was her swiftest dismissal yet. Cara wondered if tomorrow would come with no need for Cara's truck. She shrugged as she started the truck. She wouldn't think about that.

Still, it was early yet. She decided to go for a drive. She drove around Leslie, taking every turn except the one that led her to Vineyard Farm. She wasn't ready to go home. After an hour of driving around Leslie, she wasn't sure when she would be.

Cara drove a little further than the "Now Leaving Leslie" sign. She drove until she reached the highway. She merged onto I-40 and just drove. She turned on her music and felt the guitars and singing interweave with familiar whispers. The whispers echoed in her ears. *No one likes you. Slut. Go away. Trouble.* Over and over, words and sentences in hushed voices that could belong to anyone. They belonged to everyone, and Cara longed to stay away from all of them.

Her longing eventually took her to Asheville. Cara blinked when she saw how far she'd gone and saw what time it was. The lateness of the hour settled on Cara's eyelids. She forced them to stay open as she pulled off on an exit to turn around. She saw the glowing lights of a Super 8 motel just off the side of the road.

The prospect of going to sleep was more appealing than the thought of driving more than five hours to get home. She pulled into the parking lot, checked in at the front lobby, and went into her room. It had an old bed and an older television set, but for that night at least, the room was hers. Her mother wasn't there. No one knew she was there — no one except the man at the front desk, and even he had only looked at her long enough to take her cash and give her a key.

Cara smiled a little as she fell into bed. It felt good to have something all to herself, even if it was just one night in a roadside motel.

She took her time the next morning. She slept late, she had breakfast in a diner where everything, even the orange juice, tasted like bacon; and then she got back on the highway.

It was dark by the time she got back to Leslie. She'd made a few stops, including a long lunch and a fill-up at a dusty gas station. She wondered as she parked in her driveway if dinner was ready.

Cara didn't smell any food when she walked inside. Instead, she saw her mother rush into the hallway, eyes angry and frantic. "Where the hell were you?" Delores shouted.

"I went driving last night," Cara explained. "I ended up in Asheville, so I stayed overnight."

"Asheville? What the hell were you doing there?"

"Nothing. I was just driving."

"And just driving until dinnertime tonight?"

"I didn't have to work today and I took my time coming home."

"What the hell is wrong with you? You've been gone since yesterday morning, I've been worried sick, and you come in like you were just running an errand!"

"It was just a drive, Mom. I'm sorry —"

"What in the goddamn hell is wrong with you? You spend all year being sullen and doing nothing —"

"All year?"

"And when you're not doing nothing, you're just disappearing in the mountains because you felt like taking a drive? Jesus Christ, Cara. What the hell is going through your head? What the hell is wrong with you?"

Delores' words were more than she'd said to her in weeks — and all of them were in anger. All Cara could hear was wrong, wrong, wrong. Something was wrong with her. Her mother thought something was wrong with her.

Even when Delores' silence was at its heaviest, Cara had trusted that Delores was someone she could count on to never add to the whispers she heard in her head. Delores was a shield against them, someone who'd tell her that nothing was wrong with her — that she was proud of her. Cara suspected with growing hurt that this had just been a lie to soothe her.

"What do you have to say for yourself?" Delores spat. "Don't stand there all quiet and sullen like you always do —"

"What do you want me to say?" Cara asked as she looked back up and glowered at her mother. "That I was wrong to go for a drive? That I was wrong for wanting to get away from this fucking farm and this goddamn town for a few hours, that I was wrong for losing track of time and staying overnight somewhere instead of falling asleep at the wheel and crashing the truck?"

"I want you to apologize for scaring me."

"I did, but you didn't hear it because you were too busy telling me how something's wrong with me and how everyone who thinks I'm awful is exactly right."

Delores softened, but it was too late to have any effect on Cara. "You're not awful —"

"Everyone says it. Awful. Trouble. Wrong. Something's wrong with me." Cara stepped towards Delores. Delores stepped back, frightened. Frightened of her own daughter. This only angered Cara further. "You're my mother. Why don't you tell me what's wrong with me?"

"Nothing's wrong with you —"

"You know me so well, know everything about me, including why everyone hates me, including you."

"I don't hate you!" Delores' shout stopped Cara in her tracks. "I'd never say that, Cara."

"But you want to, right?" Cara knew it wasn't true, even as she tried to tell herself that to keep the anger coursing through her veins and making her feel more alive than she'd felt since school.

"No, never. I know you know that."

"Fuck this." Cara spun and left the house.

"Where are you going now?"

"Out. Don't follow me." Cara knew Delores would try. She sped to the truck as fast as she could and pulled out of the driveway.

She wouldn't go back to Asheville. She wouldn't even go far. Every time she passed a sign for the highway, she avoided it. She didn't want to end up so far away that she'd just continue fighting with her mother. She knew she'd end up back on Vineyard Farm. Even in the heat of her anger, she'd be pulled back. She had nowhere else to go and nothing else to think of.

Her mother's shouts echoed in her head. They quieted, but into a hum. Wrong, wrong, wrong. Hate, hate, hate. She heard it as a whisper, but one that was distinctly her mother's. Cara felt her eyes burn. She had nothing — nothing but roads to drive on and thoughts to drive her crazy as she sped through Leslie's darkest roads.

Cara's thoughts were broken by a loud smack against the truck. Cara looked in the rearview mirror as she slammed the brakes. She saw someone standing on the side of the road — someone still upright, thank God, she hadn't even seen him — with his arm raised. He appeared to be shouting, and she saw a rock speed towards her truck and hit the back.

She turned off the car and swooped out of the truck. "What the fuck, asshole?" she shouted as she walked towards him.

"Whoa, hey." He held up his hands, and took a step back as she approached him.

"You trying to make me crash or something?"

"I didn't know you were a chick —"

"You trying to make a dude crash, then?"

"I was trying to get you to stop. I need a ride."

"Then use your thumb, not a rock."

"All the other cars were ignoring me! I've been out here for almost an hour, and I need to get to Rocky Mount."

"I'm not going to Rocky Mount." Certainly not now.

"But you could get me closer, right? Maybe out to the Triangle, somewhere with more people or a train station or something?"

"Why would I drive you anywhere?"

"Look, I'll give you some money to fix the dents. I'm sorry about the rocks. But come on …" He smiled, and even under the moonlight, Cara could see the begging begin to make way for him trying to be smooth and impressive. "You're really going to leave me out here in the dark?"

She tried not to roll her eyes — especially when she found herself no longer wanting to jump in the truck and leave him in a cloud of dust behind her. "I'll take you to Raleigh. Get in."

Cara regretted it almost as soon as they were on the road. "Can't stand this screamer shit," the man said as her radio turned on with the rest of the truck. "Don't you listen to country or pop or something?"

Cara turned up the volume.

"Come on, you're not going to talk to me?" he asked. "Long drive ahead."

"Raleigh is forty-five minutes away." Thirty if she sped. She pressed the gas.

"Still a long time."

"It'll be longer if you don't shut up."

"Damn, you got a mouth on you." His hand moved towards her leg. Cara stiffened. "A pretty one, though."

She stayed quiet. She knew that swatting his hand away would just send it to her arm or her hair. Instead, she thought about the knife in her purse, one she could use if the man overstepped.

"Pretty mouth like that should say pretty things."

Cara imagined taking the knife and slashing off his hand, chucking it out the window where it wouldn't be anywhere near her. She smirked at the thought of him looking for it, and tried not to laugh at the thought of him throwing it at another car to try and get a ride.

His fingers, woefully still intact, crept to her inner thigh. "Or do pretty things."

His hand being lost wouldn't be enough. She imagined both hands on the ground, no thumb left to hitch another ride. Nowhere to go, because he was lying on the ground, buried and bleeding into the dirt. Nothing to say, because his throat was slashed. Cara didn't feel the sense of dread she'd felt before when those kinds of thoughts entered her head. This man was a stranger. This man was a lech.

"You want to make the trip a little longer?" He unbuckled his seatbelt, moved closer to her. His hand brushed up her leg, her waist, and her neck. She kept her eyes forward as he brushed her hair behind her ear, whispered into it with hot, damp breaths. "Show me what that mouth can do?"

Cara smiled. This man could be quieted.

———

Cara leaned against her truck. She could only see a wall of black that denoted the trees against a navy, starless sky. It was enough. She knew the woods were ahead. She'd emerged from them earlier, her hands empty save for a belt with a garish silver buckle. She wasn't sure why she'd kept it; she'd simply felt the urge to do so. She'd dropped it on the ground, leaned against the truck, and stared at the woods beyond the empty pumpkin patches.

She'd been staring for awhile when she heard the gentle smack of the screen door against the house. Cara kept her gaze forward, even when she heard her mother's footsteps.

She didn't want to look at her. She wanted to stare into nothing.

"You're home," Delores said, in a voice so soft it almost disappeared in the grass. Cara glanced towards Delores. She stood to the side of the front of the truck, no closer.

Cara nodded. "I am."

Delores leaned against the truck, and stared at the woods with Cara. They watched the sky, their words from earlier rustling through the fields with the nighttime breeze. Cara wondered for a moment if Delores could smell the blood on her body. She knew that even with the glow of the porch-light, it was too dark for Delores to see her in full — and even if Delores could see her, she didn't care. Delores already thought something was wrong with her. At least now, Cara had something to show for it.

"I'm sorry," Delores said. "For what I said earlier."

"I'm sorry I scared you," Cara said curtly.

"I don't hate you." Delores walked towards Cara. Cara kept her gaze forward. "I love you more than anything, even myself."

Cara didn't speak. Her mother's words had hurt her more than she ever wanted to admit. She buried them in her thoughts, kept them buried under the whispers that had been reduced to a sputtering buzz with the dying screams of the hitchhiker.

"And there isn't anything —" Delores stopped as her foot clanged against something hard on the ground. The belt Cara had dropped. Cara closed her eyes, then opened them. She wouldn't be embarrassed.

"Anything what?" Cara asked.

"Anything wrong with …" Delores' voice trailed as she picked up the belt. "What's this?"

"Something I brought home."

"Who's it belong to?"

"Paul." Cara saw his name scrawled in ugly cursive on the belt buckle as she'd kicked him out of the truck before he could bleed all over her floor.

Delores walked as she studied the belt, whose buckle shined in the light of the porch. "Who's Paul?"

"Someone I picked up. Watch out for the passenger door."

Delores side-stepped, and looked at the truck as she did so. "What's on the buckle?" Delores asked. "Is that —"

Delores stopped when she looked at the truck. Even at night, she couldn't miss the dark streak smeared across the rusted silver passenger door.

"What do you think it is?" Cara asked in her quietest, calmest voice.

"He … he hurt you, right? You were defending yourself."

"Is that what you want me to say?"

"I want you to tell me why. I want to know why you did this."

"So he'd stop whispering in my ear." Cara turned to face her mother. Delores looked scared. It didn't bother Cara at all. She walked towards her, walked towards the small glow cast by the porchlight. Her mother could see her, could see her stained clothes and blood-smeared neck. She didn't care. She wanted her mother to see that she wasn't afraid of her or her words. She wasn't afraid of anyone.

"I always hear them," Cara said. "I hear what my class-mates say about me, people I know. People we knew at

church who'd look at us, teachers who'd sneer at me because I wasn't like Amanda —"

"Amanda? That bully from school?"

"Boys who talked instead of whispered, boys I liked to
be with until they didn't want to be with me anymore, they
just wanted to talk about me —"

"Boys'll do that —"

"And it never stops — not even when I'm at home. I hear
about how I'm trouble, how I'm hated, how something is
wrong with me."

"I don't hate you."

"Something *is* wrong with me: I can't stop hearing about
what's wrong. I can't ever make it stop." A lump rose in Cara's
throat, which choked her words. She couldn't stop it, never
could no matter how hard she tried. It was why the whispers
followed her home and found their way into her mother's
mouth. It was because they were a part of her, a part that everyone saw when they spent enough time with her, and simply spoke out loud in an effort to keep her away from them.

She lost her sneer and looked down before her mother
could see her look sad. "I can't stop them," she whispered.
"I can't stop. I can't …"

"Ssh." Her mother walked towards her and cupped her
cheek. "You can stop, Cara. You can stop hearing what they
say, and stop believing it."

"I can't."

"You can. You did." She held up the belt. "You stopped
someone whispering in your ear."

Cara looked at the belt buckle. She remembered the look
on Paul's face when she'd reached in her purse, told him she

was getting a condom; and then how he'd yelped when she unsheathed her knife. She'd felt so powerful, so alive.

"You stopped someone from whispering nasty things." Delores smiled, but it looked like a sneer. "Let me guess: he was coming onto you?"

"Yeah, but …"

"Ssh. You don't have to say anything else." Delores squeezed Cara's elbow, and looked at her with startling warmth, one that was steeped in a darkness Cara had never seen in her mother's eyes before. She found it comforting.

"Come on inside," Delores said. "We'll wash the truck in the morning."

Cara did as she was told. They walked in the house. Delores moved towards the living room with the belt in hand. "You gonna burn it?" Cara asked as she glanced at the fireplace.

"It'd take forever to burn this hideous thing down." Delores moved towards the cork board, which hadn't any new accomplishments added since the middle school science fair. She took a large thumbtack and speared it through a hole in the belt. It hung in the center of the board, its buckle glaring in the living room lamp.

"Something for you to remember," Delores said as she smiled at Cara. "For when you think you can't do anything. You can — and you'll always make me proud."

————

December 2000-January 2004

Cara resigned herself to a life at Vineyard Farm. With each passing year, it grew less bad. Not good by any means, but not bad either. Just there. Just like her.

She kept at her odd jobs, mostly connected to the truck. People often asked her to drive out of town for them, which got her away for awhile and at hours which didn't worry her mother. She relished that time away, and yet with each passing year, that too became just another part of her existence. She went through the motions, drove between Leslie and anywhere else to make deliveries, came home for dinner, and slept. That was her life, and Cara told herself it was better than nothing.

Still, Cara was able to find moments of sparks to keep her going. Sex was still a good jumpstart. Cara sometimes brought a handsome man to her truck. It was always fast and always just once. It was what Cara trusted herself to handle, something that kept her satisfied in a way that was safe for everyone involved.

Other nights, though, Cara wasn't concerned with safety — especially when the whispers became too much for her to bear. It was on those nights that men on the side of the road came to her rescue. They peppered the roads she drove back and forth on, confident that they'd be able to get to the destinations they were hitching to, or to the places they'd been walking to before Cara pulled over and asked if they needed a lift. They'd often try to talk to her, try to whisper or say something she didn't want to hear; and Cara would disrupt their whispered routines by silencing strangers. It was a quiet that wouldn't last, but when it came, Cara felt a rush that couldn't be matched.

The only rush that came close was the one that came from making her mother happy. Delores always smiled when Cara brought home a souvenir from someone who met his fate at the end of her knife. Cara kept them for herself, as reminders of what she was capable of; but she also did it for her mother, the one person who'd ever love her no matter what. It was lonely in Leslie, and home was not the quiet place it was for Cara as a girl. But when Cara saw her mother smile, heard her mother say she was proud of her as she kissed her cheek, it was a rare moment where she didn't think that everything was hopeless.

CHAPTER 4

Cara spent the next morning scrubbing Darren's blood from the inside of her truck. She wanted to get the truck clean in case her mother's coworker, Rhonda, showed up early to drive her to work. Her mother didn't mind the mess, but Rhonda would certainly have questions — ones Cara wasn't confident that Delores could avoid on their half-hour drive to the office.

The seat covers made cleanup easy, but they didn't stop a few stray spurts from smattering the window. "Fucking squirters," she muttered to herself as she threw the bloody rags in a bag with her ruined clothes, all to be disposed of in the lake before she left for work. Mornings like this made her consider switching from blades to poison.

"Cara! Want some breakfast before you head out?"

Cara's stomach growled, and she tossed the bag in the bed of the truck before heading back inside. She smiled when she saw a plate of blueberry muffins on the table.

"So," Delores said as she sat down to join her. "You gonna be at the brewery again today?"

"Yup," Cara said with a mouthful of muffin. "Just like I've been for the past two years."

"I guess I'm still used to you working odd jobs."

"The brewery's growing. It's a busy time of year."

"Maybe it's growing enough to where Keith can get you something full-time."

Cara shrugged. "I think it's easier for him to pay me here and there to fill in the gaps." There were ebbs and flows at the brewery, but even Cara noticed lately that Keith Conniff, the co-owner and head brewer of Papa's Secret Brewing Company, had been calling her more and more.

Keith had gone to Leslie High, but they'd barely known each other — he was a senior when she was a freshman. They met in Charlie's, a bar that Cara found herself frequenting on nights when she didn't feel like going for a drive. Her beer in a quiet corner was interrupted by a voice saying, "Hey, Leslie High!"

The voice was close enough to her that Cara looked up. She saw a handsome black man with a beard and a Wake Forest baseball cap. He smiled and pointed at her shirt. "You went to Leslie High?" He chuckled to himself, and Cara felt warmed at the sound of it. "Actually, if you're from around here, then of course you went to Leslie High."

Cara laughed over her beer. "Yeah. I just graduated a couple years ago."

"And you're drinking beer?" Cara set down her drink; and the man laughed again. "Don't worry, I'm not a cop — I won't confiscate whatever fake ID the bartender didn't check," he said with a wink.

Cara smiled and held out her hand. She enjoyed talking to a man in a bar that seemed genuinely interested in just talking and not being a creep. "I'm Cara," she said.

"Keith." His brow knitted in faint recognition. "Cara Vineyard?"

"Yes."

"Ah, cool. I still don't remember you from school, but I think I've heard your name before."

Of course he had. Cara sipped her beer in an effort to quell the disappointment that flowed into anger as she remembered all the mouths her name had flowed in and out of at school.

"Small school like that, you're bound to hear everyone's name even if you don't see their face," Keith added.

"Especially when everyone talks about you," Cara muttered.

"What?"

"So what are you doing back home?" Cara asked in an effort to take both their minds off of anything said about her.

"Brewing. I've been home brewing since I was fifteen."

Cara sputtered over her beer a little. "Fifteen?"

"Yeah, it was kind of an open secret around Leslie. Me and my friends would make beer in my dad's garage and sell it to the neighbors. We got good at it, and Dad started selling kegs to local bars and saying he was making it. I got a degree and got old enough to do it myself, so, here I am." Keith pulled a menu between them on the bar and pointed at a beer three listings down, called Papa's Secret Wheat. "You want one?"

"What, a pint?"

"Yeah, always happy to get people drinking my beer. Strictly a sales pitch, I promise — not trying to pick you up."

"Isn't that what guys always say when that's exactly what they're doing?" Cara said with a smile. She could tell that Keith wasn't acting on desires or on anything he may have heard about her in school. Still, it was reassuring to see Keith laugh and shake his head.

"Maybe some guys, but not me. I'm a straight shooter — you'd have known right away if I was trying to pick you up. I want to buy you a beer to show off and to make a new friend from Leslie High."

Cara enjoyed making a new friend from Leslie High, even if it was several years after he graduated. That friendship culminated into a working one, as Keith would ask her to help him make deliveries. "Gives me more time to brew," he said when she first parked her truck outside of the garage that served as his brewery.

Her truck became his go-to for delivering cans of beer, along with kegs, tools, and other things Keith needed to keep brewing. "I'm so glad I met you at Charlie's," he said after a year of working together. "Having you to help with deliveries and errands really helped the brewery grow."

Cara's job grew right along with it. People from outside of Leslie started to come by looking for Papa's Secret, and bars in other towns asked for their own supply so that those people would come back and drink there. The brewery moved out of Keith's garage to an empty building on the outskirts of town. Keith started to hire actual employees and turn his hobby into the business he'd dreamed about since brewing in secret in high school.

SONORA TAYLOR

There was always a spot for Cara, though, even on the periphery of odd jobs. "I could always use an extra truck," Keith told her. "And I've always got space for friends."

As those friends and employees grew in number, Cara wondered if Keith kept her on out of pity more than need. But work was work, and Cara wouldn't question an opportunity to earn some money and get out of the house — especially on a day like today, when Keith said he'd need her for a full day.

"Delivery day!" Keith beamed as Cara walked into the brewery. "You ready for a road trip?"

"You got me going far out, right?"

"Far as Greensboro. That far enough to scratch your road trip itch?"

"I'll make do." They both began hoisting kegs outside and towards her truck, whose rust gleamed under the morning sun.

"I don't know how your truck can stand all that driving," Keith said as they each set a keg on the grass.

"It's stronger than it looks."

"And I don't know how you can stand it either. I got you going to Greensboro today and had you out in Apex for those tap handles."

"Oh yeah, let me get those for you." Cara opened the door and grabbed the bag of tap handles she'd tossed under the backseat the day before, checking for any stray speckles of blood she may have missed before pulling it out of the truck. They both began walking back inside.

"I guess if you like doing all that driving, I won't scale you back on it."

"Please don't."

"Hey, don't worry — I'd only scale back on it so I could give you other things to do here with everyone else."

Her response was still the same, but Cara pursed her lips to keep from saying it. "I like driving," she said instead, which was also the truth. "I like getting out of town for awhile and seeing the rest of the state outside of Leslie."

"And I like that you're doing that instead of me. Helps me focus on the beer."

"Hey Keith! You want this out near Cara's truck?" Keith and Cara halted as Greg Sturdivant, one of Keith's growing band of employees, walked by with a keg in his strong arms.

"Yeah, get the Greensboro, Hillsborough, and Raleigh deliveries out there," Keith said.

"Keith and I can take those out," Cara added, not wanting Greg or the others circling her truck without her there.

"I got this. Let me help."

"Come on Cara, there's three more kegs inside," Keith said. Cara followed him reluctantly, but cast a few glances behind her to watch Greg and make sure he left the keg next to the truck, not in it.

"Cara, can you come help me?" Sadie Williams' voice rang out from her own car as she pulled into the parking lot. "I've got bags of malt and barley out the ass back here."

"I'm helping Keith with the beer," Cara called.

"Go help Sadie. Greg and I can get the kegs." Keith smiled. "I'll make sure he doesn't scratch your truck."

Cara laughed a little, but it sounded more like a sigh. She walked outside and saw Sadie opening both her back door and trunk, which were, indeed, packed with brewing ingredients.

"I swear to God, worst thing I ever did was tell Keith I lived a few miles from the supply store in Durham," she said as she rolled her eyes a little. She brushed back one of her braids, and the large bead at the braid's end clacked against the others. "Now he's got me loading my car with this every other day."

"I can get this stuff if you want," Cara offered as they each grabbed two bags and began walking inside.

"Nah, I complain, but it's nice to have a job that isn't just growler fills or bar upkeep. Can't let the boys make us do all the waitressing work." They lumbered inside with their bags and brought them to the brewing room in the back. "Did you have fun driving yesterday?" Sadie asked with a grin as they walked back outside.

"Yeah, it was pretty quiet."

Sadie's copper eyes glinted with mischief, like pennies catching the sun. "No new friends?"

Cara had known the minute Sadie called her name that she wanted her help so that they could gossip. Sadie had gravitated towards another girl in the brewery within a week of being hired, and always pressed Cara for stories about her road trips. Sadie's questions didn't bother Cara as much as she thought they would, and Cara figured it was because Sadie had grown up in Durham, away from Leslie and away from the stories of others. Cara would occasionally comply, but kept it limited to a few stories of men she'd met in bars while making a delivery. Sadie always smiled and told her to go on, a welcome change from what she'd gotten in school.

Cara didn't tell all of her stories, though. "No new friends," Cara replied. "No one at all. I just drove to Apex and back."

"Well, try picking someone up today. I'm in a dry spell and need to hear about other people having sex so I can remember what it's like."

"Cara, we're ready to load the truck!" Keith called.

"Let her help me with these last bags!" Sadie called back before Cara could set down the bag she'd begun to lift.

"I'll help you," Greg said as he walked over. Cara stepped aside.

"I'm sure you will," Sadie said with an eye roll. Greg lifted two bags and followed behind Sadie as they walked inside.

"Greg isn't working unless he's showing off what he can lift," Keith clucked.

"You said the kegs are ready?" Cara asked, eager to leave before Sadie or Greg could keep her there any longer.

"Yeah. Greg loaded them in the bed, so you can peel on out." Keith shrugged before Cara could say anything. "He insisted. I think he's subbing the brewery for the gym today."

"Whatever. I'll get these delivered for you."

"Sounds good. And if you get to Raleigh late, I'll just see you here tomorrow morning."

Cara waved, then hopped in her truck and peeled out.

The drive to Greensboro wasn't too long. Cara made it there and had time to enjoy lunch before she needed to make her way back. She did her best to take her time. Rather than rush down I-40, she stayed in the slow lane and took in the bare winter trees lining the road. They were brown against a gray and purple sky that ached to snow.

It was cold, but not too cold to make a stop at one of Cara's favorite places to be alone. Just before she reached Raleigh, she pulled off the main road and drove down a dirt path lined with dead winter grass until she reached the banks of Lake Hollow. Lake Hollow stretched across the Triangle and beyond. Its wide open banks and lack of hiking paths made it the perfect place to park. Cara had driven there on more than one occasion and seen a few beat-up cars with steamed windows parked near the water.

She always went there alone, even when she picked someone up in Raleigh. The lake was a nice place to just be, to sit and listen to her radio while she smoked a cigarette or two. Cara didn't feel like a cigarette that afternoon. Instead, she watched the water in silence. Her only company was the occasional egret that glided over the water in hopes of finding a winter fish. It was a quiet paradise, one so still that Cara didn't register the setting sun until her cell phone began to ring.

Cara rolled her eyes a little as she picked it up. Overall, she liked the cell phone she'd bought for herself with the money she'd saved from the brewery. It was a good way for Keith to call her without holding up the house phone, and a good way for her to call Keith when she was on the road and had questions. It was also a way for her mother to get in touch with her if she was worried.

This was both good and bad. Cara didn't want her mother blowing up at her again like she had after her impromptu trip to Asheville, but she also didn't like her mother calling her when she was just trying to have a moment to herself in the waning evening. Cara sighed as she answered the phone. She'd sacrifice her moment of silence in exchange for an evening of peace later on. "Hey Mom," she said.

"Hi honey. You going to be home for dinner tonight?"

"Maybe, but I might be a little late. I've got to make some deliveries in Raleigh for Keith." And she'd take as much time as possible to do it.

"Okay. I'll save you a plate." Delores hung up. Cara tossed her phone back on the passenger seat and stared back out over the water. The sunset reflected in its ripples, and another egret passed by. It was less serene. All Cara could hear was her mother's voice beckoning her to come home.

———

Cara needed to deliver six kegs to five bars. She liked making deliveries in Raleigh. It wasn't as far of a drive from Leslie as the other cities she sometimes made deliveries to, but it was bigger than Leslie and had enough to keep her mind off of her quiet home for a few hours at least. She liked driving through downtown and seeing the tall buildings, and really liked driving by NC State and seeing all the bars, record stores, and bookstores filled to the brim with college students.

She liked driving by, but she had no desire to frequent those places. The bars where she made deliveries were all loud and crowded. It helped drown out the noise in her head, but it was still a lot to take in. She couldn't imagine enjoying a meal or even a beer anywhere in Raleigh. But she could enjoy Raleigh on the periphery — a placement she was used to, after all.

It was dark by the time she reached the fifth and final bar, a sports bar called Sylvester's. The voices, music, and kitchen sounds smacked Cara as soon as she walked in looking for the owner. Even the smaller noises, like a bark of laughter or silverware hitting the plates, added to the hum.

She approached the bar and waved to get the bartender's attention. He thankfully saw her and came over right away. "What can I get you, sweetheart?" he asked with a smile.

Cara became less grateful, but kept her face straight so she could leave as soon as possible. "Where's the manager?" she asked.

"Something wrong with your drink?"

"I didn't order anything. I have a delivery from Papa's Secret."

"Victoria's Secret delivers now?"

"Papa's Secret," she shouted over the increasing din. "The brewery!"

"I know, I heard you. I was making a joke." The bartender grinned. Cara remained stone-faced. He shrugged. "Guess delivery girls don't have a sense of humor."

"I do when the jokes are funny."

"Man, you've got sass. Want me to get you a drink, temper that a bit —"

"Will you please get me your manager?"

"Fine." He walked off. Cara calmed herself by imagining him walking behind her truck as she pulled out of the parking lot at top speed.

The manager, another man but a less talkative one, met her with a nod and then a handshake. They walked out to her truck and the silence outside was music to her ears. He helped her get the keg, walked with her inside, and set it down in the back without a word. He didn't speak until he waved and said, "Thanks honey."

She'd even take an unwarranted honey in exchange for silence. She nodded and walked back out into the bar. It had somehow grown louder. Barks of laughter became roars. Cara could hear glasses being drained and pitchers hitting the table. A table in the corner was filled to the brim with men, and one of them yelled, "Get a pitcher for the birthday boy!" They laughed. Others spoke, their voices a blur that rang in her ears. The bartender caught Cara's eye and winked.

Cara needed to leave before she felt the urge to do things for which there were too many witnesses. She sped towards the exit, towards the quiet night outside that would get even quieter when she was in her truck and heading back to Leslie. Cara sighed with relief the moment she was outside. The only thing missing from her exhalation was smoke. She opened her purse and dug around for her pack. All she felt was her lighter.

She suddenly remembered smoking her last cigarette the night before, the empty carton burning in the fire by the lake. With everything on her to-do list, from work to deliveries to cleaning her truck that morning, she'd forgotten to buy more cigarettes. "Fuck!" she spat as she zipped her purse in a huff.

"Lose something?"

The last fucking thing she needed was someone else talking to her. She turned, then softened when she saw someone smiling at her behind an unlit cigarette.

A man stood alone against the side of the restaurant. He was young, maybe her age, maybe a little older; with dark brown hair that would've faded into the shadows behind him if not for the bangs hanging over his forehead. His expression was kind but bemused, a mixture of finding her frustration amusing but also genuinely wondering what was wrong. She mostly saw this in his eyes, which were dark and yet glinted with mirth. She caught a better glimpse of him as he lit his cigarette, and she found herself trying to see what color his eyes were in the orange glow of the lighter's flame.

Cara realized she was staring instead of speaking. She smiled and tried to play things cool so she wouldn't sound smitten. "Out of something," she said. "Cigarettes."

He took a long drag, one that Cara knew was meant to tease her. Even so, she couldn't get upset, not when she saw how his lips pressed gently on the end, then how they puckered when he blew out the smoke. Cara didn't know what she wanted more, his mouth or his cigarette.

"Tough break," he said, speaking around a puff of smoke.

Cara moved a little closer to him. She saw his eyes flit down to her collar, then right back up. "You wouldn't happen to have a spare, would you?" she asked as she crossed her arms just enough to give her some cleavage. He wasn't the only one who could tease someone with something they obviously wanted.

He kept his eyes on hers as he reached into his back pocket. Cara could almost see the muscles in his eyes straining to keep their gaze up. She tried not to laugh.

"I might," he said, producing a silver cigarette case. He opened it, and his smile fell as he turned the empty case towards her. "Then again …"

Cara felt a wave of disappointment, but less over the cigarette than for losing an excuse to stay in his company. "Shit. I was looking forward to smoking with you."

He smiled at her again, the slyness returning to his eyes; and a rush of tingles swam from her hips to between her legs. He held out his cigarette.

"You still could," he said. "If you wanted to."

————

His name was Jackson, he was 27, and he'd moved to Raleigh from Pinesboro almost three years ago. That was all she got to know about him, as he spent most of their shared cigarette asking her questions. By the time the cigarette was a nub passed between their fingers, he knew her name, her age, that she worked at a brewery, and that she lived on a farm out in Leslie. "Leslie?" Jackson asked. "Where's that?"

"Way past here," Cara said. "Middle of nowhere."

"Ah, I'm familiar with nowhere. Lived there for nineteen years."

"Is that why you're here now?"

"Yes." They both chuckled, and Cara was about to take a drag when she noticed that it would be the final one.

"Take it," Jackson said, nodding towards the cigarette.

"It's your cigarette, though."

"Go ahead. It'd live a better life if it died with you."

"Huh, that's … kind of pretty, actually."

Jackson shrugged, and Cara was surprised to see him look a little sheepish — and further surprised by how much that turned her on. "I have some good words when I put my mind to it," he said.

Cara took one last drag, then dropped the cigarette to the ground. "Well, the cigarette's gone, but do you think you'd want to share a beer?" she asked. She'd brave the din of Sylvester's if she could sit inside with Jackson — especially if it meant sitting inside of her truck with him afterward.

Jackson hesitated, and Cara wondered if she'd misread him completely — or worse, if their conversation changed the thoughts he'd had about her when she was just someone to look at. "I mean, I figured it'd be nice to keep talking," she continued, even though talking was the last thing on her mind.

"Oh no, it would," Jackson said quickly. "I'd really like to, but —"

"Hey Jack!" The shout came from behind Cara. She turned around and saw a man in a Tar Heels hat and a rumpled Godsmack shirt amble through the door. "Jack," he repeated when he turned and saw them both.

"Jackson," he replied curtly.

"Jackson," the man said without missing a beat, "you done smoking, man? James wants another round."

"Yeah, I'll be in in a minute."

The man smiled at Cara, but before he could say anything, Jackson said, "Goodbye, Steve."

Steve shrugged, then ambled back inside. Cara turned back to face Jackson, and she held in the laugh that had formed the minute she saw Steve when she saw how humiliated Jackson looked. "What, you think I wouldn't enjoy drinking with Steve?" Cara teased.

"*I* don't enjoy drinking with Steve. I don't know how anyone does, really." Jackson laughed a little. "But he's my coworker's friend, and we're all here for my coworker's birthday."

"Gotcha."

"So as much as I'd rather stay with you, I don't think you'd want a beer with me, Steve, and a bunch of guys like Steve sitting around a table pounding pitchers of Bud."

"I understand." Cara remembered seeing that table, and knew that leaving would be the best thing for her sanity and for their throats, even if it meant leaving Jackson behind. "I should probably get going anyway. I don't want Mom worrying about me."

"Your mom?" Jackson smiled at her. "She keeping tabs on you or something?"

"No, I still live with her." Cara didn't share her home life with men, mostly because it didn't come up. Now that it had, she felt oddly embarrassed — a feeling she didn't like at all.

"Hey, that's nothing to be embarrassed about."

"Who says I'm embarrassed?"

"Your face."

Cara looked down, but felt a small smile cross her lips in spite of herself. She was a little unnerved at how quickly he not only got her to tell him things about herself, but at how quickly he made her feel okay with that. Still, it was better than feeling embarrassed.

"Well, I would like to have a drink with you sometime," Jackson said. Cara looked back up. She felt a dueling sense of wanting to keep him at a distance so she could leave, and a pricking at her hands to take him by the jacket and bring his mouth to hers more closely than a shared cigarette ever could. "Somewhere without Steve," he added with a grin.

Cara chuckled. "I'd like that too."

"How about Sara's Glass, on Friday night? It's quieter there, and they let you smoke inside."

"That sounds good — though I liked being able to smoke outside with just you tonight."

"We still can. I'll want some time alone with you for sure."

Cara would too. She wanted that now, and she tried not to squeeze her thighs or curl her fingers at the thought of running her hands all over his skin as she straddled him inside of her truck.

"Well, in the meantime —" Jackson pulled a cell phone out of his pocket — "can I get your phone number?"

Cara furrowed her brow. She wasn't used to exchanging numbers, mostly because she saw men the same night she met them and had no need for further contact. "I'll see you Friday, right?"

"Yeah, but you know, just in case anything comes up." He smiled at her. "Or in case I just want to call you."

His smile, she learned, could bring forth words like a whistle could bring forth birds. Cara recited her number, then asked for his. She cursed under her breath when she remembered her phone was in the truck.

"It's okay," Jackson said as he pulled one more item out of his pocket. "I can do this the old-fashioned way."

Cara drove home alone, but with a smile on her face; one her mother could see even with just one lamp on in the living room. "You're home late," Delores said as she set down her magazine. She gave Cara a sly smile. "Got another souvenir?"

"Not tonight," Cara said. None she'd show Delores. She walked up the stairs, fingering the rumpled receipt that contained Jackson's scribbled phone number.

CHAPTER 5

Cara woke up the next morning thinking of Jackson. Her dreams hadn't held him — any she remembered were flickers of roads driven or trees she walked by, destined to fade with each moment awake — but as her eyes fluttered open and she turned off her alarm, she found her thoughts fixing on the image of Jackson leaning against the wall of Sylvester's and smiling at her as he smoked.

He had a strange hold on her, even though she'd known him less than twelve hours. She had a few explanations for this already. He was kind. He was funny. He had a nice voice. He was handsome. God, he was handsome.

But Cara had known plenty of men who were all those things. Jackson was a little bit more, and Cara could only explain it in how he made her feel. She'd felt a crackling between them the moment their eyes met, and with each word they spoke, she'd gotten a sense that the crackle was different, one that could result in a slow, lingering burn as opposed to the burst of flame that she usually got when she hooked up with a man.

That didn't mean she didn't want that burst. She wanted it. In fact, she ached for it. Cara was certain that some of the sexual energy that Jackson gave off was intentional on his part, but she also suspected that some of it was just his manner, just the air that surrounded him as he gifted someone with his presence. It didn't matter if he gave someone a sly glance and a matching smile, or if he chuckled softly as he did something as mundane as pulling out his lighter. It would make someone want him.

Cara wanted him, and she wanted him as soon as possible. She remembered his phone number in her jeans pocket, remembered his fingers grazing hers as they passed a cigarette back and forth. She remembered him as she dipped her fingers into her panties. She couldn't wait, and until their date tomorrow night, her memories of him would suffice.

————

Cara missed her mother before she left for work. She found a blueberry muffin and a note on the table: *Please get me some aspirin on your way home.* Cara pocketed the note as she grabbed the muffin and headed to work.

It wasn't a delivery day, so Cara did her best to find solitary corners in the brewery. It was in the middle of a field surrounded by woods, and Cara offered to set up — and clean — animal traps on the outskirts. She also found errands to run, any excuse to stay on the periphery of her coworkers. "We could use some canning supplies," Keith said as the afternoon grew late. "You can bring them in tomorrow if you want to take off after getting them."

Cara nodded and felt relief once she was in her truck. She drove to the supply store in Durham to buy some time before going home. It still wasn't enough. She got off the highway in Raleigh, drove up and down the roads surrounding the fairgrounds and NC State's campus even though she had nowhere to go. She knew she'd be going for a drive that night, could feel it in her bones the moment Keith gave her an errand. Nothing far, and nothing which would give her something to hide; but just a chance to disappear for an hour or two before going home.

She remembered the errand her mother had given her, and decided to do that before she got back on the highway and became lost in her journey. She drove until she saw a Walgreens, then pulled into the parking lot.

Cara squinted in the glare of the fluorescents as she walked inside. She lowered her baseball cap over her eyes and walked in silence, grabbing her mother's aspirin and adding a few items of her own. Once her basket was full — due in no small part to an abundance of Reese's products — she wandered up and down the aisles, waiting for the line up front to dwindle so she wouldn't have to stand between a bunch of people. She made a mental note to not forget to buy cigarettes once she checked out. The night ahead held a drive, candy, and smoking. Nothing could make it better.

"Cara?"

Cara figured she was hearing things — she didn't know anyone in Raleigh. If she was hearing things, she figured it was probably time to be alone in her truck. She turned towards the cash register and decided to brave the line.

She was two people away from being able to leave when a sound she'd never heard before — and thus couldn't imagine — rang from her pocket. It was a single chime, and Cara furrowed her brow as she took her cell phone out of her pocket. She saw that she had something she'd only heard the man at the cell phone store mention: a text message.

Her curiosity became delight when she saw that it was Jackson. She flipped open her phone and read his text: *You in Walgreens?*

Cara kicked herself for ignoring her name. It'd been him calling her, and she could be talking to him instead of waiting in line to spend the evening alone in her truck in the middle of nowhere. She looked around but saw no sign of him. Cara typed carefully and hoped her slowness didn't mean that he'd be halfway down the road by the time she reached him: *Yes where r u.*

"You gonna move forward or what?"

Cara looked behind her and saw a short elderly woman sneering up at her. Cara narrowed her eyes and said nothing. She didn't need to. The elderly woman kept her sneer, but Cara saw a flash of fear in her eyes. Cara smirked as she got out of line to let the woman move ahead.

Being out of line still didn't bring Jackson into view. She wondered how he could disappear as quickly as his call rang in her ears. Had he seen her on his way outside? Did they just keep missing each other in the aisles?

A single chime answered her questions. Cara almost dropped her basket as she flipped open her phone and saw his message: *Pharmacy.*

Cara walked as quickly to the pharmacy as she could without looking harried. She was excited to see Jackson, but knew enough about dating to know when excitement crossed over from flattering to off-putting. Her first view amidst aisles of aspirin and band aids was of no one, and she wondered briefly if he was on his way. It was brief because, when her eyes fell on a white countertop and shelves of other people's medicine behind it, she saw Jackson.

"Hey!" she said. Her grin widened beyond her control, but she no longer cared. Either way, Jackson didn't seem to mind.

"Good to see you," he replied. "I thought that was you wandering around, but I didn't want to keep calling your name and creep out a stranger."

"What are you doing here?" she asked. It was out of habit, and she couldn't catch it in time before embarrassing herself. Jackson stood behind the counter and wore a white lab coat with his name printed on a plastic tag. He looked down at his sleeves, then looked back up at her with an expression that kindly asked if she was serious.

"I've been pretending to work here to get free codeine," he said with a smile. "But don't tell anyone, you'll blow my cover."

"Yeah, yeah." Cara rolled her eyes, but laughed a little as she did so. "I didn't know you were a pharmacist."

"Yup. Been one for four years now."

"And you smoke?"

Jackson laughed, and Cara wanted to pluck it from her ears and let it weave through her fingers like soft linen. "We all need a vice," he said.

"Just one?"

"At least. Why, do you have more than one?"

"None I share without dinner first." And others she'd never share at all. Still, she felt a strange sensation to share more than usual as they flirted under the fluorescents. He was more clearly in view than he'd been the night before, and Cara took the opportunity to take him in. He mostly looked the same, even in his work clothes and with his hair brushed back. It was his eyes that struck her the most. They were brown, flecked with hazel and encircled by an amber ring. They looked like a cave in a blinding desert, one whose darkness beckoned to Cara the more she stared.

A voice behind her, though, pulled her right back out. "Excuse me."

Cara turned as Jackson looked over her shoulder. She saw a woman smiling with dwindling patience.

"Can I get my prescription refilled before you close?" the woman asked.

"Sure," Jackson replied. "Carson, right?"

"Right."

"It'll be ready in ten minutes if you want to wait over there," Jackson added as he gestured to the side.

"Thanks. I'll just shop and come back." The woman walked away, and Cara knew that she should do the same. "I'll let you get back to work," she said.

"I guess I do have a job to do," he replied with a playful shrug.

"So I'll see you tomorrow?"

"Actually —"

"You're not cancelling on me already, are you?" Cara teased, though her heart did a quick and panicked jump at the thought that he might be.

"No, the opposite. I get off work in twenty minutes. If you don't mind waiting, I'd love to hang out with you."

"Really?"

"Yeah, if you're not busy. Otherwise we can meet up to-morrow —"

"I can hang out tonight."

"Great! I didn't drive in today, but we could walk some-where —"

"I can drive you if you want. I don't mind."

"Sure, that'd be good. I'll wrap up here soon and then I'll find you."

"Sounds good. I'll wait for you outside."

"Great. Maybe we can get dinner." Jackson smiled slyly as he moved to get the woman's pills. "I want to know more about those vices."

"Sure. I'll tell you a few," Cara teased.

"It's the ones you can show me that I want to know about." He turned and walked away. Cara was grateful his back was turned and that he couldn't see her cheeks grow-ing warm. She remembered her unpurchased wares and walked back towards the checkout line, adding a box of condoms to her basket on the way there.

———

Cara leaned against her truck. Her only company was people getting into cars and a man against the wall, who spoke on his phone in a low voice before hanging up and staring ahead into nothing. She forced herself to not smoke as she waited outside. She wanted to wait and smoke with Jackson. She was going to be with Jackson that night. She'd been thinking about him all day, and now he was here. She'd have to thank her mother for needing aspirin.

Cara paused at the thought of her mother. She wondered if she should call her and let her know she'd be late. She

frowned a little at the thought of having to explain why —
that she was going out with a pharmacist she'd tried to pick
up the night before outside of a bar, and while she didn't
know if she'd be out very late, she had a strong feeling she
would be.

Jackson exited the pharmacy, and all thoughts of her
mother disappeared. "Over here," Cara called as she waved.

Jackson turned towards her, then smiled as he began to
walk over. Before he reached her, though, he noticed the
man standing against the wall. "James?" he called. The man
looked up, and Cara wondered if this was the same James
whose birthday had delayed her and Jackson getting a drink
at Sylvester's the night before.

James smiled, but only a little. "Hey Jackson."

"I thought you took off already."

"I did, but my mom called me on the way out."

"How's she doing?"

"She …" James' already-faint smile disappeared completely. "Dad died. This morning."

Cara's eyes widened, and Jackson froze completely.
James continued, "It was peaceful — it was during a nap,
and at home, but …"

James looked down and took a breath. Jackson touched
his elbow and gave it a squeeze. "I'm sorry," he said. Cara
heard a crack in his voice.

"Thanks." James looked up, then glanced over at Cara
before looking back at Jackson. "I should probably go," he
said. "I probably won't be in tomorrow."

"I can tell Riya," Jackson said. "Just take care of yourself
and your mom."

"Thanks. I'll email Riya with my leave schedule and the funeral details and all that, but …" James swallowed, and Jackson squeezed his arm again. "I'll be okay," James added with a nod. "I just need to go home."

"Are you sure?"

"Yeah. It's hard, but — well, we knew this day was coming. It was just a matter of when." James removed his arm from Jackson's hold, then nodded at him. "Have a good night."

"Thanks. Call me if you need anything."

James nodded, then turned and walked to the other side of the lot. Cara watched him leave, then looked at Jackson. She was about to ask if he was ready to go, but stopped when she saw him standing with his eyes closed. His hands were in his pockets, but she could see through the fabric that they were clenched. He took slow, long breaths, ones that sounded more like he was scared than sad.

"I'm … I'm sorry," Cara said. She knew it wasn't Jackson's father who had died, but she didn't know what else to say.

Jackson opened his eyes and looked up at her. He seemed to be noticing her for the first time that night.

He smiled a little. The fear and pain slowly disappeared from his eyes. "Thanks," he said. "For James, I mean. He … his dad had been sick for awhile, but …"

"I'm sure it's still hard."

"It's hard for him, yeah."

It seemed hard for Jackson as well, but Cara decided not to mention that — especially when Jackson appeared to have calmed down.

Jackson walked towards her, then paused. Cara wondered if maybe he hadn't calmed after all, and prepared herself to hide her disappointment if their date was put off yet again.

"This is your car?" he asked.

Cara nodded towards the truck. "Yup."

"It runs?"

She laughed as she realized the source of his hesitation. "I know it looks like a piece of shit, but yes — it runs, and runs well."

"If you say so."

"I know so. I drive it all over North Carolina making beer deliveries. Hasn't broken down yet."

Jackson smiled — a full one, one without sadness — and Cara warmed at seeing him happy again. "So naturally, it'll break down in the middle of nowhere tonight and we'll have to 'keep warm' while we wait for hours for a tow truck, right?"

"If you're promising me hours, we can 'break down' in the parking lot."

"Let's get away from where I work at least. Kind of a mood killer." Jackson's stomach interrupted them with a small growl. "As is hunger."

"Let's get some takeout. And I know a great place to get away from more than just work."

"I like it — and I'll buy."

———

Cara drove down the road, two bags of Cook Out between them on the seats. They ate their burgers, listened to music, and talked about their workdays. Apart from the news that Jackson received from James — news that Cara was careful not to bring up — they'd both had a mundane day, one that, for Cara's part, would be significantly improved by the promised evening ahead.

She pulled onto the banks of Lake Hollow and saw with relief that no one else was there. "I like coming here after long days," she said as she turned off the truck. "I just sit and smoke and stare at the water."

"Sounds nice." Jackson pulled out his cigarette case and took out two cigarettes.

"Oh, I bought cigarettes," she said.

"You'll get the next round, then." Jackson placed both in his mouth before she could protest. He lit them, then handed one to her as he smoked the other.

Cara took it with a smile. "Cigarettes and hush puppies. You know how to treat a girl on a date."

Jackson smiled back as he lifted out his fries. "I do my best." The truck soon became a haze of smoke and grease, a combination that Cara found rather delicious. She smoked with one hand and ate her hush puppies with the other.

"So did you come here a lot in high school or something?" Jackson asked as he ate his fries. "Seems like a spot where you'd find a lot of kids parking."

"I talked about me during yesterday's cigarette. Talk to me about you."

"What do you want to know?"

"More. I know your name is Jackson and that you moved here from Pinesboro. I only know you work at Walgreens because I ran into you." Jackson chuckled, and Cara asked with a smile, "Why'd you move away from Pinesboro? What'd you do there?"

"Nothing, really." Jackson leaned back, setting aside his uneaten fries and focusing more on his cigarette. "I lived in Pinesboro most of my life, which is about as boring as it sounds. Not much to do except go to church, help take care of my grandma before she died, hang out with my friends, and go to college."

"Where'd you go?"

"NC State. It's why I moved back here again after going to Pinesboro after graduation. I liked Raleigh more."

"More friends here or something?"

"It's just better than Pinesboro. I don't have a lot of close friends here, actually; but I don't mind that."

"What about James?"

Jackson looked down, but before Cara could apologize and change the subject, he said, "Yeah, he's a good guy."

"Is he your best friend or something?"

"No. My best friend lives in Pinesboro. James and I are just work friends."

Cara thought of Jackson's sorrow upon James' news, and the way he'd held James' arm. She was work friends with Keith, and she wasn't sure if she'd ever feel as close to him as Jackson seemed to feel with James. "You guys just seemed pretty close for work friends," she observed.

Jackson appeared uncomfortable, and Cara decided not to press. Before she could change the subject though, Jackson said, "Well, if I'm being honest, we were pretty close before. We ... James and I used to date."

Cara's eyes widened before she could stop them. Jackson looked away, and Cara quickly touched his elbow. "I'm just a little surprised," she said. "I didn't know you liked guys."

"You did say you wanted to know more about me." Jackson laughed, but it disappeared as quickly as it came. "But yeah," he said. "I'm bisexual."

Cara nodded. "Okay."

"Okay?"

"Yeah. Okay. You like guys and girls." Jackson raised his eyebrows, and Cara smiled. "I know what bisexual is — I'm not that backwoods."

"Oh, it's not that," Jackson said with another small laugh, but one that lasted a little longer than before. "You just reacted better to hearing that on a first date than some people do on the fifth — or even just some people in general."

"People in Pinesboro?"

"People here too, but yeah, definitely in Pinesboro. I kept pretty quiet about it around there. Still do here — it takes some getting used to, knowing who I can tell and who I want to tell."

"You told me pretty quickly."

"I felt comfortable telling you. I feel pretty comfortable right now — more than I usually do around new people." Jackson smiled at her. Cara realized her hand was still on his arm. His own hand, though, stayed on his leg. She removed her hand, but only after giving him a gentle squeeze.

"Well, I'm glad you feel comfortable," she said. "I know the evening didn't start too great."

"What do you mean?"

"Well, hearing that your ex's father died … I mean, it was sad news, and I knew why it upset you, but now I understand more why it upset you so much."

Jackson stared out over the dashboard, watching the lake as he smoked in silence. Cara looked down at her hands. "I'm sorry," she said. "I shouldn't have brought it up —"

"That's not why it upset me."

Cara looked back up. Jackson added, "I mean, that was part of it, but … it upset me because news like that reminds me of Pinesboro."

Cara furrowed her brow. "Pinesboro?"

"Yeah." He sighed, letting out a stream of smoke as he did so. "Going back to Pinesboro after graduation reminded me why I left. It was full of something that I could see more starkly than I thought I could in a bigger place like Raleigh."

"What?"

"Death."

Cara watched Jackson in silence.

"Pinesboro reeked of death as far back as I can remember," Jackson said. "Ever since I was a little kid. My grandma lived with us, and my only memories of her are of her being sick. She had an oxygen tank, she barely walked, she coughed after every other word. She died when I was eight, and I wasn't even surprised. But she wasn't the only one. Our town was full of death. Our neighbor beat his wife into a coma, and she never woke up. People OD'd, people committed suicide, people got cancer … people died, and while I know people die everywhere, it seemed like everywhere I turned in Pinesboro, someone was falling into their grave." Jackson stubbed out his cigarette, and Cara noticed that his hands shook a little as he did so. "And I really, really didn't want to be a part of that. So, I came back here — somewhere people blended together, and where the deaths stayed anonymous and out of bored, gossiping mouths. Somewhere I could keep it at bay — or at least, keep it from my doorstep. As best as I can, anyway. I'm not sure I can even do that."

Cara continued to watch him in silence, breaking her stare only to take one last drag before her cigarette became nothing but ash. She had thoughts on death, many thoughts — namely how it was nothing to fear, and how it was both something she could control and a way she could control other people and their whispers. She knew better than to say so.

Cara needed to remember not to say so, because she felt a strange pull to say something to Jackson. Not everything, of course, but just a piece, a little piece of her that made her feel better in the hopes that it would make him feel better too. She wanted to comfort him, even if that meant opening up to him. She'd never felt that way before — and was disconcerted to feel it now.

Jackson sighed a little, which pulled Cara out of her thoughts. "Not the best opening conversation, right?"

"No, it's not that," Cara said. "It's just … that was really honest."

"Yeah, and really dark. I'm sorry —"

"Don't be. It's fine."

"I'm normally much better at what to talk about on first dates."

"But you said earlier you were pretty comfortable. Maybe it's better you're talking about what you want to instead of what you think I want to hear."

Jackson finally smiled. "You really want to hear about all my irrational fears?"

Cara smiled back. "Sure. For all you know, it's a huge turn-on for me."

Jackson gave her a playful, sexy look; one that Cara only registered as sexy. "I'm also afraid of mice," he said in a low voice that poured over her body like a warm shower after a walk in the snow.

"Ooh," Cara teased in an effort to quell her growing arousal. She walked her fingers up his arm. "Are you afraid they'll crawl on you?"

"I'm afraid they'll bite. I got bit when I was four and tried to play with one I found in the backyard. My mistake for picking it up."

"You just gotta know how to hold them when you pick them up."

Jackson laughed a little, and a sheepish expression crossed his face. Like the night before, his expression turned Cara on even more. "If I say something about knowing how to hold you after picking you up, you'll just dump me in the lake and drive off, right?"

Cara laughed as well. "I'd be tempted to, but no. I think I picked *you* up, though."

"I got your attention yesterday, and shared my cigarette with you."

"I asked you for a cigarette, and drove you here today."

"Okay, we'll call it even."

Cara glanced at her hand, which still rested on his shoulder. "It's not even in who's holding who, though," she said as she moved her fingers closer to his neck.

Jackson scooted closer and moved one arm to the seat behind her. Before Cara could say that didn't count, he circled his other arm around her waist. His fingers moved up and down the small of her back in gentle strokes.

"How's that?" he asked.

"Better," she replied.

Jackson lifted his hand and cupped her cheek. Cara tried not to close her eyes as he touched her. He moved his thumb towards her mouth and traced it over her bottom lip.

"Do you bite?" he asked.

Cara knew it was an invitation, not a question. She smiled, then gently nipped him. Jackson closed his eyes and breathed deeply.

"Do you do more than hold the people you pick up?" Cara asked.

Jackson opened his eyes and leaned closer to her. She barely had the chance to tilt her head before he kissed her. She cupped his cheek and did what she'd wanted to do since she saw him smoking the night before.

Cara didn't bother to kiss him gently at first. She flicked his lips with her tongue, savoring each little taste she received while kissing him deeper, harder, and more closely with each movement. Jackson kissed her back in kind, pulling her close by her waist before running his hands up her back. He broke her kisses with his tongue, and she savored that as well, holding him close as she straddled him. Jackson took off her hat and threw it in the back. His hands became entangled in her hair, hers in his, and they kissed over and over while his hands unraveled themselves from her hair and made her way to her breasts.

Jackson broke away from her with a gasp. "Wait," he breathed.

"Why?" Cara leaned forward to kiss the top of his head. Doing so brought the skin exposed by her shirt collar against his cheek, and he leaned against her. "I want you."

"I want you too. Jesus God, I want you." He succumbed to her skin, kissing her neck and collar line. Cara grabbed her jacket, and Jackson enclosed her hands, stopping her before she could remove it.

"But the minute you take off your clothes, I'm going to want you in this truck," he said with a smile, the same mischievous smile that made Cara want him so much. "And I've got a bed at home that would be a lot more comfortable." Cara laughed, then sighed as Jackson nibbled her earlobe. "You want to come home with me?" he whispered.

"That depends. How far away is your house?"

"An apartment. It's small, and a bit of a mess since I wasn't expecting anyone tonight —"

"It could be a condemned shack in the woods for all I care, so long as I can fuck you inside of it in under fifteen minutes." Cara cupped her hand around his stiffened cock, and Jackson breathed deeply. Cara moved her lips to his ear and whispered, "I've wanted to do this since yesterday, and I'm tired of waiting. How far away is it?"

"About fifteen minutes. Ten if you speed."

Cara slid off of him and started up the truck.

———

The drive to Jackson's place took a little less than ten minutes. Cara slammed the door when she got out, and her speed walk towards his building was only slowed by Jackson grabbing her and beginning to kiss her again. He pressed her against the truck, and they kissed over and over, Cara's hands tangled in his hair and Jackson's hands going further and further up her shirt.

They slowly moved towards his apartment, taking turns between kissing each other and watching where they were going. They only stopped kissing when they reached his door, and even then, Jackson kept his arms around her as he unlocked it.

They started up again as soon as they got inside, slowing down to relish every kiss and every touch. Their jackets fell to the floor. Cara flicked her tongue across Jackson's lips, then gripped his ass through his jeans before sliding her hands across his chest and back.

"So," she said in a playful whisper. "Tell me, Doctor …" Her voice trailed as she tried to remember his name tag. "… whatever your last name is …"

Jackson smiled as he kissed her. "Price."

"Tell me, Doctor Price: what would you prescribe for my condition?"

"No one calls me Doctor Price."

"Come on, work with me." They both laughed and kissed as they moved through the living room. Jackson lowered himself on the couch before Cara could suggest they skip the bed and fuck there instead. "Besides," she said as she straddled him, "Pharmacist Price doesn't really roll off the tongue."

"So show me what does," he said as he pulled her down by her shirt.

"Doctor Price …" She traced his lips with her tongue before kissing him. "Jackson Price …" She brushed her lips across his cheek. "Jackson …" She moved towards his ear, and he sighed as her lips touched his earlobe. "Jack …"

"Please don't call me that."

She felt his body stiffen a little as he spoke. "You don't like that?" she asked as she kissed his temple.

"No." Still, he relaxed with her kiss.

"No nicknames?" She kissed his forehead. "Not even Doctor Jack?"

Jackson placed his fingers on her lips. While he looked at her with kindness, Cara saw a flicker of warning in his eyes.

"Please don't call me that," he repeated.

Cara smiled against his fingers and hoped he didn't see her confusion about why it was such a big deal. She'd just wanted to have some fun, to tease him a little. But she wanted him more than she wanted either of those things. "Okay," she promised, taking his hand and kissing his fingers. "I won't, Jackson."

He smiled, all warning and annoyance gone from his face. "It's Doctor Price," he said. Cara giggled, then sighed as Jackson pulled her close and began to kiss the tops of her breasts. "And as for your condition, Miss …"

"Vineyard."

"Miss Vineyard." He paused from kissing her. "Cara Vineyard?"

There was no way in hell Jackson had heard about her all the way out in Pinesboro. Cara tried to stop herself from spiraling into assumptions on how he'd heard her name before. "Yes," she said.

"That's a beautiful name."

Her spiral slowed, and she relaxed. "Thank you." Cara kissed a trail from his neck to his chest. "I came to talk to you about my condition, though," she whispered as she unbuttoned his shirt and kissed each new bit of skin that became exposed. "What do you think I should do, Doctor Price?"

"Well, Miss Vineyard —" Jackson gasped a little as she neared the fly of his jeans and kissed his stomach — "I can't tell you what to do until you tell me what you have."

"I'll tell you, then." She rose back up and repositioned herself so that she sat more securely on his lap. "I have this insane, compulsive desire to fuck you."

"I see. When did this start?"

"Last night, when I first saw you." She peeled off her shirt and dropped it to the floor. She kept her eyes locked on his as she unhooked her bra. "It's compulsive ..." She pulled down one bra strap. "It's constant ..." She pulled down the other. "And it's all I want."

She slid off her bra and let it fall from her hands. Seeing the look on Jackson's face in the living room light was worth the wait she'd endured to drive them both there from Lake Hollow. He ran his hands up her waist and ended their journey at her breasts. He cupped them and ran his tongue in circles around her nipples before kissing and sucking them both. Cara sighed with pleasure as she arched back, then leaned forward again to hold him close.

"So tell me, doctor," she whispered. "What should I do?"

Jackson pulled away. He looked up at her, and Cara felt herself weaken under his gaze. He looked like a devil who knew he didn't need to offer any conditions for her soul. He just had to tell her where to sign.

He shifted, and Cara slid off of him, allowing herself to be lowered beneath him. She lifted her hips as he unzipped her jeans and slid them down her thighs. Once they were gone, he moved his hands back up her legs, then back down again over her bare skin. She curled her toes in response to the tingles left in their wake.

"I think I can help you, Miss Vineyard." Jackson slid off his shirt, and Cara breathed in as she touched him. She ran a finger over his chest, his stomach, the scant line of brown hair that disappeared beneath his pants.

He lifted her hand, kissed her knuckles, then released her as he moved his fingers to his belt. "I think you should stay off your feet for the rest of the night." He unhooked the belt and slowly slid it through each loop. "I think your only movement should be touching me, wrapping your legs around me, and kissing every inch of my skin."

"I'll try," Cara said, trying to keep her seductiveness while trying not to become lost in the journey of his belt.

"And I'll try my best to treat you." His eyes stayed locked on hers as he pulled the belt through the last loop with one sharp flick. "I'm going to touch you and taste you, and really look over you so I can see what we're dealing with here."

"I'd appreciate that." Cara curled one leg around him as he dropped his belt on the floor. "I know how thorough you are."

"I need to be thorough to treat the condition you have." He slowly unzipped his fly. "And just so you know —" He pulled down both his pants and his underwear, and Cara didn't even try to keep eye contact with him — "I'll need to get in really deep in order to be able to treat you."

She looked back up at him and smiled. "I'd expect nothing less." She pulled him close and he began to kiss her. Cara wrapped both legs around him and grew even more aroused as his erection brushed against her through her underwear.

"Oh, and one more thing, Miss Vineyard."

"What?" She tried to sound patient, but her interest in anything but fucking Jackson's brains out was disappearing faster than a heavy stone dropped in a pond.

"After we're done, I'm going to insist that you stay overnight for observation."

Cara grinned as Jackson began to slide down her underwear. "Whatever you say, Doctor Price."

CHAPTER 6

Cara and Jackson made it to the bedroom, but only to sleep. Cara fell into his bed, almost dissolving into the comfort of its sheets. Jackson followed right behind and curled against her. She immediately turned and wrapped her arms around him, burying her face into his chest as he pulled her close.

She woke up the next morning removed from Jackson's hold. She turned to face him and watched him sleeping. She gently traced her fingers across his back, careful to avoid the scratches she'd left there the night before.

Jackson rolled onto his back, a motion that made Cara move her hand away. His eyes lifted open. He looked at her, and the faintest of smiles crossed his face.

"I didn't mean to wake you," Cara said.

"It's a nice way to wake up," Jackson replied as he rolled towards her.

A gentle morning kiss took two seconds to become a make out session. Cara wasn't sure how long they'd been entangled by the time his alarm went off, but it was short enough for Jackson to groan and bury his head in his pillow at the sound of it. "You can't call in sick?" Cara teased.

"Not the morning of," Jackson said as he turned off his alarm with a smack. "Not without pictures of me throwing up or something."

"What time do you have to be in?"

"In a couple hours, but the bus comes in an hour and a half."

"You don't have a car?"

"It's in the shop."

"Oh, so you give me shit about my truck when it's your car that needs repairs?" Cara said with a grin. Jackson snorted.

"All cars need maintenance. That truck needs to be put out of its misery."

"It works fine!" They both laughed as they sat up. "Worked fine last night anyway," Cara said as she traced her finger up his arm. Jackson closed his eyes as he shared her memories of the night before.

"You know, I could give you a ride to work if you want," Cara offered. Jackson raised his eyebrows in thought, and Cara kissed his cheek. "If you want to sleep in a little more," she added, tracing her fingers down his chest and landing on his morning wood. Jackson breathed in as she enclosed him in her palm.

"That'd be great," he said, "if you don't mind."

Cara slid over top of him. "Not at all."

———

They showered together afterward, keeping anything physical to just quick kissing sessions under the stream of water. Cara relished the feel of the cold shower tile on her back as hot water soaked them both. They managed to keep it demure for breakfast, likely aided by the fact that they were dressed.

"I can't find your hat," Jackson said as they prepared to leave.

"I think that came off in the truck," Cara replied.

"I thought it came off in here with your jacket." He held her jacket out to her and she took it.

"Well, if it did, I can get it next time. I know you have to go."

Jackson paused on his way out the door. Cara furrowed her brow as she zipped up her jacket. "What?"

"Nothing, just ..." He smiled softly. "You said 'next time' even though we haven't set up a second date yet."

"Oh." Cara looked down and wished she had her hat to cover her warming cheeks. "I mean, I can get it later ..."

"No, you can get it next time. I just liked that you said that without even thinking about it." He moved close to her and held her by her elbows. Cara smiled as he kissed her neck. "No questions about whether or not I'll see you again," he whispered.

"You'll see me again."

"Good." Jackson pulled her closer and added her shoulders to his line of kisses.

"How else can I get my follow-up treatments if I don't?" she added. "I haven't been cured, Doctor Price."

Jackson laughed as he moved back up to her neck and cheek. "We'll set a follow-up right away, Miss Vineyard," he said.

She smiled as he kissed her, but didn't laugh. Good memories of the night before came rushing back, but those memories included the brief moment that things hadn't gone well.

"What's wrong?" Jackson asked as he pulled away.

"Why did it bother you so much last night when I called you Jack?" Cara asked. She hated to say it again, especially when he stiffened a little. "Do you just not like it?"

"I mean, no. People sometimes call me that even though I never introduce myself that way. I say my full name and go by that because that's what I want."

Cara nodded, even though it was an answer that didn't explain his reaction. Jackson seemed to know it. He added, "And it doesn't help that you get characters with that name a lot. My life was a living hell when *Titanic* came out."

Cara chuckled. "I can see that — though don't worry, I'd die before doing any *Titanic* role-playing."

"Wouldn't *Titanic* role-playing require dying?"

"Not if you end it before the ship does."

"Fair." They laughed, and Cara felt satisfied with that answer. She was about to open his door when Jackson said, "It's not that, though."

"I mean, if that's all you want to tell me —"

"No, it's fine. The main reason is that the only person who calls me Jack is my mom."

Cara snorted, and Jackson looked at her curiously. She got the sense too late that he didn't find it as funny as being compared to movie heartthrobs. "I'm sorry," she said. "I just figured it bothered you because when I called you that, it was the last time you'd want to be thinking about your mom."

Jackson laughed a little, and Cara relaxed. "That didn't help," he said. "But even when I'm not having sex, I'd rather not hear people call me what she calls me. We … we don't really get along."

"Okay." Cara wondered if his answer was an understatement, but she didn't want to pry.

"We're not like you and your mom, from the sound of it," Jackson added as they finally walked out the door.

Cara almost froze. Her mother had no idea where she was — and while Cara wasn't sure if her baseball hat was in the truck, she knew that was where she'd left her cell phone.

"Everything okay?" Jackson asked as he glanced back at her. "You look like you forgot something."

"Yeah, it's fine," Cara lied. "I just thought my shift started earlier, but it's actually at ten."

"Lucky you." They got in the truck and Cara stopped herself from checking her phone. She knew it would have a bunch of missed calls and maybe a frantic voicemail. She could deal with those later.

They planned their next date as they drove to Walgreens, deciding once again on Sara's Glass. "Next Friday work for you?" Jackson asked as Cara turned into a parking space.

"Works great," Cara said. It was partially true — she would've been happy to see him tomorrow, or even that night. But she didn't want to push it.

"Perfect. I'll see you then." He leaned forward and kissed her, then kept his lips against hers afterward. "I can't wait," he whispered before kissing her again.

"Me either," she replied before kissing him back. *Why wait?* she wanted to add. But she didn't. Instead, they kissed a few moments more before Jackson slipped out of the truck and disappeared into Walgreens.

————

Cara could almost hear her mother scolding her for using her cell phone while driving, but it wasn't as bad as what she was going to hear on voicemail. Sure enough, when she'd grabbed her cell phone, she saw six missed calls. "Fuck," she breathed.

She waited until she was out of the parking lot before making any calls — she didn't want Jackson to wander back outside and think that she was staking him out — but she knew better than to wait until she was back in Leslie before trying to call the house. She awkwardly dialed her home number once she was further from Raleigh and could talk and drive without dirty looks from other drivers.

Her mother wasn't home — or at least, she wasn't answering. Cara glanced at the clock on her stereo. It was almost 9:30. Delores was probably at work.

Cara waited until she was in the parking lot of Papa's Secret before trying to call her mother's office. Rhonda's cheerful voice zapped Cara's ear like a whistle. "Good morning, Schuster and Sullivan!" she chirped.

"Is Delores there?" Cara asked.

"Cara? Is that you?"

"Yes. Is Delores there?"

"Yeah, I picked your mother up this morning."

"Can I talk to her?"

"She's out getting coffee for the board meeting."

"Oh."

Cara sat in silence. She'd expected to be able to talk to her mother. As she thought about what to do next, she wondered if Rhonda's eternal smile was starting to waver.

"Do you want to leave her a message?" Rhonda offered.

"Yes." Cara blinked and shook her head. "Yes, just — just tell her I'm at work and that I called."

"Sure. Want her to call you back?"

"No, don't worry about that. Just tell her that I called and that I'm back in Leslie."

"Okie dokie! Back in Leslie? Were you on a trip or something?"

"Thanks. Goodbye."

Cara hung up, but not before she heard "Bye, Cara!" trill from her phone. She wondered if her mother's sour mood each day after work was due to sharing space in Rhonda's tiny VW Bug to and from the office.

Even if Rhonda talked Delores' ear off on the way home, Cara knew that anything Delores felt that evening would be because of Cara. Cara frowned as she got out of the car. Even though Delores would likely demand to know what happened last night, likely yell and huff about where she was and why she hadn't been back at the farm at a decent hour, Cara wouldn't yield. Where she was, what she did, and who she spent her evening with was her business.

Thankfully, she could start the morning with people who minded their own. "Morning Cara," Keith said as he walked out of the parking lot with a keg in hand. "Ready to make some deliveries?"

"Yes," Cara replied; and only she knew how much of an understatement that was.

"Awesome. I don't have you going too far today —" Cara tried not to let her shoulders drop too much — "but I've got you going to a lot of places in the Triangle. Kegs *and* cans today."

"Perfect." Keith disappeared back inside as Sadie came out with a stack of six-packs. Sadie smiled at her. Cara nodded, but followed Keith inside before Sadie could start talking to her.

Her truck was loaded to the brim with beer, to the point where packs were in the back seat and passenger side. "Oh hey, you lose your hat?" Keith asked as he ducked back out of the truck, her discarded baseball hat in hand.

"Oh. Right. Yeah." Cara took it and put it back on.

"Thought you looked different today," Keith said with a grin as he walked back inside. Cara tried to laugh, but it came out more like a cough.

"That's complete bullshit," Sadie said. Cara turned to face her. She stood by the driver's side door, and Cara knew Sadie wouldn't let her leave without a little conversation. "Keith didn't notice you looking different. He just noticed the hat."

"So?" Cara asked as she put it back on.

"So, if he actually *did* notice anything, it'd be that you're wearing the exact same clothes as yesterday." Sadie grinned as Cara looked at her shoes. "Meet someone in Raleigh yesterday?"

"I need to make the deliveries." What Cara needed more, though, was for Sadie to mind her own business. She pursed her lips as she busied herself with the cans in an attempt to send Sadie away.

Sadie didn't budge. "It's 10:15," she said. "You've got all morning. Talk to me about last night. Who was he?"

"Can we talk later? I can't work as late tonight as I did yesterday."

"I bet you can't. Did you even sleep?" Sadie laughed and Cara looked up with a glare.

"Why do you care so much?" Cara asked.

Sadie stopped laughing. "I'm just making conversation."

A conversation where she was the butt of a joke — just like most of her conversations at school. Cara frowned as she remembered the words of others. "It's always about my sex life, though. Why don't you talk to me about anything else?"

"I don't know anything else about you. You want to talk to me about deliveries or your farm or something?"

"I'd like to talk about something where you're not making fun of me."

"I'm not making —"

"You are. You always laugh and grin at me like I've done something wrong when there's any possibility I went out with a guy. I fuck after work, okay? It's not a big deal."

Sadie's smile fell, and Cara turned to face her truck. "I should go —"

"Wait, just real quick before you go."

Cara paused, but stayed facing the truck.

"I'm not trying to embarrass you. I'm sorry. I was teasing you but not because I think what you're doing is wrong. I thought we were just having fun."

"How is it fun?"

"I don't know, because at work you're so quiet and just going about your business, and then you drive off somewhere and fuck a guy and then come back and act like it's all part of your day. It's kind of cool. I wish I could do that."

"You could if you wanted to."

Sadie laughed again, but this time, she sounded embarrassed. Cara glanced at her. "Maybe. But I wasn't trying to be mean, really."

"Okay." Cara could never be sure — Sadie teased more than she spoke — but believing Sadie meant she could get going sooner.

"Some friendly advice, though?" Sadie added.

"What?"

Sadie smiled and pointed at Cara's neck. "If you don't want to get teased at work the morning after, at least make an effort to cover up the bite marks before you show up."

Cara whipped her head towards the sideview mirror and saw a purple welt beneath her ear. Sadie chuckled as she walked away. Cara watched her leave in the mirror and sighed with relief.

————

Cara got home in time for dinner, but waited a few minutes before going in. She knew her mother would read her the riot act the minute she walked inside. It didn't matter if she was sixteen or twenty-two — being scolded by her mother always made Cara feel as small as when she was five.

Cara walked inside and smelled hamburgers. "Hey Mom," she called. Part of her hoped her mother couldn't hear her over the skillet's sizzle.

"Hi," Delores called back. Curt, but not angry. Cara walked into the kitchen. Delores kept her back turned.

"Dinner smells good," Cara said, smiling weakly even though her mother couldn't see.

"Figured you'd want something filling after a long day — and night."

Cara knew she wouldn't get off so easily. Delores turned off the burner, then placed the burgers on two plates beside her that already held waiting buns and a mound of potato chips. Cara stood up to take them, but Delores nodded towards the table as she turned around. "Sit down," she said. "I've got it."

Cara did as she was told, and forced herself to wait to eat before Delores joined her. Delores took her time finding ketchup and mustard, then brought them to the table and slowly dressed her burger. Cara tried not to roll her eyes at Delores making her wait. It was better than being grilled.

At last, Delores began to eat. Cara watched her as she ate some chips.

Delores wiped her fingers, but kept her eyes on her food.

"I know you're an adult," Delores said with a voice Cara knew she was struggling to keep steady. "And even though you live here, I don't expect you to live like you're sixteen, always checking in or coming home at a certain hour. But when you say you're just making a delivery for work, and then you don't come home for dinner or even before I go to bed; and I don't hear from you and you don't answer your mobile phone, I really have no choice but to worry about you."

Cara nodded as she took a solemn bite of her burger. "I'm sorry," Cara said. "I'll call next time."

"Thank you. That's all I ask. I don't even need to know why you're out, just that you're out." Delores' eyes glinted as she ate another chip, and Cara knew what she was hoping for before she even opened her mouth. "I don't suppose you have something to put downstairs?" she asked.

Cara shook her head. "Nope. I was just out late."

"Okay." Delores shrugged. Cara felt a nagging on her tongue, an urge to be more honest about where she was last night. She was an adult, and an adult didn't sneak around with a boy behind her mother's back.

"I was out with someone," Cara continued.

Delores raised her eyebrows. "Out with someone?"

"Yes. On a date."

"A date?"

"Mom, you don't need to repeat everything I say." Cara grinned. "Unless you bugged the place and plan on turning me into the cops."

"Never." Delores rolled her eyes as she took a sip of Coke, but Cara saw her smile behind the glass. "So, was this with someone from the brewery?"

"No. It was with a man I met in Raleigh while making a delivery. Jackson. We ran into each other at Walgreens while I was picking up your aspirin, and we decided to get dinner." Even adults didn't need to share every detail of their dates with their mothers.

They didn't need to share every detail, because their mothers already knew without being told. Delores gave Cara a pointed look as she returned to her food. "Pretty long dinner," she said.

Cara nodded, and they left it at that.

———

Friday became Saturday. A boring weekend lay ahead, so boring that Cara called Keith to see if he needed any extra help. "Nope, we're good," Keith said.

"No deliveries or anything?" Cara asked.

"Not yet. Bars and stores are all stocked. Take the weekend off."

Cara sighed as she hung up the phone. There were always chores around the farm, she supposed; and then watching television with her mother at night.

Her cell phone rang, and Cara picked it up with excitement — maybe Keith needed her after all. She looked at who was calling and smiled even more. It wasn't Keith. It was someone even better.

"Hey Jackson," she said.

"Hey Cara. How are you?"

"I'm okay. What about you?" Cara smiled mischievously, even though Jackson couldn't see her. "Did I leave my underwear at your apartment or something?"

Jackson laughed a little. "Not that I've found — though if I did, I'd probably keep it and not tell you."

"Well, you just told me, so —"

"I told you I didn't find anything, though."

"So that means you did and you're not telling me by telling me?"

"Yeah, exactly. I'm being sneaky by feigning incompetence." They both laughed, and Cara kept the smile on her face once they stopped. "I didn't find any underwear," Jackson continued. "But I wanted to call you. I know we talked about seeing each other next week —"

Cara's smile vanished. "You still can, right?"

"Oh yeah, of course. I can't wait. And …" Cara imagined Jackson looking sheepish, which sent a rush of tingles to between her legs. "And that's why I'm calling you."

"Because you wanted to talk about seeing me next week?"

"No, because I want to see you tonight."

Cara uncrossed her legs. "Tonight?"

"If you want to. I'll understand if you're busy, and I don't want to come on too strong or anything, but … I'll be honest: I haven't stopped thinking about you since yesterday. I'm not working today, and I'm not busy tonight, so if you're free and want to get together, I'd like to see you sooner than next week."

"I would too," she said. "I'd love to see you tonight."

"Great! Want to come by my apartment first? Then we can ride in the same car to wherever we go."

"Sounds good — almost as good as what'll happen at your place."

"Almost, yeah. But no matter how good that is, you're not getting your underwear back."

"You said you didn't have it."

"Shit! I'm really bad at this."

"Don't worry, you're good where it matters."

"So are you." Jackson's voice trailed a little, and he repeated, "So. Are. You."

Cara felt her body warm at the memory of his hands and lips all over her skin. Soon, it wouldn't just be a memory. "I'm looking forward to seeing you tonight," she said.

"I'm looking forward to seeing you too. See you tonight."

"See you." Jackson hung up, and Cara held the phone open a few moments longer before snapping it closed.

"Who were you talking to?"

Cara jumped a little as she turned and saw her mother. "Were you listening?" she asked.

"I just heard the end," Delores replied. "Who was it?"

Cara decided against a repeat of the other night — and telling her now meant she'd avoid the embarrassment of checking in later that evening while she was out with him. "Jackson. I'm seeing him tonight."

"You're going out with him again?"

"What's wrong with that?"

"Nothing, just —"

Cara tried to keep her growing impatience down. "Just what?"

"You just saw him the other night. That's an awful lot of time with someone you just met. How long until you're spending whole weekends with him, or weeknights, or every night?"

"It's a second date. I'm not thinking about any of that, and neither should you — especially because it's my business."

"Fine. But I know the way you look when you're excited for your future, and plan to keep a good thing going." Delores gave a small, sly smile. "I saw it after your first kill."

Cara shrugged — and tried not to smile at their shared memory.

———

Cara spent the rest of the day feeling better than she had all morning. She felt better than she had since dropping Jackson off at work the morning before. Part of her discomfort before had come from being nervous about talking to her mother, but most of it came from not being near him despite her wanting that more than anything.

Cara felt a little trepidatious about that wanting, one that gnawed at her heart and stomach alike. One that caused her fingertips to touch each other in lieu of touching him, caused her to stop from walking or moving and take a moment to create a picture of him in her head, one she could do whatever she wanted to with, because they were alone in her thoughts. It was a feeling she recognized, even if her resulting thoughts and actions weren't quite the same.

Delores was right about one thing: Jackson excited her in ways she hadn't felt in four years. The excitement was different, of course — she wasn't aroused by killing, even if it sparked life into her. Sparks that with each passing year grew harder to come by despite repeated strokes of her knife against the whetstone of a stranger's neck. But sparks that came, nonetheless, and made her feel like there was something worth getting into her truck for each morning.

Jackson propelled her this way as well. Yet in many ways, he excited her in ways she'd never felt at all. He brought something to the surface that a score of men before had never brought forth. Or maybe they had, and their sparks had faded too with time.

Cara shook her head. She didn't need to think about them right now. They were gone, flickers that faded into the night as they became one with the smoke and the sky. Jackson still burned within her.

————

Cara thumbed through the clothes in her closet with a frown on her face. While Jackson already knew what she looked like, she still wanted to look a little nice for him, show she'd put some thought and effort into their meeting.

The effort, though, was increasingly frustrating. Cara had settled on a skirt and tights, but was stuck on what top to wear. She looked through all her shirts and didn't think any of them were right. She dropped each one onto a growing pile of clothes on the floor, then continued to dig through her closet in the hopes of finding something good buried in the back.

"You going to Goodwill on the way to your date?"

Cara kept looking without a word. Delores walked into her room. "I figured I would've seen this scene more in high school," she remarked as she stood by Cara's side.

"I want to look nice," Cara said.

"He's already seen you. What're you worried about?"

"I'm not worried." Cara held up a pink blouse, then dropped it on the ground with all the others.

"Well, at the rate you're going, you're either going to show up in a dirty work shirt or your bra — and while I'm sure he wouldn't mind the bra, I can't let you leave the house in your underwear."

Cara rolled her eyes. Delores ignored her and began to pick through the pile of clothes. "This one's nice," she said as she pulled a red cotton shirt from the bottom.

"I've had that since I was fifteen. It's too old."

"You barely wore it in high school. It's almost like new."

"You think it'll fit?"

"One way to find out." Delores held it out. Cara sighed and took it. Trying it on was better than thumbing through more clothes. She pulled it on. It still fit, though it was a little snug around her breasts. She looked at herself in the mirror, and felt a small sense of calm. She looked nice.

"There," Delores said. "You can stop destroying your closet now."

"Thanks," Cara replied. She checked her phone to see if it was close enough to their date for her to go ahead and leave. As soon as she picked it up, it rang — and unfortunately, it wasn't Jackson. It was Keith. Cara wondered to herself what he wanted before answering with a curt hello.

"Hey Cara. Got a quick job for you to do if you're still available."

"I'm kind of busy —"

"It's a fast one, I promise. Sylvester's ran out of Papa's Pale, and they asked if we could send another keg over for the Saturday crowd. Can you drive out to Raleigh tonight? I'll pay you extra."

Cara was about to say no, then paused. She could take the beer to Sylvester's on her way to see Jackson — and she didn't mind the chance to make a little extra money. "Just one keg, right?" she asked.

"Only one, I promise."

"Okay. I can do it." She hung up without saying good-bye and walked out of her room.

"Cara, don't leave all your clothes on the floor," Delores called after her.

"I'll pick them up tomorrow," Cara called back. She thought she heard Delores sigh, but she didn't care. She grabbed her coat and sped out the door. The sooner she could deliver the beer, the sooner she could begin her evening with Jackson and Jackson alone.

———

"Where's the keg?" Cara called when she walked into the brewery.

Keith smiled as he walked from behind the tap station. Sadie stood behind the bar, cleaning glasses. "What, no 'Hi Keith, where's the keg?'" he asked.

"I'm in a hurry."

"Got a hot date or something?"

"I bet she does," Sadie said with a smile.

"What makes you think that?" Cara said, looking away in the hopes that neither Sadie nor Keith would see her flush.

"I can't think of what else you'd be busy with on a Saturday night," Keith called. He'd disappeared into the backroom to grab the keg.

"Or why else you'd be wearing that outfit," Sadie added with a devious smirk. "Taking the girls out for a ride?"

Cara zipped her jacket up over her chest with lightning speed. "Do you need help?" she called after Keith.

"Nope, I've got it," Keith said with a grunt as he reappeared with the keg. "Let's get this outside so you can go on your date."

"I'm —" Cara was about to protest, then decided to keep quiet. It wasn't worth lying about why she was in a hurry, especially when lying meant more time talking and less time getting on the road.

"Have fun tonight!" Sadie called after them. "I want to hear about it on Monday!"

"Sadie gets to hear about your dates?" Keith asked with mock jealousy as they walked towards her truck with the keg.

"Why would you want to hear about them?" Cara asked.

"I don't. Well, I mean, if you want to tell me about them, you can, but I just meant that I like talking to my employees like they're people. People with lives. I almost never hear about yours."

"There isn't much to tell."

"Then why do you make such a big effort to not talk about it?"

Cara looked at Keith in irritated surprise. He set the keg on the ground and held up his hands. "I'm sorry. It's not your job to tell me about your life."

Cara nodded, then opened up the bed of the truck. "Well, I have somewhere to be tonight — somewhere in Raleigh — and I'd like to get there before dinner."

"You got it." They hoisted the keg into the truck, and Keith gave Cara an apologetic smile. "Thanks for doing this, Cara — and I'm sorry if I made you uncomfortable."

Cara softened just enough to nod once more and say, "It's okay." Keith could be nosy, but in general, he minded his business and was nice to her. He never picked on her about much, and he talked to her like a person, like an employee he trusted, like a friend. Cara figured he'd continue to do so as long as what he already knew was all he knew about her. Sadie was certainly proof of that theory. She'd found out more, and only ever teased her.

Cara felt herself grow irritated again at the thought of Sadie — and knew she needed to get going before the cloud in her mind became an electric storm. "I'll see you on Monday," Cara said with a wave as she hopped into her truck.

———

127

Cara made her way towards Raleigh, but felt no better than when she'd left the brewery. The drive gave her a chance to stew as opposed to the chance to let things go. Sadie's teasing got her started, but Sadie was a distant flicker in her mind. All she could see and hear were the voices of Amanda and Dominic. All she could hear and feel were the laughs and touches of various boys, the ones that made her name a joke in their mouths. She even heard her mother, joking about thinking she'd have seen more of Cara planning for dates in high school. Of course she'd expect that — her mother expected what everyone else expected of her once they got to know her better.

She drove and saw nothing but empty roads ahead of her. There was no one who could absorb her fury, no one she could slice open and allow her anger to pour into as it seeped from her skin like the blood from their throats. Cara hoped her anger would dissipate but with every turn onto an empty road, she only had more time to hear the familiar buzz and feel the fire turn into a blaze.

Cara parked with a slam of the brakes in the parking lot of Sylvester's. She'd deliver the keg, get back in her truck, and drive around until she no longer felt so terrible. She'd drive aimlessly if she had to — anything to dispel her anger before she saw Jackson. Cara didn't want him to see her in one of her moods. She calmed a little at the thought of seeing him later that night. She'd be with him soon — just as soon as she made this delivery.

Sylvester's was even louder than it had been three nights before. Cara wasn't too surprised, given it was Saturday, but that did nothing to temper the blow of the noise to her senses. She shoved her way through crowds of people in

Wolfpack shirts. She guessed there'd been a basketball game that day, and while she couldn't tell if NC State had won or lost, she saw multiple empty pitchers of beer that said the crowd was taking the result in drunken stride.

There was a line three people deep to get to the bar. Cara tried to move to the corner to get the bartender's attention, but to no avail. Impatient customers leaned in front of her to hold their place in line. "I'm not buying beer," Cara said when one man rudely cut her off on her way to an empty space. "I'm just —"

"Getting a guy to buy you one when he notices you?" He grinned stupidly. Cara glared at him and walked off.

"Hey, I was just kidding!" he called.

Cara ignored him and made her way to the manager's door in the back. Like magic, she caught the bartender's attention. "No customers in the back," a woman with a brown ponytail said with a frown as she approached her.

"I'm here with a keg."

"You can't buy a whole keg."

"No, I'm delivering a keg!" Cara shouted. The woman rolled her eyes and went to get the manager. Cara didn't care what her problem was. She just wanted to get out of Sylvester's, and fast. It was loud and hot. She didn't dare remove her jacket though, in case she got any more comments like she'd gotten at the brewery. Cara closed her eyes as the whispers of others in her head began to overtake the shouts of the bar patrons.

Cara felt a tap on her elbow. Cara snapped open her eyes, and the manager held up his hands. "You okay?" he asked.

Cara softened her glare. "Yeah. It's just really loud in here."

"That's Saturday for you."

"The keg's in the truck." Cara didn't have the time or the patience for banter. They walked outside and moved towards the truck.

"Yeesh. Aren't your legs cold?" he asked with a glance at Cara's outfit.

Cara felt her cheeks burn. "No," she said as she opened the back of the pickup. "I'm wearing tights."

"Never knew how much good those did in the winter." Cara hoisted one leg up, and the manager stopped her by holding her arm. "No sense ripping your tights to get that," he said.

Cara moved her arm out of his grasp. "They won't rip —"

"I'll get one of the guys to help. Hang on." The manager went inside before Cara could protest. She fumed by the side of the truck. She was tempted to bring the keg in herself — she was used to a little heavy lifting, after all. Limp bodies could be rolled onto the ground much easier than kegs, though. Cara smirked at the thought of rolling a keg into her lake. She wished she were there now, watching someone disappear beneath its surface.

"Keg's in the back of the truck there." The manager's voice disrupted Cara's daydreaming. She saw a young man with nice arms by the manager's side. Cara moved to help them, but they both moved towards the open pickup, blocking her from helping. It was like having two Gregs in front of her.

"We'll get this inside," the manager said. He winked at Cara. "Hope you're meeting up with someone who's gonna keep your legs warm."

Cara didn't reply. She knew she'd say something that would sever Keith's business ties with Sylvester's if she did. She turned towards her truck and pressed her palms against the driver's side window. The cold glass did little to comfort her. She took a breath, closed her eyes, let it out. Her breath fogged the window and she felt the moisture touch her palms. She needed the water of the lake. She needed the trickle of blood.

She needed to go for a drive.

"Hey there!"

Cara looked up. She saw a man ambling towards her from the direction of the nearby bus stop. No car. Nothing to leave behind.

Cara stopped herself from getting too excited. She needed to find someone out on the road.

The man smiled as he neared her. "You ain't sick, are you?" he asked as he leaned against her truck.

"No," she replied. "Just need some fresh air."

"I need bar air. I need beer and pretzels and beer —"

"You already said beer."

"I need a lot of beer."

"I think you've had a lot of beer already."

The man laughed, then burped a little. "I might've been celebrating today, yeah. Big win for the boys."

"Yeah, a real big win." Cara would agree to anything if it meant getting him to leave and her getting on the road all the sooner.

"Wanna go in and celebrate with me? Hate to celebrate alone."

Cara perked up. "You're alone?"

"Yup. Friends aren't around, and ain't got a woman to drink with." He leaned closer, and Cara could smell a keg's worth of beer on his breath. "Not yet, anyway."

Cara smiled sweetly. "I'd like that. But why don't we go somewhere else?"

———

The water felt icy on Cara's palms. She rinsed her hands and picked at her nails to get any extra flecks of blood out from underneath. She'd take care of her neck and her chest when she got home. She felt better than she had all night. She walked to the truck with a smile on her face, one that grew as she felt the drunk's bottle opener keychain that hung from her back pocket tap against her butt as she walked.

Cara opened the door. The sound of her phone in mid-ring emptied out of the truck. Cara furrowed her brow as she pulled her phone out of her purse. Keith had promised it was just the one keg, and she didn't know why her mother would call when she knew she had a date.

Cara's eyes snapped wide open. She cursed to herself, then cursed again when the phone stopped ringing. She saw a missed call from Jackson, and when she opened her phone, she saw two more. She called him back, careful to not get the phone near any stray splashes of blood on her cheek.

"I'm so sorry," she said as soon as he answered.

"Hey. Where are you?" Jackson asked.

"I'm sorry," Cara repeated. "I got called into the brewery to make a last-minute delivery, and it took longer than I thought."

"Oh. Well, do you still want to go out tonight?"

Cara looked down at her chest and shirt, both soaked with blood. She'd have to shower, then change, then explain her detour to Delores. It was too much, no matter how badly she wanted to see him.

"I … I don't think I can," she said.

Jackson was quiet for a moment. Cara swore she could feel his disappointment through the phone. Then again, that disappointment could have just as easily been hers. She felt it seeping through her body like the blood that had trickled down her chest only minutes ago.

"Okay," Jackson said. The disappointment in his voice made Cara's heart drop a little in her chest. She wanted to try and fix it, and jumped right into an effort to make things right with him.

"I'm really sorry," she said. "I wanted to come out to-night, I just can't."

"It's okay."

"I'm sorry I didn't let you know about work."

"It's fine, really."

"I thought I'd be done in time, but I lost track of time, and —"

"Really Cara, it's okay. I'm bummed I won't get to see you, but I know these things happen."

He didn't know, and he couldn't know — and that was exactly why Cara couldn't see him. She hated that she'd been so overtaken by anger that she'd forgotten that. She'd taken for granted that she could just go on with her evening after making someone disappear. She could only do that when the only place she had to go was home. She looked at the farmhouse in the distance, its one porchlight shining like a star. Cara frowned at its brightness.

"What about tomorrow?" Cara asked. "I'm free then."

"I can't do tomorrow," Jackson replied. "I'm filling in for James while he goes to his dad's funeral."

"Oh." Her own disappointment faded to the background as she remembered how much James' father's death had affected Jackson. "Is that going to be hard for you?" she asked.

Jackson was quiet, and Cara wondered if she'd asked the wrong thing. After a moment, he said, "Yeah. Yeah, it's a little hard."

Cara felt an urge to hold him and to try to dispel all of his sadness into the air, to make it vanish like secondhand smoke in the wind. "I wish I could be there and make it less hard."

"I wish you could too."

Cara closed her eyes.

"But again, don't beat yourself up over it. Thanks for calling me back."

"Of course."

"And let's see each other soon."

"Absolutely. How about next week, like we planned before?"

"Yeah, next Friday works. Want to come by my apartment after work?"

"I'll do that." Cara would make sure of it, even if it meant telling Keith to make Greg do a late-night delivery instead. "See you then."

"See you Friday. Good night, Cara."

"Good night."

Jackson hung up, and Cara slammed her head against the driver's seat. "Fuck," she breathed. "Fuck, fuck, fuck." She put her head in her hands and groaned. Leaning forward caused the bottle opener to dig into her butt. Cara pursed her lips, then yanked it out of her back pocket. She got out of the truck, returned to the lake, and threw it into the water to sink alongside the body. She didn't want to remember this kill.

CHAPTER 7

Cara sat in her truck in the driveway while she waited for the blue glow of the television to disappear from the living room window. She knew she couldn't avoid telling her mother the date was off — not without sleeping somewhere else that night. It was too cold to sleep in her truck, and she knew that the staff at even the seediest of motels wouldn't ignore the blood stains on her body. It seemed, though, that her mother was staying up for *Saturday Night Live*. Minutes became an hour, one cigarette became two, and the light of the television continued to glow.

Cara sighed as she stepped out of the truck. If her mother spotted her as she came inside, she'd dart upstairs as fast as she could. Delores would have questions, just like always — and the biggest one she'd have would be why Cara didn't bring home a souvenir. Cara wasn't sure what she would tell her. She could tell her the truth, but something told her from the way Delores turned cool at Cara mentioning a second date, she wouldn't like to hear that Cara was changing her behavior already because of Jackson.

Cara walked inside as quietly as she could. She heard the television, and then a loud snore. She peered into the living room and saw her mother sleeping on the couch.

Cara smiled as she walked up the stairs. With everything that had gone wrong that night, it was nice to get even the tiniest bit of a reprieve.

———

Cara would've slept late the next morning if Delores hadn't come into her room at 7 a.m. "What are you doing home?" she asked as she shook her awake.

"Good morning to you too," Cara mumbled.

"Weren't you going out with that boy?"

"I came home while you were sleeping on the couch."

"I didn't sleep for that long. Did your date end early?"

"Jackson had to work today." Cara was grateful for answers that didn't require an elaborate lie. She was too tired to come up with a story.

"Oh. Well, when you decide to get up, I'll make us breakfast."

"Mm." Cara turned her head and closed her eyes. Going by the lack of comments from Delores, the bag of her ruined clothes must have gone undetected. She smiled a little before falling asleep.

———

Cara's mood continued to improve as the week began — mostly because each day that went by meant that she was one day closer to seeing Jackson again. Cara thought of seeing him all week long, to the point where she was even quieter at work.

Keith, Sadie, and Greg took her silence as par for course; though they noted that she at least seemed happier. Cara seemed so happy by Thursday that Sadie had to ask what was going on as they loaded cans in her truck. "You look like Greg got a new job," Sadie remarked.

Cara laughed and, in spite of herself, gave an answer: "I'm seeing that guy again tomorrow — the one I met last week."

"Wow, three dates in one week? You must really like him."

"It's only our second date."

"Didn't you see him on Saturday?" Cara paled, and Sadie added with a smile, "Or was that *another* guy?"

Cara furrowed her brow. "There isn't another guy."

"Hey, no judgment if there is, I swear. Play the field if it's not exclusive, that's what I say." Sadie leaned against Cara's truck. "So, is the guy you're seeing tonight — the one you obviously like a lot, whether or not you saw him last week — your boyfriend now?"

"Boyfriend?" Cara closed her eyes at the sound of Keith's voice. Of course he had to appear the moment she'd let her guard down and shared something with Sadie against her better judgment. He smiled as he approached them with one last package of cans. "I take it Saturday went well?"

"He's just someone I met in Raleigh," Cara said as she took the cans from Keith.

"Hey, no need to be shy about it. That's great. Bring him by the brewery sometime."

"So you can sell him beer?" Sadie cracked.

"That, and so we can get a brewery spouse that isn't just Greg's girlfriend."

Sadie rolled her eyes. "I'm sure your boy would be a massive improvement, Cara. Greg's girlfriend gets on my nerves."

Cara hadn't realized Greg had a girlfriend. She also didn't care — she wanted to get going. "Well, maybe sometime," she said, as she knew an outright refusal would only encourage them to keep needling her.

Cara sighed with relief as she left the brewery. Alone in her truck, she was free to just think about Jackson.

————

Cara also thought about Jackson at home, something her mother was less thrilled about than either Sadie or Keith.

"Think about him later," Delores remarked that evening. "You've barely spoken at dinner all week."

"How do you know what I'm thinking about?" Cara asked as she pierced her green beans with her fork.

"I doubt you're getting that dreamy look over beer."

"I'm career-oriented." Cara smiled, but Delores didn't see it. She was frowning over her mashed potatoes.

They spoke, but in small asides about their days, almost like they were coworkers. After dinner, they watched TV, a time Delores was quiet anyway. Still, it was time together, time Cara could buy ahead of the weekend so she'd be free to see Jackson as long as she wanted without her mother being able to say she hadn't been home in ages.

"I'm seeing Jackson tonight," Cara said on Friday. "I probably won't be home —"

"Until tomorrow. Got it." Delores waved as she sipped her coffee. "Have a good day."

"You too. Love you." Cara didn't hear her mother say it back, but she told herself it was because she was out the door before Delores had a chance to answer.

————

Friday at work went by in a breeze, with just a few errands to run around town. Cara stopped at the brewery before going to Raleigh to drop off an order of empty kegs. Keith handed her a six-pack of Papa's Pale before she could leave. "I want you and your date to have a drink on me," he said with a smile. Cara took it, even though she and Jackson planned to go to a bar. The beer would keep in the fridge, and taking it meant getting to his place all the sooner.

Cara was so excited to get to his place that she arrived fifteen minutes early. She thought about waiting in her truck, then shrugged and got out. She'd waited long enough to see him. She reached his apartment, knocked, and took a breath so she wouldn't look as excited as she felt when he opened the door. She wanted to look normal and maybe a little happy, but not crazed.

Jackson opened the door and grinned when he saw her. Cara did the same. "Hey!" he said as he stepped aside to let her in. "You're early."

"Figured I'd make up for being a no show last week," she said as the door closed behind her. "Again, I'm really sorry."

"Don't be." Jackson cupped her face and kissed her. One kiss became two, then three, then a continuous stream as Cara wrapped her arms around his waist. "I almost don't

140

want to go out," Jackson whispered with a smile once they pulled apart.

Cara pulled back her arm and held up the pack of beer. "Nothing says we have to."

"Oh, nice." Jackson smiled as he took the beer from her. "This from where you work?"

"Yeah. Keith insisted I take some, mostly to make up for making me work last week."

"He's too kind. Both of you are." Jackson set the beer on the coffee table as they both sat on his couch. "Really, last week wasn't my first time having a date cancel on me. At least you had a reason."

"It wasn't a good one, though — and I shouldn't have left you hanging."

"It's okay."

"I hate that I did that." Cara felt a small wave of the guilt she felt the week before creep up her skin and into her heart. She put her hand on Jackson's knee. "I wanted to see you last week, but mostly, I wanted to be better for you. You deserved better than that."

"That's sweet of you." Jackson smiled softly as he put his arm around her. Cara leaned on his shoulder. All of the bad things she'd felt before — the worries, the guilt, the frustration and anger — faded and quieted until they became silent whispers that flickered faintly in the dark.

"I'm glad you're here now," Jackson added. "I've been looking forward to seeing you all week."

"Me too," Cara replied. She leaned forward and kissed him. Jackson pulled her closer, and soon, he was between her legs, the beer on the table forgotten. They made out, then had sex on the couch, a mess of clothes and limbs as they kissed, bit, and touched each other the way they'd wanted to all week.

It wasn't enough. Cara sat in her underwear and t-shirt while Jackson, clad in his boxers, searched for a DVD. She watched him, and grew tired of simply watching. Cara sauntered over, spun him around, and began to kiss him. Jackson shoved her against the wall, pulled down her panties, and thrust into her with so much vigor that she needed to cling to his DVD rack.

They repeated this in the kitchen as Jackson got a bowl of popcorn, except against his counter and with Jackson taking Cara from behind.

After making it thirty seconds through the movie without kissing each other, they moved into his bedroom. They didn't have sex again, but they stripped off the scant clothes they wore and remained in a huddle of moving limbs on top of his comforter. Cara relished the feel of his skin, cold with the sweat of their past three fucks, moving against her as he kissed her over and over again. She did the same, pulling him closer and closer with every kiss, and kissing the parts of him she could reach when he moved to kiss another part of her.

"I can't stop kissing you," Cara whispered.

"I don't want you to stop," Jackson murmured.

"Good, because I can't."

"Are you trying to?"

"No." Cara giggled and Jackson smiled against her chest. "It's just that I —" She sighed as he began to kiss a line from her stomach to her neck — "I feel like I can't. I feel —"

"A constant, compulsive desire to kiss me?"

Cara laughed at the memory of the week before. When she told him that, she'd picked a word that simply came to mind in a game she played in jest. Now, though, she wasn't so sure. It had only been a week, and her craving for him — one she thought would at least dissipate when they were together and he could scratch all of her itches — seemed to only grow with each moment they spent together. Saying yes to him wasn't enough. All she wanted to say was more.

She could say that, though, and get it. "Yes. I have a constant, compulsive desire to kiss you — and more."

"It's the 'and more' I like to hear," he whispered in her ear before nipping at her earlobe.

"Even though you got 'and more' three times out there?"

"We've got the whole night ahead of us. I'm nothing if not ambitious." They laughed, and Jackson rolled over and pulled Cara on top of him. He kissed her fingers as she kissed his cheek. "But I have to be honest with you, Miss Vineyard …"

"What is it, Doctor Price?" she said with a smile, though a part of her worried about what condition he was about to impose. Maybe some sort of boundary would be better to keep them both — especially her — in check. She just hoped it wasn't one that meant their night satisfying each other's cravings would be the last, or the last in a long time.

Jackson released her hand, and Cara's heart sank — but only for a moment. He wove his fingers through her hair and began to kiss her neck.

"I've got the same compulsion," he whispered. Cara closed her eyes and smiled as he moved his kisses to her shoulder.

"You must've gotten it from me," she teased.

"I got it the minute I saw you outside of Sylvester's." He shifted so that they were facing each other. He pressed his forehead against hers and stroked the back of her neck with his thumb. "And I don't think it's going away anytime soon."

"Not even with all the treatment we've been doing?"

"Especially with all the treatment we've been doing. It's just making me want more."

Cara smiled softly. "Then I think it's working fine."

Jackson began to kiss her. Cara pulled him closer, content to stop speaking and to just kiss him, as long as she wanted, and know that she didn't have to stop.

CHAPTER 8

Cara's days as she knew them ceased to exist. Instead, she lived in moments with or without Jackson. There were moments when the line was blurred, when she wondered if those moments truly held him — a truth thankfully acknowledged when she felt his breath on her shoulder as they slept, or his fingers through her hair as they woke — or when she wondered if she'd ever had moments without him, and what they had possibly been like. Empty. Devoid. Waiting for him.

She wasn't sure what to make of her obsession with him. She knew she was diving too deep, too soon. She kept waiting for Jackson to push her to the surface and make her feel less like she was drowning. But he didn't push her up. When she was with him, she felt him pull her down and keep her alive beneath the water, the only breath she needed being his as his lips met hers and his hands pulled her deeper and deeper.

Jackson's pleas to see her were becoming a constant, beautiful refrain. Fridays at his apartment became weekends. Even those were proving to be too short. "Stay again tonight," he said one Sunday morning as they kissed in bed. "You're not working today, right?"

"Right, but I should get home sometime. I've been gone since Friday."

"Just one more night, though; before we go back to work. We can hide out in here —" He rolled on top of her — "stay under the covers, and I can kiss you all over." He began to kiss her as he spoke, punctuating each word with a kiss on her neck and shoulders. Cara tried to keep her resolve, but it grew harder as Jackson nestled between her legs and continued to kiss her.

"I can stay all day, at least," she said. "But not all night."

"Then we'll make the day count." Jackson gave her a deep, sensuous kiss on the lips, one that made Cara's toes curl as she wrapped her legs around him. "Though as much fun as this is, I like falling asleep next to you," Jackson added as he traced a finger along her cheek.

Cara kissed his finger as he traced her lips. "Me too."

Jackson smiled a little. "I don't suppose your room at home is a separate room above the garage?"

"No, sadly." Cara laughed a little, and Jackson slid off of her, keeping his arm around her waist as they went back to cuddling. "Staying over with me means rooms with thin walls and my mother down the hall." And a basement she'd have to keep him out of.

"She goes out, right? We can sneak around like high schoolers. I'll climb up the drain gutter and through your window. She'll never be the wiser."

"Look, just because I live with my mom like a high schooler doesn't mean I'm going to sneak around like one."

"Does she know you're with me now?"

"Of course she does." Cara ran her fingers through Jackson's hair. "But if we're going to make the day count, I don't want to spend it talking about my mother."

"Fair. But I do think it's nice you get along with your mom so well."

Cara shrugged. "We do, but I'm still a 22-year-old living at home."

"Big deal. I meant it when I said there was nothing wrong with that. Some people take longer to leave home. At least you and your mother talk, and you feel welcome when you walk in the door."

Cara knew even before Jackson looked down that he was thinking more about his own home life than hers. "You don't feel that way when you go home?"

"I'm home now," he said, almost too quickly. Still, Cara pressed on.

"When you visit, I mean. Do you ever go back to your old house in Pinesboro?"

"Not if I can help it."

"What about after school? You moved back home then, right?"

"I moved back to Pinesboro, but I didn't move back into my old house. I lived with Moira."

"Moira?"

"Oh, right, you wouldn't know her. She was my best friend growing up."

Cara began to imagine what this other woman was like, while trying to avoid asking questions that made her sound jealous. "So I guess you were more than friends for a bit?" she asked.

"No, we were just roommates. I can't even imagine dating her."

"Sorry. I shouldn't have assumed."

"Don't worry, you and everyone else in Pinesboro assumed the same thing." He smiled mischievously. "I fucked her brother a few times, though."

"Ah, so that's why you lived with her," Cara teased.

"He was long gone when I was living in Moira's guest room — living in another city, I mean. Not, you know, gone."

"Right."

"But living with her, even without Chris, felt just like old times. Her family's house was a nice escape, especially after my grandmother died. Gave me somewhere else to be."

"And your parents didn't guilt you into coming back to live with them?"

"It was just my mom. My dad died in a car accident before I was born."

"Oh, I … I'm sorry."

"It's okay. I never knew him."

Cara could almost see the landmines cropping up in their conversation. She still felt compelled to make her way through the field. Jackson had told her more about Pinesboro that morning than he'd said since they started dating. She wanted to know more about him, even if the information only came out in curt sentences. "So you didn't want to move back in with your mom?" she asked. "Not even for a little while to get on your feet, or —"

"She didn't want me there. She said, verbatim, stay away from my house."

"Oh." Jackson kept his eyes on the ceiling. Cara tried to process a parent who put up such a barrier. Her mother almost wouldn't let her leave. "Why?" Cara asked.

Jackson turned and dropped his feet to the floor. He nodded his head towards the doorway and said, "I want to show you something." Cara followed him, grabbing his discarded shirt from the floor and slipping it on as he pulled on a pair of flannel pajama bottoms. They walked into the kitchen, and Jackson searched through a pile of things on a table propping up his phone, answering machine, and mail. He picked up a blue shoebox on the bottom shelf of the table.

"You remember what I told you about Pinesboro, and how it's filled with death?" he asked.

"Yeah?"

"Mom agreed with me." Jackson set the box on the table and sat down next to Cara. "She saw it too, felt in her bones that there was something in Pinesboro that caused all the death."

"Sounds like a conspiracy theorist. Did she think the government was poisoning the water or something?"

Jackson didn't laugh. Cara made a note to keep her jokes to herself.

"It wasn't just that people died," he said. "It's that the deaths were so close to us. She was pregnant twice before me, and both died in utero. They were far enough along that she had them buried in graves afterward."

"Jesus. I'm sorry."

"But it wasn't just them. Dad died while she was pregnant with me. Grandma got sick after I was born, and died when I was eight. After I was born, Mom read about more death in the news, saw more stories of death on TV —"

"It's everywhere."

"But it was everywhere around her when I showed up."

A chill settled on Cara's skin as she processed how often Jackson referred to himself when chronicling the many deaths of Pinesboro. "She ... she didn't think it was you, did she?"

Jackson's silence told her everything even before he closed his eyes. "What the hell?" Cara breathed. "How could she —"

"She thought I brought something with me when I was born," he said. "Something that struck Dad, struck Grandma, struck the town, and struck the people I was close to. She thought that death followed me like a shadow, one she said would cast on others and settle in their hearts until their hearts gave out. One that settled even before they saw the light of day. She ..." He swallowed, his expression more pained than she'd ever seen. Cara found herself imagining a woman who looked a little like Jackson, a woman who could be his mother, a woman who smirked as she hurt Jackson. It was a smirk that Cara could smack right off, smack over and over until she bruised and bled.

"She said it was such a part of me that it started in her womb," Jackson added. "Started even before I was formed. That I brought it to my brother and sister before they were born, and sent them to their death before they had a chance to live."

"She said all this to you? When?"

"All the time, ever since I was little. She was always aloof, and when I was little, I didn't understand. I'd ask her what was wrong, and she'd tell me. She'd say it was me, that me being alive was killing everyone around us. She also took me to see my brother and sister. Their graves. Little ones in the cemetery outside of church, buried near her grandparents. She'd tell me about how badly she'd wanted them, and how they'd been taken away no matter how much she prayed. Grandma used to call me her little miracle, but she told me that Grandma was wrong. Mom told me I was her curse. She didn't know what for, but I was proof her prayers were intercepted and answered by the devil. That he swapped out her wishes for me, to remind her of death wherever she went."

"That's crazy!" Cara snapped. How anyone could say something like that to someone as wonderful as Jackson, especially his own mother, was beyond her comprehension. She took his hand and squeezed his fingers. "You didn't believe all that, did you?"

He shook his head, but slowly enough for Cara to know that it was an effort. "Jackson, it's not true," she said. "You're not some spirit of death. It's sad that so many people close to her died, but you had nothing to do with it; and your mother is an awful person for saying that to you."

He looked up at her in mild surprise. "Well, she is," Cara added. "How could she say that to her own son?"

"It was what she believed."

"But that doesn't give her the right to hurt you. It doesn't give her the right to be so … evil."

"She … I don't know what it was, evil or awful or what, but she was like that my whole life. Grandma would try to make me feel better, tell me to just ignore the things she said and remember at the end of the day, she was my mother and she loved me. I'd try, but it was really, really hard."

"Especially when she made it so hard." Jackson nodded, and Cara looked at the shoebox. She couldn't help but joke, "So, is what you wanted to show me her remains?"

Jackson burst out laughing. "No," he said with a smile as he lifted the lid. "These are letters Mom sends me. She likes to show me what I've left behind."

Jackson scooted the box towards Cara. She saw newspaper clippings and a few handwritten notes, all of which were brief. All of them also had one thing in common.

"You weren't kidding about all the deaths Pinesboro," Cara said as she lifted up a large handful of obituaries. "Did you know all these people?"

"No. I mean, some of them — and a lot in passing. Some I didn't know at all."

Cara studied them, ranging from kids who died in car accidents to grandmothers who died peacefully in their sleep. Handwritten notes peeked out from under each folded article. One slipped into her palm, and she saw what she presumed was his mother's scrawl: *It's still here, even if you aren't.*

She lost interest in the articles — she'd gotten the point, people died, they died every day — and focused on the notes. *At least this one went in her sleep,* one note said, with an article about an elderly woman with no kids who was better known for her bingo winnings and complaints from the neighbors about a lawn filled with flamingos in compromising positions. *No children to curse her with death.*

"I can't believe she really thinks you brought death to her," Cara said as she sifted through the shoebox. "Or to anyone, from the looks of it. This one isn't even in Pines-boro." She lifted a clipping printed off the Internet which detailed an overdose in Virginia.

"Yeah, even Pinesboro runs out of bodies after awhile. But Mom sends me those because of my job."

"At Walgreens? She's mad you're working at a drug store?"

"For being a pharmacist. She likes to send me stories about people dying from prescriptions. Says it's only fitting I sell something that kills people."

Cara read the handwritten scrawl on the printout: *Found another death related to what you sell. How strange that you got into medicine to help people, and all I read about is people dying from it.*

"Did you tell her that?" Cara asked, trying to keep her mounting temper down. "That you wanted to help people?"

"I did." He nodded, and looked embarrassed. "I do. A lot of the people I knew who got sick needed medicine more than anything. I didn't want to be a doctor, but I could help with the part that makes the day-to-day between doctor's visits bearable for people like Grandma. She used to pay me to count her pills and sort them in her pill box. I was always so careful to get the right ones and the right colors and the right amounts. She used to call me Bean, because I was her bean counter."

"She sounds wonderful." Certainly better than the night-mare that was his mother. "I bet she would've been proud of you."

"Maybe. But she isn't here." Jackson sighed as he placed the lid back on the shoebox. "Mom is, and she just sees this as further proof of death being a part of me, following me wherever I go and sitting on the doorsteps of the people I touch."

"Well, she's wrong. People dying from accidental over-doses has nothing to do with you. People in Pinesboro dying has nothing to do with you. Did you go up and murder those people? Did you force all those pills down their throats, or make them sick, or —"

"I get the point, and no, I didn't."

"You're not a killer, Jackson. Trust me, I would know."

Jackson smiled a little as he cocked an eyebrow. "You would?"

Cara figured he was teasing, but she balked a little all the same. "Well, I've killed some unlucky critters on the farm," she said with her own smile, one she hoped wasn't as shaky as she felt.

"Critters? I thought you didn't have any crops anymore."

"Doesn't stop possums and such from sniffing around our yard."

"You get mice too?"

"Sometimes, but I just catch those and take them to the woods. They don't get near the house."

"Well, I'm glad I know someone who can deal with mice if I ever get them."

Jackson smiled as he squeezed her hand, and Cara finally calmed. "Absolutely," she said. She would protect him from anything. She kept that to herself, though, as mice were the last thing on her mind when she thought that.

"But the things that happened to your mother — your dad, your grandmother, her unborn kids — none of that has anything to do with you," Cara said.

"I know. I know it doesn't. Even when I have to tell myself that to make myself believe it, I know." Jackson folded both hands over hers. "But even though I know that, it's hard. If it were anyone else, I'd be right there with you. But she's my mother. Even on the days I'm able to completely remove myself from what she's said and done to me, it'll always be hard knowing that the one person who's supposed to love me without condition just hates me."

Cara kissed his cheek, then looked down at the shoebox and the smattering of notes beside it. They almost seemed to sneer up at her. "Why do you keep these?" Cara asked. "All they do is remind you of that hatred. Doesn't that make it harder for you?"

Jackson let go of Cara's hand. He began to put each note back in the box, one-by-one. "Mostly," he said. "But just like I can't ignore what she says to me because she's my mother, I can't ignore the ways she keeps in touch. In its own way — its own twisted way, I know; but its own way all the same — it's how she makes sure we're still connected. That we're still family. I like to think that if she really hated me, she wouldn't go to the trouble to write."

Cara watched him with pity as he picked up the final note and dropped it in the box. She read its words before he replaced the lid: *Someday all this death will catch up with you. Maybe then we'll be safe.*

She felt a familiar sense of anger start to course through her veins. Instead of letting it flow, she said once more, "I'm sorry."

"It is what it is," Jackson said as he put the box back in its spot.

"And I'm sorry I upset you in bed before," she continued as he returned to the table.

"That's okay. You didn't know."

"I wish I hadn't made you think you needed to show me all this, to think about it when you just wanted to have a nice Sunday together."

"Really, it's okay. Honestly, I … I'm glad it came up. That I could tell you this now."

"Were you waiting to tell me or something?"

"I hadn't thought about it a lot, but yeah — it'd crossed my mind." He scooted closer to her, and placed his hand on her knee. "I feel like … and first, I know this is an awkward segue, hopefully not too awkward for you …"

"What is it?" Cara said with a small smile. It always got her when Jackson got sheepish, the way he looked down and to the right and gave a half smile, the only kind that revealed the small dimple on his left cheek.

"It's just that with you, with each day, each week, I don't feel like we're just dating or just fucking or just something in passing. I feel like we're something more than that. Like we're getting serious." Jackson took her hand. "And I like that. I'd like to keep going, and see where we go. But I don't want to do that without you knowing this about me. It's just about me — not you, not us, just me — but it's part of me, and as much as I want to keep it away, there's going to be times like this morning where I get hit with memories, or days I'm going to bury another letter in that shoebox, and you'll see it. I don't expect you to solve it and I don't expect you to deal with it, but if you like where you and I are going, you should know it's there."

Cara did like where they were going. She wasn't sure, though, that Jackson would want to go with her if he knew the parts of her she'd bring along. Parts her mother was proud of, but that no one else alive knew, that no one else could ever know. They were things she kept buried, things that were her secret.

Things, though, that she hadn't felt compelled to do in months. Jackson hadn't filled a void in her life. He'd created a whole new sense of being. It was a sense she'd keep by being with him — and by staying quiet.

Cara lifted Jackson's hand and kissed it. "I like where we're going," she whispered. She kissed his knuckle. "I like you."

Jackson smiled, and moved his hand from her grasp so he could stroke her cheek. "I like you too," he whispered. He leaned forward and kissed her. She felt everything around her and everything inside of her cease; giving way to the feel of his lips against hers, the stroke of his fingers along her arm. Everything disappeared when he was there. She'd keep him there. She'd keep the parts of her he didn't need to see in the void where they belonged.

A sudden rush of rain unfurled itself against the window. Cara got up, looked outside, and sighed when she saw her truck blurred from view. Jackson joined her at the window. "It'll be a fun drive home later," Cara said. She knew an April shower like this one wasn't just a quick burst. It'd probably last through the night.

Jackson slipped his arms around her waist. "Guess you'll have to stay a little longer."

Cara smiled, and closed her eyes as Jackson kissed her neck. "Guess so."

———

"Glad you made it home through the rain."

Cara smiled as she hung up her keys. "Waiting until morning was the right call," she said.

Delores leafed through a magazine, but Cara saw her roll her eyes a little. "I'm sure it was a real inconvenience for Jason —"

"Jackson."

"To let you stay." Cara began to walk up the stairs, and Delores called after her, "There's a blueberry muffin in the kitchen if you want it."

Cara pivoted and went towards the kitchen. She saw the muffin waiting on a plate.

"Bought some yesterday." Delores walked in behind her, and they both sat at the table. "When I thought I'd have company for breakfast."

"Mom, you said you didn't care what I do as long as I tell you where I am." Cara began to peel the muffin liner off ridge-by-ridge. "Sounds like you care quite a bit."

"I'm just teasing you." Delores topped off her coffee as she spoke, but Cara knew from her voice that she was only somewhat telling the truth. Cara shrugged to herself, and began to eat.

"So are you going to move in with him?" Delores asked.

Cara set down her muffin. "What's wrong with you?"

"Nothing's wrong. I'm asking a simple question."

"You're interrogating me."

"I'm asking a question. You have a boyfriend —"

"He's —" Cara stopped before she denied it. She and Jackson had never called each other boyfriend and girl-friend, but she supposed such titles came with what was growing between them — and getting stronger every day.

"One you see a lot," Delores continued, "more and more each week; and one who lives almost an hour away."

Cara had never had a boyfriend before. She smiled a little at the thought. She thought of Jackson, and smiled more.

"What are you smiling about?" Delores asked.

Cara dropped her smile. "I just like the way that sounds, me having a boyfriend."

"You're just now aware of it?"

"It's nice to say it out loud. I never have before."

Delores chuckled a little as she sipped her coffee. "I think you've had plenty of boyfriends."

Cara felt her cheeks grow hot. "They weren't boyfriends, they were just guys I saw."

"Whatever they were, there's nothing wrong with dating around."

"You make it sound like something's wrong with it."

Delores' expression softened as she set down her mug. "I didn't mean it that way. I was just teasing you."

"Right. Just like everyone else."

"If you mean everyone else like that little bitch who picked on you in school, then don't think that way. But I'm sorry if I reminded you of her, or of any of them."

Cara shrugged and left it be. Her mother would never understand what it'd been like for her in school.

"I should know better, really," Delores continued. "I used to hear my name all the time in unsavory ways back home."

Cara looked at her with raised eyebrows. "You mean in school?" Cara asked.

"At school and at home. My brothers and parents weren't too thrilled to have me around. Always said I was getting into trouble, even before I knew what trouble was. Uncle

Leo was the only one who didn't mind me being around, even when I arrived in Leslie knocked up and out to here." Delores traced an arc around her flat stomach.

"What did you do — in Egret's Bay, I mean?" Delores almost never brought up her hometown. Cara wanted to hear more while she had the chance.

"Anything I could to get into trouble, really. Figured I was already in it, so why not enjoy it?" Delores abandoned her coffee and took out a cigarette. Cara tried not to roll her eyes at her mother feeding her lines instead of information. She knew Delores didn't like to talk about Egret's Bay. What she didn't know was why.

Instead of asking about Egret's Bay, she asked about one specific thing she hadn't asked since she was a child: "Who was my dad?"

Delores took a drag and looked out the window.

"I'm not gonna go look for him," Cara continued. "Not to talk to him or demand any answers or even to kill him." Delores laughed a little and exhaled smoke in spurts as she did so. "But can't you tell me who he is?"

"No."

"Why not?" Cara threw up her hands. "What's the big deal? Who cares if you fucked some guy when you were seventeen and got pregnant?"

"A lot of people cared."

"They're either dead or they've moved on. Everyone in Egret's Bay probably forgot you, and people in Leslie talk about me, not you."

Delores finally looked at her, though with narrow eyes. "Everyone here has moved on from you too, Cara. Stop thinking about what people said about you in school."

"How can you say that when you're so caught up in what everyone said about you in Egret's Bay that you won't even tell me who my dad is?"

"It wasn't just Egret's Bay and you know it."

"Of course I know it. I had to hear about it all the time."

"And I hate that fact every day." Delores stubbed out her half-smoked cigarette and blinked rapidly as she looked back out the window. "I hate that the minute you got off this farm and went anywhere else, you had to hear about me and then hear about you. I hate that Uncle Leo died before he could give you the armor, as little as it was, that he gave me when he told me he wanted me here and made me feel good for something other than people's insults and men's pricks. I hate that Terry left when you were so young, and I really hate that whenever either one of us leaves this farm, we're swarmed with what everyone says and it's all because of me."

"It's not all you," Cara said, her voice softer.

"And what I hate most of all is that in many ways, they're right."

"They're not."

"They are. I — I can't tell you who your father is because I honestly don't know." Delores sighed as she leaned back against her chair. "I was seeing too many people when I got pregnant with you. I don't know which of them is your father."

"That's it? Mom, that happens all the time. They have whole talk shows about that."

"And they're all about how those women are sluts or idiots or both."

"The men don't get off so easy — especially when they keep saying they aren't the father and it turns out they are."

"But you know as well as I do that only men get to reap the benefits of sex, including the benefit of the doubt." Delores took out another cigarette, and Cara held out her hand.

"If you're going to waste your cigarettes, at least give me one so they won't all be half smoked."

Delores chuckled as she handed Cara a cigarette. They each produced their own lighters. "I had an idea who your father was," Delores said. "But I knew I could never get him to believe me. It would've gotten us both in trouble."

"Why? Did he have a wife or something?"

"Give me some credit. I stayed away from married men — no matter how often they looked down my shirt. Their wives just blamed me for that, though," she muttered.

Cara cut her off before she could go on another tangent. "Why do you think my dad would've gotten in trouble?"

"Because I think your dad was my science teacher."

Cara's eyes widened as she smoked. "You fucked your teacher?"

"I fucked a lot of my teachers. If the teachers at Sea Glass High weren't sending me to detention, they were driving me home from detention and stopping in the woods on the way there."

"Wow."

"It's not impressive. What they did was wrong. I didn't know that then, but they did, and they didn't care. But around the time I got pregnant with you, I was sleeping with a few people — a couple of classmates, an actor who was filming a movie in Wilmington —"

"An actor? Who?"

"And Mr. Parker. I only slept with him once, but that's all it takes."

"So it could be any of those people," Cara said. "Maybe even the actor."

Delores smirked as she gave Cara a pointed look. "Even if your father was the actor, it's no one who went on to do anything famous. His big role was Man at Beach." Cara pretended to sigh in disappointment, and Delores laughed. "But I'm pretty sure it was Mr. Parker."

"Why?"

Delores smiled warmly at Cara — the first time she'd done so all morning. "You didn't get your beautiful eyes from me," she said as she tapped her finger near her own grey irises. "All the girls in my class loved Mr. Parker's baby blues. One girl said he must've gotten them from the shores of the Outer Banks."

"Isn't the Atlantic green?" Cara asked.

Delores laughed again. "And there goes Lucinda's poetry. You know she went on to be a pretty famous poet in the area."

"I hope she improved her metaphors."

"I hope so too. But, there's your answer. I think your father is Thomas Parker, former science teacher at Sea Glass High."

"Former? What happened to him?"

"Nothing macabre." Delores knew Cara too well. Cara supposed Delores always would. "He married a woman from California and moved out there to teach."

"I thought you didn't keep in touch with him."

"I didn't. The principal told me when I called Sea Glass High and asked about him. Fortunately it was a new principal, one who didn't remember me. Otherwise I might never have called at all. And before you ask —" Delores stubbed out her cigarette, and Cara closed her mouth — "I called in a brief moment of bravery where I was going to reach out to Mr. Parker and see if he'd take a test and maybe pay some child support if he was in fact your dad."

"What made you do it?"

"Terry leaving. With Uncle Leo gone and Terry out in Apex, I was worried I wouldn't be able to take care of you myself. But Mr. Parker disappearing on me told me that I'd have to. I knew that anyway — I didn't even know if he was your dad — and I just figured that him being gone was a sign from God telling me that you were mine and mine alone to take care of."

Cara remembered Jackson's mother's thoughts on how children were signs from God. Her thoughts strayed strictly to Jackson, and she kept quiet as she chose to spend some time with her thoughts in lieu of being with him.

"Do you want to see him or something?"

Delores' voice snapped Cara out of her thoughts. "Jackson?" she asked.

"No. Your dad." Delores chuckled, but it didn't sound kind.

"Oh. No." Cara decided to send Jackson a text and pulled out her phone.

"You're thinking about him, aren't you?"

"Mr. Parker?"

"Jackson!"

"Oh." Cara didn't bother to try and say no. Her mother knew. She always knew.

"Well, some dating advice from someone who knew her way around the block: stop checking your phone so much. Men can sense when you're desperate to hear from them."

"I'm not desperate. I just — you know, figured I'd let him know I was thinking about him."

"He probably knows. Desperation seeps from women like bad perfume. Men catch a whiff and suddenly they're busy with other things."

Cara's phone chimed before she could protest. Cara flipped it open with a smile as she read three words from Jackson that did more for her that morning than her mother's many words: *Thinking about you.*

"Or, they write and let you know they feel the same," Cara said as she texted back, *u 2.*

"Watch out for them too. It's almost worse when men detect desperation and see that as their cue."

Cara snapped her phone shut and smirked at Delores. "So the answer is no men at all?"

"It's working out for me!" Delores shrugged playfully as they both laughed. "I just want you to be careful," she added.

"There's being careful and there isn't trusting anyone."

Delores shrugged, but this time it was in silence.

"So I *can't* trust anyone?"

"Of course you can. You can trust me." Delores smiled. Cara tried to keep hers, even though she felt slightly unsettled, like she'd been brushed by a breeze that only moved one or two strands of her hair out of place.

Her phone chimed again. "I need to go to work," Cara said, figuring there was no better way to leave the table gracefully.

"I know that's not Keith calling you."

"I'll see you for dinner." Cara waited until she was in the hall to flip open her phone.

"I'll see you then." Cara sighed with relief at the lack of jokes or needling about whether she'd see Jackson that night. "I love you."

"I love you too." But it was automatic, said by default without even thinking. Cara was too busy replying to Jackson to think of anything else.

CHAPTER 9

Cara was back at Jackson's by Friday night. She went straight to his place after finishing her deliveries for Keith, deliveries which had her out as far as Burlington and thus had her at his door after dark. Jackson didn't mind. He'd ordered Chinese food before she arrived, and they were able to sit on his couch, eat, and watch TV with only each other. They would spend the weekend with only each other, and Cara looked forward to every minute.

Their minutes alone, though, appeared to be short-lived by Saturday morning. Both were awake, lying in bed and talking to one another, when they were interrupted by a loud knock.

"Who's that?" Cara asked.

"I don't know," Jackson replied. He turned over and held Cara closer instead of getting out of bed to find out. "Probably a solicitor or some Mormons or something."

Another knock. "Are solicitors usually that persistent?" Cara asked.

"The Mormons are, but only when you open the door." Jackson smiled as he got out of bed. "I'll see who it is and remind them it's morning."

"Well, almost morning," Cara said as she looked at the clock on his bedside table. "It's almost eleven."

"That's definitely morning on Saturday terms." Jackson disappeared down the hall. Cara stared at the ceiling, and hoped that whoever it was would leave as quickly as they appeared.

Muffled voices broke through the silence. Cara thought she heard an exclamation from Jackson, but while she couldn't hear what he said, she could hear that he was happy. She briefly panicked at the thought that his mother was here, but then common sense got the better of her. Even if Jackson kept his mother's letters in the hopes of keeping a connection, he'd made it clear that he had no desire to see her — and that if she came to see him, he wouldn't be thrilled.

As the moments became minutes, curiosity about who was there beat out Cara's desire to stay out of sight. She rolled out of bed, pulled on one of Jackson's shirts and a pair of his boxers, and walked out of the room.

Cara approached the living room slowly, and saw Jackson with his back turned. Past Jackson, she saw a tall woman standing in front of the kitchen table. She wore a faded black jacket, a maroon t-shirt with a rumpled collar, jean shorts that rolled and tore where they'd been cut off, and black-and-orange striped stockings with a hole in the knee. Her bobbed hair hung against her cheeks and was topped with uneven bangs. Everything that made her up seemed frayed on its own, yet came together neatly as herself.

When she turned her head and noticed Cara, she flashed a grin that was only broken by two crooked teeth in the top row. "Am I interrupting something?" she asked, winking at Jackson as she spoke.

Jackson turned, and Cara stepped back sheepishly. "I'm sorry," Cara said, "I didn't mean to —"

"No, don't be," Jackson said as he walked towards her. "I should've gotten you before." He slipped his arm around her waist and turned back towards the woman. "This is my girlfriend, Cara."

"Girlfriend!" The woman moved forward and held out her gloved hand, the fingertips missing and the bare threads around her fingers showing that the gloves hadn't been made that way. "I'm Moira."

"Oh!" Cara smiled as she shook Moira's hand. "Jackson told me about you. It's nice to meet you."

"Well, I'm glad he told *you* about *me*." She grinned mischievously at Jackson. "I can't believe you didn't tell me you had a girlfriend."

"How would I? You don't stay home long enough to get letters, you never check your email, and you refuse to get a cellphone."

"Get a carrier pigeon, or learn how to make smoke signals."

"Or get a cellphone, like a normal person who travels all the time would."

"And lose my luddite charm? No way." Both Jackson and Moira laughed like old friends who found each other funnier than anyone else would. Cara simply smiled.

"Well, you guys want to get some food or something?" Moira asked. "I'm starving."

"You want to?" Jackson asked as he looked back at Cara.

"Oh, I can head out if you guys want to go," Cara replied.

"I said 'you guys,'" Moira said with a grin. "I want to take you both out. My treat."

"Well … sure. Sounds good." Cara was a little hungry, but it was the small look of pleading that Jackson cast in her direction that convinced her to go with them.

They went to IHOP, for Moira insisted on getting pancakes even though it was close to noon. Cara tried to ignore the clatter of pots and the hum of voices in the small, crowded restaurant. Those were easier to ignore as Moira chatted happily over it all, filling Jackson in on the goings-on of Pinesboro and beyond, while interjecting explanations of who people were on the side to Cara. Watching Moira speak was like watching a one-woman tennis match. Still, it was nice to hear names out of Pinesboro that weren't on the obituaries in Jackson's shoebox, and more so, that made Jackson smile or laugh upon hearing them.

"Chris says hi, by the way," Moira said as she poured more syrup over her half-eaten short stack. "Stayed with him in Carrboro on my way here. You should visit him sometime."

"Sure," Jackson said without any sort of commitment.

"C'mon, he'd love to see you — as friends, of course. He's living with —"

"Michael, I remember."

Moira looked at Cara, and Cara shifted her focus from her breakfast. "Do you know who Chris is?" Moira asked.

"Yes," Cara said, relieved to actually know one of the many names Moira rattled off.

Moira's grin turned devious. "You know everything about him?"

"Yes," Jackson answered for her.

"Well, I didn't want to make things awkward if she didn't know — though I'd hope your girlfriend would know you like guys sometimes."

"Not sometimes, all the time."

"Right, right, you like both." Moira shrugged. "It was hard enough getting my folks to understand that Chris liked guys. They'd never get someone liking both. They'd be like, well, pick one!"

"He doesn't have to, though," Cara said, and Jackson smiled at her.

"Of course not. We're learning, but we're trying," Moira said as she patted Jackson's arm.

"You succeed," Jackson said as he smiled at her. Cara almost felt like a voyeur intruding on their friendship, that she should be at the booth across from them and letting them catch up while she ate her eggs and said nothing, with no one expecting her to say anything.

"So tell me more about you guys," Moira said, fixing her eyes on Cara. "How'd you meet? How long have you been seeing each other?"

"A few months," Jackson said. "And —"

"You've talked enough, Jackson," Moira said as she playfully waved her butter knife. "Let Cara speak."

Cara shrugged, feeling nervous to be put on the spot. "A few months," she repeated. "We met at a bar."

"Ah, a classic pick-up. He buy you a beer or something?"

"Not really. We were outside and I asked him for a cigarette."

"Well Jackson, at least your nasty habit had one good side effect: getting you a woman."

"It's no nastier than all that weed you smoke," Jackson retorted.

"Smoked. I quit last year. Got too expensive."

"I have to go to the bathroom," Cara said as she stood up.

"Eggs went right through you, huh?" Moira asked as Jackson glanced in her direction.

"Here's some money in case they bring the bill," Cara said as she fished out a ten from her pocket.

"You think you'll be gone that long?" Moira asked. "You get food poisoning or something?"

"Moira, stop," Jackson said, though in a friendly tone. "Let her pee in peace."

"Fine, but I just wanted to know if she had food poisoning so we could get the bill comped if she did."

"We'll see you outside," Jackson said with a smile. She wondered if a part of him knew that she'd deliberately take a long time, that she needed a minute away from Moira's chatter and from feeling like she was invading their space as they caught up.

Cara did have to go, but stayed seated after she was finished. She took deep breaths, and focused on how muted the noises at IHOP were within the bathroom stall. The only sounds were other women and the occasional child coming in and out.

After a few minutes, Cara figured she'd been gone long enough. She washed her hands, then looked in the mirror. She smiled, then quickly dropped it. Trying to smile was worse than not smiling at all. She looked in her own eyes.

She didn't look agitated or sad or alone. She looked neutral. That was best.

Cara left the bathroom, and saw that their booth was occupied by a family of five. Relieved that they could go, she walked outside. Jackson and Moira weren't by the door.

She spotted Moira's car, but saw neither of them inside it.

Cara furrowed her brow as she looked around. Maybe she'd looked at the wrong booth, or otherwise missed seeing them inside. Her gaze fell on a scant line of pine trees lining the parking lot. She saw the backs of Jackson and Moira's heads behind one of the trees. Cara smiled and walked towards them.

As she neared them, she saw that their heads were low and their voices were even lower. They looked like they were whispering. Cara's smile fell as she wondered if they were whispering about her. She shook her head and tried to stop imagining what they were whispering about.

Moira noticed her first. She looked up and immediately stopped speaking, which didn't help.

Jackson looked up at her and smiled. "Hey, we were wondering where you were," he said as he walked towards her.

"Is that what you were talking about?" Cara teased, though she worried that it didn't sound like a joke.

"Nah, we were just sharing secrets in the woods," Moira said with a smile that made Cara wonder what it was concealing. "Well, the 'woods,' I guess," she added while creating quotes with her fingers as she looked at the single row of wilting pine trees behind her.

"Moira's family lived near a patch of woods. We had a fort back there and it was the one place in Pinesboro we could talk and no one bothered us," Jackson explained. Cara felt a sharp sting at Jackson saying they'd been bothered, then reminded herself that he meant people in Pinesboro.

"But it's Pavlovian now," Moira said. "I see some trees and suddenly I want to spill my guts. We outgrew the fort but we'll still walk in the woods and talk."

"About what?" Cara asked.

"They're secrets!" Moira widened her eyes and placed a finger to her lips while laughing a little. Cara found her antics less amusing now that they weren't new — and done in an effort to hide things from her.

"Let's go home," Moira said as she moved towards her car. Cara stayed quiet and tried to fight the growing murmurs in her head. Murmurs telling her to think about it, to not think about it, to not think at all. She just wanted silence, but the more she wanted it, the louder her thoughts grew.

Jackson put his arm around her. Her thoughts quieted. They didn't vanish, but even quieter was enough.

"Moira's just having fun," he said in a low voice, even though Moira was far ahead of them. "But just say so if she's being too much. She'll stop."

"She doesn't need to," Cara said, and it was the truth. She was the one that needed to stop.

"It's one thing when she's teasing me, but you guys just met. If it makes you feel any better though, she's only like that around people she likes."

Cara nodded. It helped a little, but she also figured any liking Moira had for her was residual from being with Jackson.

They reached the car, and Jackson moved straight towards the back. "Go ahead, sit up front," Cara said. "I'll be fine back here."

Jackson shrugged and sat in the front. Cara felt better sitting behind them as they talked, and being able to watch the trees and sky in silence as they did so. Her bubble was only broken by Jackson occasionally reaching back and stroking her leg. Cara smiled at his touch.

"So where are you staying?" Jackson asked as they got out of the car.

"Probably one of the motels near campus," Moira said. "I'm just here for a couple days."

"You're not checked in yet?" Jackson asked, and Cara briefly feared that he'd ask Moira to stay with him. She shook the fear off. Even if he did, it was his apartment and his couch. She thought of everything they'd done on that couch and tried not to smirk at the thought of Moira sleeping there, oblivious to what those cushions had gone through.

"I will be," Moira replied. "It's not graduation season yet. I'll drive out and find something if there isn't anything around here. But I figured we'd hang out a little more and catch up before I did." She smiled at Cara, and Cara felt uneasy at the attention. "Unless I'm interfering with any plans for today"

"You're not," Cara said, "but I actually think I should go."

Both Jackson and Moira's faces fell. Cara tried to keep her conviction especially under Jackson's gaze. "I've got some stuff I need to do back out in Leslie," she said. "My mom could use some help around the farm —"

"You live on a farm?" Moira asked.

"A pumpkin farm," Jackson answered.

"It's not Halloween yet," Moira said with a smile.

"We don't sell pumpkins anymore," Cara said. "But there's still stuff to do, like fixing things around the house and cleaning out the critter traps —"

"Oh my God, I love that you say 'critter.'" Moira giggled as she clapped her hands, and Cara pursed her lips. "Reminds me of my granddad out in Tarboro. He'd catch 'critters' and send their skins as hats to Chris, but I always stole them from him and wore them around. Mom called me Moira Crockett."

"Well, if you like possum hats, I'll send you one," Cara said in the hopes that a joke would quiet her thoughts that began to equate Moira to everyone else that laughed and whispered about her before.

"Sure, it'll match my rabbit belt and squirrel-skin boots." Moira laughed again, and Cara smiled a little. "Well, if the critters are calling, I'll let you answer," Moira added — almost too quickly, Cara thought. She tried to ignore the thought.

Moira walked towards Jackson's apartment. Jackson stayed behind and pulled Cara close. "You sure you need to go back?" he asked. "You can hang out with us."

"No, you should be able to catch up with Moira without me around," Cara replied. "You haven't seen her in ages. You don't need to worry about including me."

"I don't worry about including you. I want to."

"Well, include me later. She's just staying a couple days. I'll see you the rest of the days."

"Alright, but I hope you're not leaving because you think we don't want you around."

"I know you want me around," Cara said as she wrapped her arms around him. "But I also haven't been in Leslie for

SONORA TAYLOR

the past few weekends. I do have some stuff I need to do
—" Stuff that she wouldn't have minded putting off if Moira
hadn't shown up — "and I know my mom will be happy to
see me." That she knew was true, but Cara wasn't sure how
much that feeling would be shared.

"Okay." Jackson kissed her, and Cara tried not to focus
on how good it felt, so she'd keep the will to go to her truck
afterward. It was a will that wavered as he pulled away and
kissed her neck, her cheeks, and her ear. "See you soon," he
whispered. It was a much more pleasant whisper for Cara
to take home with her.

———

Cara took her time driving back to Leslie. She drove
under the speed limit, and took as many back roads as she
could. She still felt a little sick by the time she approached
the worn sign for Vineyard Farm. She turned off of the driveway and drove as quietly as she could towards the woods.
Her mother didn't need to know she was home — not yet.
She parked by the trees, hopped out, and went for a hike. All
that accompanied her were birds and the rustle of leaves.
It was calming — so calming that, every time she thought
of turning back and heading to her truck, she turned down
another hiking path. When she grew tired of walking, she'd
lean against a tree and smoke, or walk through the brush to
find new paths.

As the sky behind the branches went from blue to yel-
low and pink, Cara decided to head back. She grew sadder with every step closer to Vineyard Farm's empty fields.
Cara hadn't planned on being home that night, and her
mind was having trouble accepting her change in plans. She

177

wondered if stalling just a little longer — perhaps with a beer — would help.

Once she approached the clearing, she hopped in her truck and quietly drove away. She headed to Charlie's for a beer and one last effort to clear her head before returning home. She walked inside and saw a few patrons. Most of them kept to themselves, nursing beers with one other person or concentrating on a game of pool. Cara sat in a corner barstool. The bartender had barely said hello before she said, "Papa's Wheat, please."

The beer was delivered. Cara sighed as she sipped it. She could do this. She could calm herself.

The calm was short-lived. The door thwacked open and a chorus of feminine voices rushed in like rapids in a river after a thunderstorm. Cara closed her eyes and took a bigger sip of beer than before.

"Get some beer for the bride!" Cara couldn't help herself and glanced in the direction of the voice. She saw one woman in a neon pink sash that said "Bridesmaid" in looping cursive, holding out money towards the bartender as he filled a glass with beer. Another woman stood next to her in a short white dress, cheap veil, and white sash that said "The Bride, Bitches" in the same font.

The bride turned her head before Cara could look away. Cara's curiosity became panic, but it was too late to duck back down and go unseen. Jennifer's eyes widened in time with her smile. "Cara? Cara Vineyard?"

"Yeah," Cara said weakly.

"Oh my God! How are you?" Jennifer walked over as fast as she could in her white stilettos. Cara knew she couldn't escape, even if she could outrun her. "I haven't seen you since graduation! You still living in Leslie?"

"Yeah."

"I can't believe I never see you. Come on, have a beer with us. I'm getting married!"

"Really? I couldn't tell."

Jennifer actually laughed, and Cara found her resolve weakened just enough to stand up. "At least come say hi," she said as she nodded towards a table of girls all wearing sashes and assorted cheap costume jewelry.

The girls waved at them — at Jennifer, most likely, but their eyes traveled to Cara to be polite — and Cara found herself walking with Jennifer. She figured she could stay standing, say hi, shotgun her beer, and then go smoke in her truck before going home. These were girls she knew in school. They'd have no problems letting her leave once they'd said hi and gotten a few digs in. She took another gulp of beer.

"Come on, sit down," Jennifer said as she pulled up a chair. Cara sat, but on the edge and without scooting towards the others. "Guys, look who I found!"

"Hey Cara!" An Asian woman Cara vaguely recognized from homeroom — Lisa, her name was Lisa — waved at her. Cara held up her fingers in greeting.

A woman Cara didn't remember at all waved as well. "I'm Shante," she said. Cara nodded in her direction.

"Still wearing baseball caps all the time, huh?" It took all of Cara's will to look in the direction of the voice, one attached to a name she'd never have trouble remembering. Amanda smiled at her over a beer. Cara looked for the malice behind it. It wasn't there, but Cara knew it was lurking in the shadows.

Cara shrugged. "I like them."

"You love them," Jennifer said. She looked at Shante and added, "She wore them all the time and all the teachers would try to get her to stop. 'Cara, remove your hat please' was almost part of the Pledge of Allegiance."

Shante and Lisa laughed, and even Cara found herself smiling a little at Jennifer's description of the memory. In school, it had just been one more way her teachers hated her. Hearing it now, though, wasn't so bad — it was even sort of funny.

"So who are you marrying?" Cara asked.

"His name's Greg," Jennifer said as she waved her ring finger over the table.

"Wait, it's not Greg Sturdivant, is it?"

"Yes! You know him?"

"If he's a guy who lives in Leslie, Cara knows him," Amanda joked.

"Hey, that's my fiancé you're talking about," Jennifer said with a glare that pleasantly surprised Cara.

"I didn't mean now, I meant in high school. You didn't even know him then."

"Still —"

"I only work with him," Cara interjected.

"At the brewery? Wow, I'm really surprised I haven't seen you!" Jennifer said. "I love going there and visiting Greg while he's working."

"I usually don't hang around the brewery." And Cara had never been more grateful. Seeing Jennifer and all the memories she brought with her on a regular basis would be more than any deliveries or any drives could ever erase. "I make deliveries for Keith around the state."

"You ever come to Raleigh?" Shante asked. "There's a lot of bars there, and I always see Papa's Secret on the menus."

"I'm in Raleigh a lot, yeah."

"I'm still living there," Amanda said, even though Cara hadn't asked.

"Amanda just got married," Jennifer said with a smile.

"Yeah, I saw her ring." Cara couldn't miss it with the way Amanda kept her left hand facing the table as she drank. "Congratulations," she said with as much sincerity as she could muster.

"Thank you."

"Do you guys ever see each other?" Jennifer asked. Cara wondered if she was serious. Cara and Amanda were never friends and never would be.

"No, I'm usually just in and out of the bars," Cara said.

"You don't stick around and meet any cute guys?" Amanda asked with a smile that was far from kind. Cara almost took comfort in its familiarity.

"Please, all the guys she sees there are probably drunk frat guys," Shante said with a playful eye roll. "Why would she bother?"

"Some guys are better than none," Lisa added. "There're maybe five men in Leslie that aren't married."

"Four, starting in June!" Jennifer said as she raised her glass. The others toasted her and laughed. Cara smiled a little and barely lifted her beer.

"And three right here."

All of the women looked in the direction of a man's voice. Three men stood near their table, all with the shit-eating grins Cara recognized as ones that came with a terrible pick-up attempt. She took a large gulp of beer and noticed with relief that she was three good gulps from finishing it.

"Heard you talking about single guys," the one on the right, the one who'd spoken before, said. The growing chill emanating from the women at the table did nothing to deter him. "You all looking for a few to join you?"

"No," Jennifer replied without looking at them.

"Not even for tonight?" another man, the one on the left, asked. "Ain't this your last night being single?"

"Fuck off."

Cara admired Jennifer's audacity. The men only ooh'd and held up their hands. "Man, her husband's got a hell of a marriage waiting for him," the one on the left said.

"Not all of you are getting married, though," the man in the center observed.

"But all of us are leaving," Lisa said as she grabbed her clutch.

"Come on," Shante added, "let's get to Cary."

"We're not all leaving," Amanda said with a pointed glance in Cara's direction. "You want a date tonight?"

Cara looked Amanda square in the eye and mustered up as much hatred as she could in the hope that Amanda would feel it, even a little. It was the best she could do with so many witnesses around them. "No," she said curtly. "I have a boyfriend," she added in the direction of the men in a vain attempt to get them to leave.

"Oh, like that matters," Amanda said with a laugh.

"Amanda, cut it out or they'll never leave," Jennifer said with a rude glance in the direction of the men. Her eyes briefly caught Cara's, and Cara thought she saw an apology within them. It wasn't enough. Cara's anger was already settled in, and sipping her beer only made it crackle, like water thrown on a skillet to test the heat.

"*Does* it matter?" the one in the center — the one that, up until now, Cara had hated the least — said with a sly glance that almost made bile rise in her throat. "Your friend seems to want you to have a good time."

"She's not my friend," Cara said. She slammed down her glass and swirled towards the men, all three of whom finally stepped back. "And the only thing I want all three of you to do is get hit by a truck."

"Something wrong here?" The bartender walked towards them and the man who'd spoken first narrowed his eyes.

"This bitch just threatened us," he spat as he pointed his finger. Cara imagined cutting it off and using it to stir his friend's drink. She didn't realize she'd smirked at the thought until the one in the center glowered at her.

"What are you laughing at, bitch?" he huffed.

"Get the fuck out of here," the bartender said, shoving all three men toward the door.

"We didn't do anything!" the third man shouted.

"Get out before I call the cops."

"Fuck you!" The man who'd first spoken to all of them looked at Cara as he and his friends were shoved out the door. "Fuck you, you cunt!" The security woman at the front door followed them out. A few patrons clapped as the bartender walked back towards Jennifer's table.

"You all alright?" he asked, looking only at the women seated — not at Cara. Cara took a breath.

"Yes, thank you," Jennifer said with a smile. The bartender left.

"Christ, you can really hold your own, can't you?" Shante said with a glance in Cara's direction. It did nothing to temper her anger.

"Should we bring her as back-up for the other bars?" Lisa added with a laugh.

"I think we should just go," Amanda said as she strung her purse over her shoulder. "Get to Cary before Cara causes any more trouble by not going home with a guy for once."

Cara could do many things that, at worst, would get her kicked out of the bar. She could throw her last swallow of beer in Amanda's face. She could slap her. She could call her every name she'd had for her as they grew up together.

She didn't do those things, but she imagined them. She imagined them and imagined more, imagined what she'd never do to Amanda even if they were alone. She wouldn't do them to Amanda, because Amanda couldn't disappear without a trace the way the hitchhikers did. People would look for her — and worse, Cara would remember her. Cara would still hear Amanda pretending to whisper, still hear Amanda say things about her along with everyone else. She could hear it now, and now had new words to add to her memory, words that swirled and foamed in a cesspool that Cara kept contained to clenched fingers in her pockets and a silent stare.

Amanda looked for a moment in Cara's eyes. Her smirk disappeared. A flash of fear darted across her face. It disappeared into a smug smile and a shrug. "Men are the worst," she said. The other girls laughed.

Cara smiled, but not at Amanda's joke. She smiled at the brief moment of fear, the moment Amanda felt a piece of what Cara was capable of. A moment where Amanda wondered if she wasn't untouchable, if all the shit she'd heaped on Cara since they were five, had heaped on her even after she moved away from Leslie, would finally have a consequence she could feel.

Like any happiness Cara had in Leslie, it was fleeting. "Thanks for making the night interesting," Amanda said with a curt nod in Cara's direction.

"Nice to meet you!" Shante said with a polite wave as she and Lisa turned to follow Amanda.

"Nice seeing you," Jennifer said with a smile. "Maybe I'll see you at the brewery sometime."

Not if Cara had anything to say about it. "Congratulations," she said again. She stood and watched as all four of them left.

The mixture of anger and triumph continued to churn in Cara's stomach. She heard all four girls' laughter as she looked at their vacated seats. She especially heard Amanda. She heard everything Amanda said to her, and everything she imagined Amanda had said behind her back. She played it deliberately like a CD on repeat, skipping back to each track and keeping each song's effect pulsing through her brain, her head, her fingers.

Cara needed to go — she wasn't sure where, but she knew she needed to leave.

———

Cara left the bar and hopped into her truck. She sped out of the parking lot and onto the road. A horn blared at her, and she screeched to a halt.

"Watch it!" the woman in the other car shouted. Cara flipped her off, then continued on without so much as a second thought.

The hum that started in Charlie's turned into a blare as she got onto the highway. She turned on the radio, but her memories sounded over the music. She thought of names and faces she hadn't thought about in months, some she hadn't thought about in years. Thinking of one grade led to another, one memory into the next, one student into another student. Amanda became girls, who then became Moira. Men she met on the road became boys she kissed behind school, who became boys that talked, who then became Jackson.

Jackson. Her thoughts quieted a little at the thought of him, but didn't cease. She swallowed and tried to think of him instead, to bury her thoughts like she'd done so many times before. Maybe the problem before was that she'd tried to bury them alone. Now she had the thought of Jackson to help her hold them down.

Her memories, though, were insistent. She'd hear a whisper of something Amanda or Lucas or Mr. Murphy said. She'd replace it with Jackson whispering in her ear. She'd imagine Jackson pulling her close and breathing "Good night" as they fell asleep. She'd fall asleep and her dreams would be about the people she knew saying awful things about her, things that everyone said once they got to know her more. Things that Moira knew to say right away.

Cara shook her head. Moira hadn't said anything to her. Unlike Amanda, her teasing really was in jest, and anything not in jest was just awkwardness from getting to know her. Once Moira got to know her, the teasing would be real.

Cara shook her head again and pressed her lips together. She wouldn't get to know Moira. Moira was just visiting. She'd be gone soon. She'd be gone, and she and Jackson would be alone again. They'd be together, and could speak freely to each other, the only whispers being what Jackson sighed in her ear. Whispers she could enjoy before he got to know her more and began to whisper her name to other people.

Cara gripped the steering wheel and bit her lip. Jackson would never do that. That she was certain.

But could she be certain? She'd only known him for a few months.

It usually only took a few weeks for the whispers to start — sometimes a few days.

Cara let her thoughts go and imagined him saying the things she'd heard other people say. She gave Jackson their expressions and taunts, but kept his voice and his eyes. She imagined him calling her a slut, a whore, a bitch. She imagined him saying he never cared for her, or that he stopped caring for her once they spent more time together.

Imagining everything she imagined before, but in Jackson's voice, brought her a strange sense of peace. She imagined some more, gave Jackson some of the worst things she could ever think to say about her, things that Cara often heard from people like Amanda but usually made up herself.

She calmed further. She began to hear the music on the radio. A song she loved in high school came on, and she found herself singing along. She didn't understand her calmness. Jackson was the last person she wanted to hear say those things. Jackson was the last person she wanted to lose. Maybe she was comforted by them because when he inevitably said those things, when she inevitably lost him, it wouldn't be so hard on her because she'd already known it was coming.

Something, though — something soft and with weight, like the first drop of rain on a windshield — told her that maybe she was comforted because she knew Jackson would never say those things, and knew she'd never lose Jackson. He wouldn't disappear.

Cara felt her truck slow, and realized her foot was easing on the gas. She pulled to the side of the highway, nothing but trees in front of her or behind her. She turned down her music so she could hear Jackson better. She imagined him holding her close in his apartment, in his bed, on his couch. She imagined him in her truck, pulling her towards him, both of them alone and only whispering to one another, only saying what they felt about the other to the other. Cara closed her eyes.

A loud knock made Cara's eyes snap back open. She turned and saw an older man outside the passenger window. He smiled and looked pleased. Cara couldn't even try to look happy. She was about to peel off when she heard him shout, "Can you give me a lift?"

Curiosity overtook her fear, but she only rolled down the window. "A lift?" Cara asked.

"Yes! I've been trying to get a ride for over an hour."

Cara looked at the trees she thought were the only things around her on that stretch of road. A truck whizzed by them, followed by several cars. She'd barely noticed them. Apparently, she hadn't even noticed the man.

But he'd noticed her. "Can you take me to Eden?" he asked.

"Eden? Kind of far, isn't it?"

"Less than an hour. We're almost in Greensboro."

"Greensboro?"

"Yeah, a couple miles or so. I was about to walk there when you showed up." Cara looked around again, and the man's brow furrowed. "You okay, miss?"

"Yes, yes." Cara took a breath as she held the steering wheel. "I've just been driving awhile and must've lost track."

"Well, if it isn't too much trouble to take me to Eden, I'd appreciate it. I'll even buy you some food or something —"

"You don't have to. Get in."

The man beamed and hopped in the truck as soon as Cara unlocked the passenger door.

————

It was near dark when Cara dropped the man off at a local Sheetz. "My buddy works nearby, he can drive me home," the man said with a grin as he hoisted himself out of the truck. "Not that I don't trust you to take me there. Just don't wanna inconvenience you."

"No problem. Have a good night," Cara called before the passenger door slammed shut. The man gave a quick wave, then disappeared into the shadows behind the streetlamps. She made her way back to the highway and smiled at the thought of the man assuring her that he trusted her — ironic, given that he was the rare person she picked up that made it to his destination.

Cara's fingers twitched a little at the thought of holding her blade and making someone's eyes widen as they touched their throat and realized their last whispers had been in her ear. She couldn't imagine that with that man, though. He'd been like a kind grandpa, just minding his business and trying to get home. He hadn't even told her his name, nor asked for hers. He just looked out the window and hummed nonsensically with the music in the car, even though Cara doubted he had any idea who Incubus or The Offspring were.

Cara drove by a streetlight along I-40, and something glinted at her from the passenger seat. She looked down quickly and saw a quarter where the man had been sitting. She smiled as she picked it up and tucked it in her pocket. He may have left alive, but she still had a souvenir she could take home.

Her smile fell. Home, where her mother was probably sulking because Cara was spending the weekend with Jackson again. Delores kept assuring Cara that it was her life and she could do what she wanted, but Cara could practically see the asterisk at the end saying Delores wished she wanted to stay at home with her, and stay in a life dotted with farm chores, television, day jobs, and the occasional kill.

Cara thumbed the quarter in her pocket, rubbing it like a worry stone. She imagined telling her mother she'd gotten it through less savory means, and smirked at the thought of her mother's pride in a left-behind coin. "But there isn't any blood on it," she'd say.

Still, it'd sit next to the belt buckle, the hat, the key rings and pocketknives and the multitude of other items Cara collected over the years. "At least you did something," Delores would say as she set it on the table.

Cara's brow furrowed. Her mother had never said that before — not after a kill. But she heard it in Delores' voice as clearly as the full moon shining over the highway.

"You're spending so much time with Jackson, you're not doing anything else," Delores' voice continued.

"Yes I am," Cara muttered.

"I want to be proud of you, not covering for you."

"Stop it." Cara wasn't sure if that was for her mother or herself.

"If you're not gonna do anything or bring me anything home, at least stay here and don't disappear on me."

"No!" Cara startled herself with her shout. She looked around, even though no one was in the truck. A deer disappeared from the side of the road into the trees. Cara chuckled a little at the thought of it telling its deer friends about the crazy blonde truck driver who was arguing with herself. She forced herself to keep the smile on her face even when she stopped laughing. She turned the radio up. Her mother's words and voice became a hum that blended in with the music. Yet another hum she'd have to ignore.

Cara grew a little sad.

She became sadder still when I-40 showed more signs of life as she neared the Triangle. Soon she'd be past the airport, then Raleigh, then back to trees and darkness as she approached Leslie. Maybe her mother wouldn't say the things she'd imagined when she walked in the door. Maybe her mother would just be happy to see her. After all, she wasn't expecting her that night — she was supposed to be in Raleigh with Jackson.

Cara's eyes widened. She was supposed to be in Raleigh. Her mother wasn't expecting her to be home. She wasn't expecting anything of her. She wouldn't even be expecting a phone call, because Delores already knew where Cara was supposed to be.

But Cara wasn't there — and only Cara knew that. Jackson knew she was gone, but thought she'd be in Leslie.

Cara could be in Leslie — but she didn't have to be.

Cara felt a sense of happiness she hadn't felt in years. Everyone thought they knew where she was, but no one knew where exactly — and for that night at least, she decided to keep it to herself. She pulled off on an exit in Durham, drove in search of a motel before deciding against that and following signs for Mallard Lake. When she got there, she saw signs warning against boats and trespassers, but no cops or cameras — and more importantly, no other cars.

She pulled a little ways towards the lake — far enough in to not be seen on the road, but close enough for an easy departure if anyone came by and gave her trouble — and parked. Everything clicked off. She moved to the bed of the truck and lay against a folded blanket. The only hum was the sound of crickets and frogs. It moved through her ears like a pulse, one that beat against her cheek as she fell asleep.

CHAPTER 10

Cara woke up to the hum of birds. She realized with the periwinkle glow of morning that she'd parked under a tree, one whose blossoms were starting to burst and which housed a bunch of birds that were looking to fill its branches with eggs. She sat up, rubbed the sleep from her eyes, and started up her truck.

Cara slowly made her way back to Leslie, taking the back roads instead of the highway. She had breakfast at a rundown Waffle House, and stopped at a hardware store to pick up more critter traps. Most of her procrastinating, though, was spent on the road, driving by long stretches of trees that pointed to a distance she would follow.

Like all distances, though, she eventually followed them back to Leslie. It was after lunch by the time she parked in her dusty driveway. Cara noticed with a little disappointment that Delores sat on the porch smoking a cigarette. She'd hoped for just a few more moments alone before walking inside.

"You're home early," Delores called.

"I bought some more traps," Cara called as she lifted them out of the back of the truck. "Want to set them up now?"

Delores was already on her feet and stubbing out her cigarette on the porch rail. Cara smiled a little as she nodded towards her mother's hand. "You could've left me some of that," she teased.

"Get your own cigarettes," Delores replied, but Cara saw a small smile on her lips as she walked down the stairs.

Cara and Delores moved across the property, setting up new traps and cleaning out old ones. Most were empty. "Give it time," Delores observed. "The possums and rabbits and other critters'll be having babies and they'll all be wandering in here looking for shelter soon enough."

"Well, maybe we can go for a walk around the lake before going back in," Cara offered as she looked out towards the woods bordering the farm. *Like we used to*, she added in her thoughts — an addition that surprised her.

It was a surprise she only shared with herself. Silence answered her. Cara turned around and saw that Delores had already begun walking back towards the farm.

Cara felt more stung, then more sad, than she anticipated. She stood still and watched her mother walk away, then shrugged and followed behind.

———

Cara stayed at the farm that night. She and Delores shared a quiet dinner and Delores watched TV. Cara tried to watch it with her, but she was mostly distracted. She'd think of driving, then think of Jackson, then think of Jackson naked and think about masturbating, but knew that claiming she was ready to go to bed at 7:30 would only arouse Delores' suspicions or, worse, arouse nothing because Delores wouldn't suspect what Cara was up to, she would know. So Cara stayed on the couch, ignoring the laugh track on some sitcom her mother merely smirked at, while wondering if Moira had maybe gone home early.

Cara's phone chimed once, signaling a text message. She smiled as she picked up her phone. *How's your weekend?* Jackson had written.

Cara kept her smile as she slowly typed back, *Good. Have fun w Moira?*

He wrote back within seconds, barely any time after she'd set her phone back on the coffee table. *Yeah. Miss you though.*

Miss you too, she replied.

The sitcom ended and became a cop drama before her phone chimed once more. "Can you at least turn the sound off?" Delores said with a frown. "It's interrupting my show."

"It's one chime," Cara said as she picked up her phone. "And it's the first ten seconds of your show."

"It's important. I'll miss something."

"If you're so concerned about that, then why are you talking over it?"

Delores kept quiet, and also kept her frown. Cara did the same even as she read Jackson's message: *Moira leaves tmrw. Wanna come over after work?*

Cara typed faster than she'd ever texted, and not just because her message was short: *Yes.* Her mood improved with each moment she thought of going back to Jackson's the next night. She considered going that night, but tempered on that thought when she thought of running into Moira before she left for her hotel. She didn't want to interfere, not on Moira's last night there. She also didn't want to feel like she was on the periphery, though she was already getting that experience by spending the night with her mother and their television.

Deep down, though, Cara knew she was on that periphery because she was spending less time on the farm. Her home was feeling less like her home, and Cara almost felt like a guest her mother had to entertain — and reluctantly at that. With each passing moment of silence, Cara felt the weight of the silence between them settle on her like a quilt. Talking wouldn't help. Delores would probably break her phone if she kept texting.

Cara stood up and stretched a little. "I think I'm gonna go to bed," she said. She knew she wouldn't be asleep for at least an hour, but she could read or even just stare at the ceiling. Anything was better than sitting next to her mother's silence and feeling the gnawing mix of sadness and annoyance that she could only get at home.

"Night," Delores said absently. She didn't care. Cara didn't know why she'd even bothered to try and stay downstairs.

————

Cara's shift at Papa's Secret was set to start late. She used the extra time to lay in bed and avoid breakfast with her mother. She didn't even stir until she heard Rhonda's car pull out of the driveway.

Cara walked downstairs and saw one muffin waiting for her on the table. She felt a little bad as she began to eat, but not bad enough to not enjoy her breakfast. The sun shone over their fields. Cara thought about taking a hike before driving out to the brewery.

The hike moved further and further away as the morning stretched on. She showered for a long time, and lay in bed for even longer after she was done. The weight of last night's silence still draped over her. She thought of her mother watching television, how the only things she'd said to her had been pithy asides about her phone or her shows.

"I wish you wouldn't leave so much," she heard Delores say — even though she hadn't said so last night.

Yet in a way, she had. Delores' remarks and silence were all a product of her disapproval. Cara knew it, even though she also knew her mother would deny it if she said so. She wished Delores would just say so.

In lieu of hearing it, Cara could imagine it. She imagined arguing with her mother. The weight of last night's silence was replaced with a blanket of slow, simmering anger that Cara recognized from school. She wrapped herself in it anyway. She'd hear those things at home, because Delores said and thought those things no matter how much she assured Cara she didn't.

Cara closed her eyes and breathed in rhythm with the hum, a hum that now followed her home. It followed her no matter how far she ran away and no matter how deep she buried a stranger who whispered. She supposed she'd have to get used to hearing it everywhere.

Everywhere except with Jackson. The hum came in flickers around him, but died as soon as he touched her. Tonight. She'd be with him tonight, and she wouldn't have to think about what everyone else thought anymore.

Her phone began to ring, and Cara was a little disappointed it didn't chime with a text. She picked up her phone and furrowed her brow when she saw who it was.

"I'm not coming in until noon, remember?" she said as she answered.

"Good morning to you too," Keith answered. "I was going to at least ask how your weekend was."

"It was fine, and it's technically still going."

"Yeah, I remember. But someone's in here looking for you."

Cara's eyes widened. She thought for a moment it was the cops, then paused. No cops had found any bodies. If they had, they'd come to the farm first.

She wondered if it was someone who worked with her mother, and wondered if something had happened to her mother at work, because of course something would happen to her the morning Cara was home and decided to spend it not speaking to her. But someone would call if something had happened, not go to the brewery.

"Who?" she asked as her thoughts raced to answer the question themselves.

"Hang on." Cara heard Keith's muffled voice ask for a name, and Cara wondered if it was someone she knew from school. Maybe Amanda had driven by, decided to pick up where she left off at Charlie's, and dropped in. Cara figured she hadn't, but the thought of hitting Amanda over the head with a tap and then dropping her into a brewing vat improved Cara's mood significantly.

Keith interrupted her daydreaming with the answer: "Her name's Moira."

Cara sat up. "Moira?"

"Yeah. You know her?"

"She's my boyfriend's friend." Cara regretted saying so in an instant. She could almost hear Keith's grin widening.

"She knows your boyfriend? So I can ask her anything about him?"

"Just tell her I'll be there soon," Cara said as she struggled to pull on her socks with one hand. Every moment Moira had alone with Keith and, worse, Sadie was a moment they could spend digging for information that Cara didn't want to give.

Cara was out of one driveway and in another in a seeming instant. Keith and Greg stacked kegs outside and looked up when her truck screeched to a halt. "Where's Moira?" Cara asked as she hopped out of the truck.

"Yeah, I'm doing good," Keith answered. "Thanks for asking."

"If I say good morning and ask how your day was, will you tell me where she is?"

"She's inside — and ask me after you get back from making these deliveries." Greg was already taking a keg towards the truck, and Keith followed behind. Cara was too concerned with Moira to care. She sped inside and saw with relief that Moira was in there alone.

"What are you doing here?" Cara asked. If Moira asked her to say good morning, she swore she'd punch something.

"Found you on a can," Moira replied with a smile. "I was drinking one of the beers you left in Jackson's fridge and when he said you worked here, I jotted it down."

Cara scrambled to remember if she'd ever left an empty beer can anywhere on her drives, namely the drives where she picked someone up. She shook her head and tried to focus on the situation at hand. "So, why are you here?" Cara asked, trying to ask politely. She didn't want to be rude to Jackson's friend, not when she'd already made both Moira and Jackson curious about why she'd decided to vanish over the weekend.

"To see you! I like beer as much as the next person, but not at 10 a.m."

"But what for?"

"Straight to the point — I like it, even if it's a little jarring." Moira laughed as she nodded her head towards the doorway. "I'm heading back to Pinesboro today. Since you didn't come back to Raleigh, I wanted to talk to you before I left. And before you ask —" Cara closed her mouth — "I just wanted to shoot the shit and talk to you one-on-one."

That didn't answer Cara's question, but she figured the only way she'd get an answer was to agree to walk with her. "Keith, you mind if I talk to Moira for a bit before she heads home?" Cara asked as they walked outside.

"Sure, no problem," Keith called. "You're here early, and deliveries today are just as far as Apex."

Cara felt relieved, as a shorter delivery day meant going to see Jackson sooner after work. She was surprised by that relief, but was brought out of wondering about it when Moira smiled at her.

"A delivery girl, huh? Jackson just said you worked here."

"I do what Keith needs me to do, but yeah, I mostly deliver beer and get supplies." Cara found it easier to talk to Moira the further away they got from the brewery. Cara noticed they were approaching a line of trees that began the scant surrounding wood. She wondered with a smirk if Moira was a wood sprite that beckoned people like her and Jackson to come to the trees and open their mouths. Her smirk stopped when she remembered Moira and Jackson talking in secret on Saturday.

"Ah, you know me well," Moira said with a grin. "Bringing me to my favorite place to talk."

"Why do you like the woods so much?" Cara asked.

"Everything just seems to hush when you're inside of them. I don't know if the bark can mute things or what, but all the noises within just sound quieter. One bird chirping, one snake sliding under some dead leaves. Even a breeze going through some leaves just sounds like Mother Nature telling everyone else to be quiet."

"Everyone except us."

"Well, that's why I talk quiet when I'm in the woods, and why I talk about quiet things."

Cara felt mounting frustration at Moira speaking as if she were talking to Jackson and she'd actually know what the hell she was talking about. "Like what?" Cara asked, prepping herself to hold her temper when Moira answered with another puzzle.

Moira smiled. "Like you."

Cara stopped walking.

"You're one of the quietest people I know," Moira added with a small laugh.

Cara didn't join her. "So you were talking about me on Saturday?"

"We talked about you most of the weekend, but yeah, a little bit on Saturday."

Cara tried not to remember. She didn't want to remember Moira's mischievous glance in her direction when she'd interrupted them. She didn't want to think about how Moira and Jackson were just like Amanda and Jennifer, just like Sadie and Keith, just like anyone who broke away from her and managed to steal a few moments where they could make fun of her. Why did she have to be right? Why did Moira and Jackson have to be like everyone else?

"It wasn't anything bad," Moira said.

Cara didn't want to believe her, but a small part of her did. "It wasn't?" Cara sounded more wounded than she'd intended, and she hated herself for it even as she took small comfort in Moira's look of pity.

"No! Jesus. I know I act like a twelve-year-old sometimes, but I'm not going to gossip like one and I'm certainly not going to act like a mean one — especially around someone who makes my best friend so happy."

"Is that what he told you?"

"Cara, I saw it. I saw it as soon as he opened the door on Saturday, but I figured it was because Raleigh'd been good to him. When you walked in the living room, I saw just how much Raleigh'd been good to him." She laughed a little as she kicked a stone in their path. "But yeah, when you caught up with us in the parking lot, I was needling him about you. If anyone was getting picked on, it was him. It was nice to see him getting sheepish instead of withdrawn and sullen like he always did back home."

"What'd he say?" Cara cared about that more than anything Moira had said about her, whether or not she was telling the truth about all of it being good.

"Nothing I'm sure you haven't seen already when you're with him."

Cara closed her eyes so Moira wouldn't see her roll them. If Moira was going to talk in puzzles, then Cara would move on to different questions. "So'd you have a good weekend?" she asked.

"We did. Mostly caught up on three years of happenings."

Cara stopped walking. "Three years? Isn't that when he moved away?"

"Yes. I travel around a lot, and Jackson's never coming back to Pinesboro unless someone dies or something."

"It sounds like he wouldn't have to wait long for that to happen."

Moira stopped walking and looked at her with wide eyes. Cara wondered if she'd said something wrong until Moira laughed. "Jesus, that sounds exactly like something Jackson would say."

"He told me about Pinesboro."

"Well, there's more to it than all the death that Jackson's obsessed with. But he's not too far off. I get why he'd want to leave it all behind."

Moira studied a leaf as she spoke and stroked it with her fingertips. Cara still saw a flash of sadness cross her face. "I'm sorry if that includes you," Cara said with sincerity.

Moira shrugged. "I'm not. He needed to leave more than I needed him to stay. It wasn't safe for him." She looked up at Cara, and for the first time since they met, Moira's face held no mirth and no teasing. "Has he told you about his mom?"

"Yes." Cara tried not to fume, but the quiet of the woods made it easier for her to hear everything Jackson had said and everything she imagined his mother saying to him. "Did she try to hurt him?" she asked.

"Not physically. I guess there was always a part of her that remembered he was her son."

"Didn't stop her from treating him like garbage."

"No, but with someone as awful as Mrs. Price, you'll take anything that isn't her being a total monster."

"Now *you* sound like Jackson."

Moira snorted. "I'll never sound like Jackson. He gives her too many chances, ones that only a child could ever give a parent. He actually thought about moving back in with her when he came home from school."

Cara remembered how Jackson said she'd turned him away. She couldn't say she didn't understand his reasoning, though. With all the fights she'd had with her mother, she never once thought of leaving her behind for good.

But for all their fights, her mother had never treated her the way Mrs. Price treated Jackson. She couldn't help but think of Jackson as a small boy feeding a bobcat in his backyard, trusting that this wild animal would always be his pet. "I'm glad he lived with you instead," Cara said.

"Yeah, almost like old times. Jackson was always welcome in our house, in no small part because Mrs. Price gave me the creeps. Whenever I went over there she'd give me dirty looks or yell at me and Jackson for being too loud while she prayed. It's one of the reasons we started going in the woods behind his house. It was so we wouldn't have to listen to her."

"I don't know how he can stand her," Cara said absently as she picked up a twig she'd crunched on the path.

"Well, everyone's got a breaking point, and it seems he's finally reached his. I don't think he's spoken to her in years, nor her him."

Cara was about to mention Mrs. Price's letters, but stopped herself. She suspected those letters were a secret between them, one Jackson didn't want to share with Moira. She'd keep it for him.

"And I'm happy about that," Moira continued. "She made him angry and afraid, but it was when he'd be quiet and sullen that I'd be most concerned. Anger and fear fade. He'd carry that quietness for days. He'd probably carry it forever if he'd stayed in Pinesboro."

"Well, he got out," Cara said. She conjured up a mental image of Mrs. Price so she could mentally shove her off a cliff and out of her thoughts.

"Yup. And he found you."

Cara kept her gaze away so Moira wouldn't see her blush. "Yeah, I guess so."

"And I'm glad he did. Leaving Pinesboro was good for him, but it wasn't enough. I'd see it when I'd visit him in college. He'd always be carrying a piece of what I saw when his mother upset him — never as much as when he lived with her, but it'd be there. It was something he couldn't let go of. It was something I saw even when he lived with me and not her. The only time I didn't see it was when I saw him with you."

"I don't think it's completely gone."

"Well, if it isn't, then you help him carry it in a way that isn't harmful — isn't a burden to him," Moira corrected. Cara furrowed her brow, but Moira looked at the trees. "But he's different with you, and he's different in a way I've never seen him with anybody. He's … happy." Moira looked back at Cara. "And I hope he'll be happy for a long time."

Cara furrowed her brow. "Wait — why wouldn't it be for a long time?"

"I'm not saying it wouldn't —"

"Did he say something?"

"No! Please, don't think that. He talked about you almost all weekend. He's crazy about you."

Cara was about to ask why she was concerned, and then stopped. She realized Moira was only talking about how he felt about her. "I'm not thinking about leaving or anything," Cara said. "I want to be with him."

"I'm sure," Moira replied.

"He makes me happy too."

"I'm sure he does."

"You're just sure? You can say you know, because I'm telling you it's true."

Moira gave the faintest of smiles. "So particular. Okay, yes, I know. I also know you left on Saturday because you thought we didn't want you around — that you thought you were in our way and were interfering between Jackson and me."

It wasn't the only reason, but Cara couldn't deny that it was the main one. She looked down at the ground.

"I just wanted to tell you that I saw how much you mean to him because I don't want you to think he'd ever not want you around. He does. And I think he needs you. You set him right in ways that I don't think anyone's ever done for him — not his grandmother, not my parents, and certainly not me. And I know things change, relationships go their courses and I'm not here to shackle you to Jackson —"

"You don't need to —"

"But I wanted to tell you how good you are for him — and I really, really hope you'll never doubt that."

"You almost seem afraid I'll go. You're more worried I'll dump him than either of us are." Cara grinned. Moira didn't. The mirth and teasing were completely absent from her eyes. Cara dropped her smile.

"I won't doubt that," Cara promised. "I don't doubt it." It was true. Cara remembered how comforted she'd felt when she heard how false the words of others sounded when she imagined them in Jackson's voice. She missed hearing Jackson's actual voice, and she tried not to shut her eyes and sigh at the thought of his lips and his whispers brushing her ear later that night.

"Good." Moira reached out and squeezed Cara's arm. Cara flinched, but not strongly enough for Moira to notice — or at least not enough for Moira to let go. "I'm glad he met you."

Cara felt a small chill, one she couldn't readily explain. She'd at least try to explain it away. "You make it sound like I'm all he has. He's got friends — and a really good one in you."

Moira smiled a little, then studied the leaves above her. She didn't seem to see any of them. "It's still good to know he's got someone like you in his life. Someone who sets him right and helps him know that everything isn't as bad as it was for him back home."

Cara shrugged. She had more questions, questions that only seemed to multiply whenever Moira spoke. But she knew Moira wouldn't answer them. "I just want to do what he does for me," she said.

Moira looked back at her. Cara pursed her lips a little — she hadn't meant to be quite so open — but Moira's smile helped her to relax.

"Then I'm glad you found him too," she said.

————

Moira and Cara returned to the brewery. "I was beginning to think you'd ditched work for a hike," Keith teased as he set a six-pack on top of a small tower of cans Cara presumed were for delivery.

"I kept her out there too long," Moira said. "My fault."

"Oh, then I guess I won't be giving you this to take home." Keith held out a pack of Papa's Wheat towards Moira. She took it with a smile.

"I'll buy it from you."

"Please, don't. It's a gift."

"I can't —"

"Really, take it. Where are you from again?"

"Pinesboro."

"We're not distributing in Pinesboro yet. Tell your friends, give them a beer and tell them to ask their bars for more." Keith winked at her. "But keep at least two for yourself, as a gift from me to you."

Moira smiled and Cara tried not to roll her eyes. "Will do …"

"Keith."

"Right, Keith. Thanks."

"Sure thing. See you around." Keith walked back inside, and Cara made a mental note to give him grief later for shamelessly flirting at work.

"Well, whenever you come back, maybe the four of us can double-date," Cara joked.

Moira laughed, but it was clipped, like it'd been stopped by a lump in her throat. Cara shook off the thought. She was thinking too much.

"Maybe so," Moira said. "But I better get going and let you get back to work." She opened her arms. Cara didn't think they were on hugging terms yet, but she didn't want to offend Jackson's friend — certainly not when she'd been so nice to her all morning. She leaned in and gave Moira a soft hug. Moira held her tightly — too tightly — but Cara tried not to move so she wouldn't offend her.

"It was nice to meet you," Moira said.

"You too," Cara replied as she counted the seconds she needed to keep her hold before it wouldn't be rude to let go.

Moira squeezed her, then let go. She got in her car, gave a quick wave, then left. Cara watched her car disappear down the brewery's driveway.

"Can I help you load your truck now?"

Cara turned and saw Greg. He stood by the beer cans and seemed more than eager to start lifting. At least he waited until she was there. "Sure," Cara said. While Moira's words still danced in her brain, she needed to focus on her job. Doing her job meant finishing her job, and finishing her job meant being with Jackson. Cara brightened at that thought.

She made her deliveries with a smile that widened with each six-pack gone. She returned to the brewery and handed Keith the supplies he asked for with a grin. She finished her shift around dinnertime, and just as she was about to go to Cook Out for a meal in her truck, she heard the single chime that always lifted her spirits.

Home, Jackson had texted. *Door unlocked.*

Cara bought two burgers and two fries. She smiled as she parked in his lot and sped to his door. She walked inside and saw him sprawled on the couch, absently watching TV. His expression changed as soon as he saw her. His eyes widened, his smile grew, and he got to his feet in less than five seconds. He looked as happy as she felt. They were together again. Everything felt right.

CHAPTER 11

More and more, Cara brought herself back to a sense of normalcy by going back to Jackson. Weekends with him became weeknights. Her mother became a voice on the phone who said, "Are you sure?" then "Fine" when Cara would call and say she was staying in Raleigh. Her job was the time between waking up with him and going to sleep with him. Even her drives just became the ones between Raleigh and Leslie, ways that she would get to Jackson. He was someone she returned to, someone she was supposed to be with; and everything else was something that disappeared in favor of where she should be.

Cara sometimes wondered if Jackson felt the same. She saw moments that showed her he did. He'd leave his door unlocked so she could just walk in. She found spaces in a drawer and in his closet where she could leave the change of clothes she brought. She saw a magnet on his fridge with the phone number for a local truck repair shop. Little hints he left around his apartment to show her that it was also hers, or at the very least, that he expected her to be there.

Even in the moments that were less peaceful, Cara noticed small changes. "Get any mail?" Cara asked one evening as Jackson paced in the kitchen sorting through envelopes.

"Nah, just junk." Jackson tossed a bunch of papers absentmindedly into his recycle bin. He held one envelope in his hand, which he opened as he walked towards his phone. The blue shoebox still sat underneath of it. Cara took a breath, but didn't say anything. She didn't want to let her anger at his mother cloud any need to comfort him once he read what she'd written.

Jackson stood still for thirty seconds, then opened the shoebox and tossed the letter inside. He closed it and walked back towards the couch. Cara watched him as he sat. "Was that from —"

"Yes."

"Do you want to talk about it?"

"No."

Cara nodded, then leaned against his shoulder. She didn't ask anything more. She knew that anything more was his to keep, a part of him that would only be a small part of both of them. She considered the parts of her that were hers alone to be the same.

More and more, though, the parts that were both of them became her whole. Even arriving home at the farm felt more and more like she was visiting as a guest, a feeling she had with or without her mother saying so snidely at breakfast. "I like staying with him," Cara said with a shrug.

"As long as you're being safe," Delores said as she buttered her toast.

"I've told you before that we are. You want me to bring home the condom wrappers or something?"

"I'm not talking about that. Not everyone will stay quiet and have toast with you like nothing's happened after seeing you come home with someone else's clothes and a bloody truck."

"I know. It's fine."

Delores finally looked at Cara. "It's fine because you're not telling him anything, right?"

"Of course not. Don't worry."

Delores frowned, and Cara narrowed her eyes. "I don't tell anyone, no one knows what I do —"

"Because you don't do it, right?"

"How do you know?"

"Because I know you wouldn't be stupid enough to go to Jackson's apartment covered in blood and with clothes in your truck like you usually do when you come back here."

Cara smiled mischievously, in no small part to hide the sting of hurt she felt at her mother calling her stupid. "You don't know that. Maybe he's into that."

"Please …"

"Maybe he likes watching me come home a mess. Maybe he likes how careless I am when I kill."

"I never said you were careless."

Cara took a bite of toast to try and calm her mounting frustration. It was a rare breakfast with her mother, and she didn't want to spend it arguing.

Delores added, "I just don't want you to lose a part of yourself because of some boy."

Cara set down her toast. "It's not the only part of me."

"But Jackson shouldn't be the only part of you either, especially when it's a part that's engulfing all the others —"

"Engulfing? He's not —"

"And when you're hiding all those other parts away —"

"You mean hiding them in places other than our basement?"

Delores stopped and looked at Cara with wide eyes. Cara set down her napkin, leaving her toast unfinished. "I have to go," she said as she stood up.

"I thought you had today off."

"I do, but I still need to go." Cara exited, and she tried not to sigh with too much exasperation as Delores followed her.

"Then where are you going?

"Out with Jackson. He has the day off too. We're spending it together."

"Oh." Cara could almost hear Delores' lips pursing, could almost feel her arms cross her chest. Cara rolled her eyes as she pulled on her jacket.

"You used to spend your days off going on little road trips," Delores remarked. "You still do that, at least?"

"Yes. Jackson and I are driving somewhere today, actually."

"So you do that, but not alone anymore."

"I'm staying with him tonight." Cara wasn't going to argue with her mother, no matter how much her mother wanted to.

Delores snorted a little. "At this point, you could just tell me when you're not staying with him."

"I know either way you'd have a damn panic attack if I didn't tell you."

"I don't panic —"

"Goodbye." Cara walked outside, and the thwack of the screen door behind her was much more satisfying than she anticipated. She walked with slight tension at the thought of Delores following her, but as she got closer to her truck and further away from the porch — all without any sounds of Delores — she calmed.

She calmed, but her brain didn't quiet. She kept playing Delores' words in her head and muttering her responses out loud as she drove, with nothing but a windshield and some rock music to listen to. She wanted to get it out now, before she saw Jackson but especially before she saw her mother again. Cara thought of seeing her mother again, and started arguing with her thoughts once more.

The thoughts quieted as she turned into Jackson's apartment complex. She parked the truck and took a deep breath.

She took two more.

It was a day off for both of them. It was a day that was just for them. Her mother could stay in Leslie.

———

Cara calmed completely when she knocked on Jackson's door. They got in her truck — Cara insisted it could make the drive, despite Jackson's continued hesitations that it worked — and drove to a forest out in Durham. "I used to come here sometimes when I didn't have class," Jackson said as they parked. "A way to get out of Raleigh and away from everyone without going back to Pinesboro."

"You're speaking my language," Cara said as she grabbed the Playmate that Jackson had packed with lunch from the back of the truck. "I love hiking — one of the only things I like when I'm at home." She tried not to wince at the memory of home that morning.

"You live near the woods?"

"Yeah. There's trees and a really nice lake." She stopped herself before she could talk more about the lake.

"That sounds awesome. Maybe we can hike there together sometime."

"Maybe. It gets pretty vast, even on our property. You could hike a bunch of paths before you end up back at the farm."

"Even if we end up there, I wouldn't mind." He grinned as they began to hike. "Unless you're worried about me meeting your mom."

"Heh, maybe; but you'll like the woods more."

Jackson nodded, and Cara appreciated him knowing not to press further. Cara knew that even without their fight that morning, Jackson and Delores meeting would be awkward at best.

The rest of the day disappeared in the forest. Cara and Jackson walked all the possible paths, neither of them anxious to go back when they were both in a place where nobody knew them. It was also a place with almost nobody around. While a few hikers and joggers went by, most were waiting for the weekend to take their walks.

Cara couldn't be happier, and she took the opportunity to steal many moments with Jackson behind a tree or while sitting on a large rock by the river as they ate lunch. Even the moments not in his arms were moments she liked to disappear in. They spoke to each other and only heard birds or the hush of the wind in the trees. They walked in silence, and Cara felt a comfort at their being with each other, with no need to remind each other through talk that the other was listening.

They drove home in silence, the radio on and Jackson's fingers tracing circles on Cara's leg. The other cars were a blur, the passing trees a line pointing to his apartment. She paused the journey only to stop at Lake Hollow and succumb to the quiet urging she'd felt with each kiss in the woods and each touch of his fingers. "If we don't make out now, I may crash the truck thinking about you," Cara teased as she unbuckled her belt.

"I'm not complaining," Jackson said with a grin, one that didn't break when Cara kissed him. He kissed her back, then added, "It's just weird being here before sundown."

"We'll be home before dark." Cara's words ended as Jackson pulled her close and kept her there.

They made it home an hour after dark. They ate frozen lasagna for dinner and watched TV. Cara lay curled in Jackson's hold and thought about nothing. When they turned off the TV, turned off the lights, and settled under his covers, Cara thought about nothing except how happy she was.

"This was the best day I've had in a long time," Jackson said, his voice soft but not yet quieted by oncoming sleep.

"Same here," Cara replied, her words dissolving into a sigh as he held her close and stroked her hair. The morning was a distant memory, one whose words were faint echoes that Cara ignored in favor of the sound of Jackson breathing lightly. She repositioned herself so that she was still in his arms but on the pillow next to him. His fingers stayed in her hair but occasionally moved down to her temple, her cheek. She looked at his eyes. Even though it was dark in the room, she swore she could still see their colors in the faint light shining through his window.

Jackson smiled softly at her. "I've thought that a lot lately — especially when you're here."

Cara ran her fingers across his chest, traced circles around his heart. "I like being here. I'd be here all the time if I could." She laughed a little in the hope it would distract him from her embarrassment. "Well, not every minute, but —"

"I know what you mean." He curled his arm around her and pulled her closer. Cara smiled at the warmth she felt from his body pressed against hers. "Though every minute doesn't sound so bad to me."

"What about every second?"

"Sure."

"Every waking moment, I'm here."

"Here in bed? That sounds amazing."

Cara laughed and leaned against Jackson's shoulder. "In all seriousness," he continued, his voice soft once more, "I like having you here so much. It's almost like you've always been here, and it doesn't feel right when you're not."

"It doesn't feel right when I'm not with you. It feels lonelier — and I've felt pretty lonely my whole life."

"I wish you didn't feel that way." Jackson kissed her temple, and Cara closed her eyes. "I wish I could go back in time and be with you sooner, so you wouldn't feel so alone."

"I don't feel that way now — not with you. That's all that matters. You're all that matters to me." Cara heard her mother talking about anything that wasn't Jackson disappearing. Cara quieted the thought. It wasn't true — and even if it was, she didn't care. Jackson was everything good in her life, and she had no issue with him taking over everything that wasn't.

"You're all that matters to me too," he whispered. He kissed her shoulders, her cheek, her neck. "You don't even know how much of a mess I was before I met you. Sometimes it feels like …"

"What?"

"It … this might sound weird, but it feels like I had this crazy interior, words and garbage and bullshit swirling around in my head. And I can usually keep it quiet; but when you're with someone — someone you care about — they're eventually going to see it. And whenever I was with someone I cared about, it just got worse, because I didn't want them to see it — or I'd let them see a piece of it, and they'd tell me to just stop and that I didn't have to worry around them, and that'd almost make it worse. I felt like those assurances just fed everything and made them rattle around even more in my head until they pushed everyone away."

It was like Jackson lived inside of her head. Cara wavered between fears of everything she knew lived inside of her and comfort at the thought that someone else, in his own way, shared that feeling.

"But I don't feel that way anymore," he said. "With you, it's not a rattle and it doesn't get worse. I feel like when I'm with you, and when I talk to you, or even when I just think about you, you just walk around in my head and sort everything right, get them on their shelves and tell them to shut up."

Cara chuckled. "I'm your brain's maintenance girl?"

"In a way, yes." He laughed as he kissed her. "But it's more like you make me feel like there's nothing to maintain, because when you're there, everything's just there. Everything's just so. *I'm* just so." He lifted her hand, kissed her palm. "And I'm happier than I've been in a long time."

Cara smiled and looked in his eyes. "I am too." She wished she could say more, that she could say how much she felt. It was so much of what he felt, and yet in many ways was different and in many other ways so much more. Each new feeling she had opened up a thousand more, a spiral that Cara dove into as opposed to trying to crawl out of. She was at peace so long as when she settled at the bottom, she was settled there with Jackson.

Jackson released her hand and curled his arm back around her. Despite the soft smile on his face, Cara thought he looked afraid — not frightened, like with something unknown or dangerous, but rather the fear someone had before taking a dive that they knew would send them into deep, warm, and safe waters if they would just jump.

"I love you," he said.

She smiled. "I love you too."

Her words hit her like a shock of cold water, and before she could stop herself, she said, "Oh shit!" Then she grew embarrassed, and looked away from him. "Oh God, I'm sorry."

"Sorry?"

"I didn't mean to say 'shit.' I just surprised myself."

"It's okay, don't worry."

"I do love you." The second time was less a shock, and felt like a cool ripple moving over her skin and ebbing the heat of her embarrassment. "It's just that I've never said that to anyone before."

"No one?"

"No. I've never felt this way about anyone before — and even if I had, I probably would've been too afraid, considering what happened now."

Jackson laughed kindly as he pulled her close. "It really wasn't that bad."

"It wasn't bad because you make me less afraid. I'm not afraid when I'm with you."

"You don't have to be. I don't want you to be. You can say anything you want to me."

"Really?" Cara grinned in an effort to ignore all the things she'd never want to say to him creeping up behind her and clawing at her back. "Anything at all?"

"Well, maybe just not goodbye. Not yet."

Cara kissed him, and the things she'd never say crawled back under the bed where they belonged. "Not ever."

CHAPTER 12

Cara ate her Cheerios as slowly as possible the next morning. She and Jackson both needed to go to work, but that didn't mean the morning couldn't be savored. They kept quiet, the other's company being enough; and Jackson occasionally brushed her ankle with his toe.

Cara glanced up and saw him watching her. He looked like he wanted to say something, but instead of speaking, he swallowed his words along with his milk.

"What time do you get off work?" he asked as he set down his bowl.

Cara didn't think that that was what he wanted to ask, but decided not to press. "After 8," she said.

"Ah. Kind of late, huh?"

"Keith needs me to make some deliveries out in Greensboro."

"So you'll be here around 9?"

"Probably." It took Cara a moment to realize it was just assumed she'd stay over. She smiled a little at the thought

— she had no problems staying with Jackson every night, especially when the alternative was staying with her mother. She remembered the argument yesterday that hadn't been finished. She sighed a little. "I probably can't stay tonight, though," she said.

"Really? Why not? I don't mind you coming over late."

"Because I've been here a lot, and as much as I've liked that, I need to do some things around the farm."

"And put in an appearance with your mom?" Jackson smiled, but it wasn't enough to keep Cara from looking down in embarrassment. "It's fine," he added as he squeezed her wrist.

"I just have some stuff I need to do there."

"I get it. It is where you live."

"Yeah." But it was feeling less like her home every day.

"If you've got some time before work, though …"

Cara looked back up. Jackson kept his kind expression, but his hands began to fold over one another. Cara took one in an effort to calm him. "What's up?" she asked.

"I wanted to talk to you."

"About what?"

Jackson swallowed, and Cara tried not to get annoyed. Still, her patience was wearing thin, and the silence was killing her. She kept filling it with what she could only assume he wanted to say. "You're not having second thoughts about what you told me yesterday, are you?" she teased.

"No, not at all," he said with a small laugh.

"You're pregnant."

"No." His laughter stopped short. "And you're not, right?"

"No! Jesus. I wouldn't be laughing about it if I was."

"I don't know, I know you like kidding around when you're nervous about something."

Cara tried to brush away the small sting she felt at his assessment. "I'm not the one nervous right now, though."

"I know, I know. This is just something I've never asked anyone before."

"What, are you about to pull out a ring or something?"

"Cara, please!" Her hand moved off of his with a start. "I know you're kidding, but this would be a lot easier for me if you'd stop making jokes."

Cara looked at her cereal bowl and moved her hand beneath hers. Jackson touched her elbow. "I'm sorry," he said. "It's just —"

"No, you're right. I'll stop." Cara knew she'd gone too far, and rather than feeling annoyed that Jackson was upset, she felt mounting shame. She felt as if his shortness was the first crack in a veneer made vulnerable by their openness from the night before, from them revealing so much of what was in their hearts to one another. It was a bridge between them, one that held them close but one that could be rocked by the wind or splintered with any wrong steps. She needed to be more careful.

She wasn't sure how to feel about that.

"This is hard, but I'm making it hard," Jackson said. She looked back up at him and saw him smiling softly at her. "You may be making jokes, but I'm sidestepping more than a crab on the beach right now."

Cara laughed, which rippled out her shame and smoothed it over into a calm surface. "So straighten out," she said. "What is it?"

"It's something I want to ask you."

Cara tried to keep her eyes at a normal width, even though she briefly feared her joke about a ring was coming true.

"I'm not proposing," Jackson said.

"Are you a fucking mind-reader?" Cara asked.

"I can hear your mind racing from here," Jackson replied as he playfully tapped her temple. Cara smiled as she tried not to think about how the bridge between them could lead Jackson to every thought she had, including her fears and, worse, her secrets.

"Plus, you pressed your lips," he added as he stroked her cheek. "You do that when you're nervous too."

"I think I'm spending too much time here. You're picking up on all my tics."

"Ah, so that's why you're saying in Leslie, right?"

"Of course not. I'd be here more if I could."

"I'd like that. That's … that's actually what I wanted to ask you."

"You want me to come over here more?"

"I want you to move in with me."

Cara stayed quiet. Her eyes didn't widen, and her mouth didn't move. She made sure of it.

Jackson added, "Well, let me rephrase that: I'd like you to move in with me. If you want to."

"You want to live together?"

"Yeah. I do." Jackson took her hand and Cara prayed he couldn't feel her pulse. "You're over here all the time —"

"Most of the time —"

"And I want that. It doesn't feel right when you're not here. I act as if this place is ours even on the nights you're back in Leslie. I sit on one side of the couch and I sleep on one side of the bed. When you're not here, it's like you're missing. I miss you. I want to miss you less."

It was Cara's turn to swallow as she minded her words. "I miss you too," Cara said. "When I'm at home, at least."

"I know it's a big step," Jackson replied. "I know it's a lot to think about."

Jackson had no idea how much Cara had to think about, and she hoped she was keeping that to herself.

"Just know if it's rent, we can talk about that, but I obviously have no problems paying for this place myself."

"I'm not gonna crash here for free," Cara said as she snapped out of her actual concerns. "I live with my mom, but I can pay for things."

"I know. There's utilities and a new car —"

Cara finally grinned. "Oh, is one of your conditions that I get rid of the truck?"

"I mean, if you're offering," Jackson said with a laugh. "But I was thinking you'd leave it because it's your mom's truck, right? Does she have her own car?"

"No, but she almost never drives anywhere herself." Cara thought about her mother on the farm and grew sadder than she expected. Even if Cara left the truck behind, she knew it wouldn't matter to Delores. All she wanted on that farm was Cara. And all Cara wanted to do was leave. But whenever she left, she'd leave just long enough to want to come back. She wouldn't do that anymore if she moved in with Jackson. She'd come home to his apartment, far away from Leslie and everything that troubled her.

"Well, again, those're logistics we can figure out later when — if you want to move in with me," Jackson said. "I mean it when I say I know it's a lot to think about. I don't expect an answer right away."

"Then why'd you ask me today?"

"Because I wanted us to start thinking about it. If you're ready now, I'd love for you to move in. If you're not ready, I'll wait. But I wanted to ask you because it's something I want. I want to live with you, and I want you to know that on the chance that you want to live with me too."

Cara did want to live with him. She thought she did, anyway. There was a lot to think about, so much to think about, and so much swirling in her head as a result. She would think of her mother, her job, of Leslie. Then she'd look at Jackson and think about how none of those things mattered to her more than him. She knew she should think about it, and believed him when he said she could for as long as she wanted. But she found herself wanting to say yes, to pull him close and tell him how much she missed him when she was at the farm, how good she felt when she walked through his apartment door, how she wanted to lie next to him in bed and tell him everything — and how all he had to do to hear everything was to look in her eyes and give her a small smile.

She pressed her lips. It barely took anything from him to get everything from her — including everything she wanted to hide. Cara felt the bridge between them shortening, a distance Jackson wouldn't need to cross because they would just be connected. Cara wondered if living with him would still allow her to keep that sense of space, that one bit of space she wanted so badly for herself, but one that the people she cared about somehow managed to bridge.

But there were new parts of her that Jackson seemed to be finding — places he led her inside of her own head that Cara enjoyed seeing. She wanted to explore that with him. Maybe if she did so, she could steer him clear of what she never wanted him to see.

"I'll think about it," she said. "I need to figure out if that works."

"I know. I understand."

"But … without promising anything, I probably won't have to think about it that long. I'll probably decide when I'm about halfway to work and I'm already missing the hell out of you."

Jackson smiled, and Cara leaned forward and kissed him. She'd tell him later. She'd probably tell him yes, but she'd still wait to say so.

———

Cara barely processed the rest of her day. She thought about Jackson the entire drive from Raleigh to Leslie, then thought about her mother the entire drive to and from Greensboro. She had to resolve things with Delores, and she also had to talk to her about moving in with Jackson. Even if she was still thinking about it, it was something Cara knew would be better to bring up sooner rather than later.

She pulled into their driveway at dinnertime, the rocks in the dirt clanging the truck doors in tune with her beating heart. She saw that it was six o'clock and figured her mother was home. She took a breath. She was home. She didn't have to be afraid.

———

Cara smelled fried chicken and green beans as soon as she walked in, and the smell was fresh enough for Cara to know her mother had had Rhonda stop at Bojangles on the way home for an easy meal. "Mom?" she called.

"I'm in the kitchen," Delores called. Cara walked in and saw Delores somberly setting a plate for herself. Cara's place at the table was empty.

"I didn't know if you'd be home," Delores explained.

"But you still got enough food, right?" Cara meant to ask it as a question and to not be snide, but Delores looked wounded all the same. Cara softened. "Don't worry about it," she said as she got a plate for herself.

They sat in silence and filled their plates. They ate quietly for a few moments.

"You staying home tonight?" Delores asked.

"Planning to."

"Hmm." Cara wondered if Delores wanted to say "Good," but was trying not to. She could see that Delores was trying with every deliberate chew.

"Might go back over the weekend, though," Cara added.

"I figured."

"And … I might be over there more." Cara felt as if a bubble grew in her throat with every word closer she got to sharing her news. But she had to get to it, no matter how hard it was.

Delores chuckled in a way that sounded like a grumble. "I don't know how you could be over there more."

"You're really saying that when I'm here right now?"

"I know, you're right. I'm sorry."

Cara's annoyance shrank the bubble in her throat just enough for her to let out, "And the way I could be over there more is if I move in with him."

Delores didn't respond. She set down her sweet tea.

"And … and I might," Cara continued, even as the bubble began to grow back. "We talked about it —"

Delores leaned back in her chair.

"And nothing's decided, but —"

"Oh, it's decided." Cara felt the chill even before Delores looked at her with narrow eyes. "You decided it weeks ago, I'm sure."

"I didn't. We just talked about it this —"

Delores rose before Cara could finish. She walked out of the kitchen.

The chill in Cara's heart evaporated. She slammed down her fork and followed her mother with much quicker steps than Delores took. "Why are you angry about this?"

"I'm not angry."

"Well, you're sure as shit ain't happy."

Delores spun to face her and they both paused from moving. "Why're you so desperate to leave?"

"I'm not desperate! I want to move in with my boyfriend like a normal adult would."

"In what universe are you a normal adult?" Cara cowered back as if she'd been slapped, but Delores took no notice. "Would a normal adult tiptoe around moving in with a man or even just seeing him, like you've done from the start?"

"When their mothers act like you, then yes, they fucking would!"

"Maybe they have to when their daughters act like you! Always yelling, always sullen, always angry and upset with everything and everyone —"

"Because everything and everyone makes me that way!" Everyone except Jackson — and, until she'd met him, everyone but her mother.

"You make yourself what you are."

"And what am I, Mom?" Cara narrowed her eyes as Delores finally pursed her lips. "Tell me: what am I?"

Delores folded her arms. "You're many things, and you're one big thing that I know you don't want Jackson to see."

"He won't see it," Cara said through gritted teeth.

"He will if you move in with him."

"Says who? I haven't done anything I need to hide in months."

"So you've had to hide yourself, then."

"Yes, Mom, I have. I've had to hide a part of me that you're so fucking proud of that you keep it hidden in our basement where no one can see."

"No shit I keep it there! You want to get arrested?"

"And a part you're so concerned with me losing that you're trying your damndest to make sure no one sees it but you!"

"If you think you need to hide parts of you to make a relationship work, then it's not going to work."

"You don't know that." Cara began to slowly cool. She looked out the window and at the woods beyond the pumpkin patch. She needed to go for a walk — alone.

"I know enough about you to know that's true. I know you think you can just keep your secrets buried here and leave me buried right along with them."

Cara turned back to her mother. "You? I wouldn't disappear —"

"You want to leave me and your secrets and everything that bothers you in Leslie behind, but it's not that easy. It's part of you and it'll follow you — and if you move in with Jackson, it'll either be a part of you both or a wedge between you both. And I can tell you now that it's a part of you he's not going to want to share."

Cara closed her eyes and tried not to think about Jackson leaving her behind. "It won't be a wedge."

Cara's phone rang from her pocket. She didn't know if it was the worst time for someone to call, or the best. Either way, she pulled it out to check, and saw that it was Jackson.

"Don't you dare answer that phone," Delores hissed.

"Why not?" Cara spat. "You want to tell me more about how I'm terrible and how Jackson will never love me?"

"I want you to put that phone away and not talk to him for one damn second."

"I haven't talked to him for several seconds. I've been talking to you, and it's been fucking great!" Cara threw up her free hand. Her phone rang again from the other. This time, even Cara wished it would stop.

Delores snatched the phone from Cara's hand. Cara's eyes widened in fear that Delores would break it. Delores saw her fear and sneered. "What, you afraid I'm gonna answer it?"

"What? No —"

SONORA TAYLOR

"You afraid I'll talk to him, tell him more about you than you'd ever want him to know? Tell him all about the things of yours I've been keeping and that I could show anyone —"

Cara narrowed her eyes. She saw Delores' anger fade. Delores knew she'd said the wrong thing and was trying to stop before she said more. Cara would drag it out anyway. "Show who, Mom?"

"Cara …"

"You said anyone. Who do you have in mind? Rhonda? The cops?"

"No —"

"You want to show them the things you've been keeping for years, things you've been telling me that make you proud, but really, you were keeping them to keep me here?"

"I wasn't —" But Delores looked down as she spoke, and that was enough for Cara to cut her off.

"If you loved me as much as you said, you wouldn't feel a need to shackle me here and have me rot alongside the old pumpkin vines. If you were really proud of who I was, you wouldn't be using my secrets to threaten me."

"I keep those secrets because I love you. I want to protect you and keep you safe. It's all I've wanted ever since you were a little girl."

"But you only want those things if in return I never leave, right?"

Delores leaned against the wall and sighed a little.

"You'll only love me if I do what you want, right?"

Delores looked at Cara. Her eyes were dotted with tears, but kept the strength and reserve that even in the peak of her anger, Cara wished she could have for herself.

"I will always love you," Delores said, her voice choked but true. "Even when you leave me or hurt me or make me try really, really hard to do it, I love you."

Cara wanted to believe her. All she could hear, though, was her mother threatening her and all the times Delores had acted wounded just because Cara didn't stay on the farm all the time.

Cara's phone chimed from Delores' hand — the single chime of a text message. She grabbed it from her mother, who made no effort to keep it.

"Then learn to do it when I'm not here," Cara said. She moved past Delores and grabbed the keys to the truck.

"Cara —"

"Good night." Cara let the screen door slam behind her. It was less satisfying than it'd felt the morning before. Even driving away and seeing the cloud of dust in her rearview mirror did nothing to make her feel better.

Cara waited until she was a few miles away from the farm before pulling over to check her phone. She didn't want to give Delores the chance to run out after her. She parked on the side of the road, then flipped open her phone and read Jackson's text: *Please call.*

Cara called right away, taking deep breaths to try and quiet the sound of her mother's shouts ringing in her ears. Delores would never move out of Cara's brain, no matter how hard Cara tried to claim that space for herself. Her mother was just like everyone else that Cara couldn't get rid of, everyone who was quieted when she disappeared or when she killed, but never, ever gone. She clenched her eyes shut.

"Cara."

SONORA TAYLOR

Cara opened them. "Jackson." She felt increasing relief at the sound of his voice. Everyone else's voices quieted. "What's up?" she asked with as much happiness as she could muster. Things wouldn't be wrong, not after she spoke to him, but until she got there, she had to pretend to be her best for him.

It didn't sound like it was enough. "Can you come over?" he asked in a tone that was both quiet and pained.

"Sure."

"I know you wanted to be at the farm tonight, but I really need you here —"

"I can come over."

"I need you, Cara, I really need you."

"I'll be there!" Cara silently cursed herself for snapping. "I'm sorry, I thought you couldn't hear me —"

"It's okay." Jackson sounded as despondent as before.

"It doesn't sound okay."

"It's not you, it's ..." His voice trailed, and Cara did her best to be patient.

"What is it?" she asked after taking a breath.

"It's Moira."

Cara wondered for a moment if Moira was there. She figured Jackson would sound happier about that, though. Maybe she called him from Pinesboro. She pressed her lips to keep from smirking as she thought that maybe someone else had died.

Any desire to laugh vanished. "What about her?" Cara asked, even though she felt she knew already.

Jackson's rattled sigh only confirmed it, even before the sigh ceased with his reply: "She's gone."

235

CHAPTER 13

Cara drove in silence to Raleigh. Jackson's voice reverberated in her head. She let it do so intentionally. She hoped that doing so would conjure up how she was supposed to feel around him once she got there.

Of course she was shocked and saddened that Moira was gone. Of course she felt sorry for Jackson. But she'd never been in a position to console someone. Uncle Leo died before she had memories, and her mother only spoke of him wistfully, like she was sorry he was gone but understood why. Her mother hadn't cried for her uncle and she hadn't cried for Terry.

Cara felt a flash of sadness at the memory of Terry. She buried it, as was her instinct; but then she tried to bring it back. Maybe it would help her understand more of how Jackson felt, and then she could be the girlfriend she was supposed to be: someone who could comfort her boyfriend when her boyfriend's best friend had died. He'd lost his friend, and so had she.

But Terry didn't die. Terry chose to leave Cara behind. Cara's sadness melted into familiar anger. She closed her eyes for a moment, took a breath. Terry didn't choose to leave. He'd gone to be with his child's mother. And he'd left Cara behind with her mother, who she was supposed to be with.

Cara wondered if Jackson's mother told him about Moira. The anger returned, and Cara let it simmer, even as she reminded herself that Jackson said that Chris had called him. Mrs. Price was not involved. Cara loosened her grip on the steering wheel. Mrs. Price had nothing to do with this. She had nothing to do with Jackson.

Cara needed to think about Jackson. The only thing she had to go on was how much she loved him. If nothing else, perhaps that would be a comfort to him. He wouldn't have to be alone. Not tonight. Not ever.

Cara let out a sigh in time with slowing to a stop in Jackson's parking lot. She would be there for him. She had to be, and she had no questions as to why. She was where she was supposed to be, and doing what she was supposed to do.

———

Cara knocked on Jackson's door. "It's open," he called.

Cara tried the door. It was locked. "No it isn't!" she called back.

She heard his annoyed sigh through the door. Cara tried to keep her resolve so she wouldn't look struck when he saw her.

The lock clicked, but Jackson didn't open the door. Cara pressed her lips and tried not to roll her eyes as she opened it.

Any annoyance she had disappeared when she saw him. Jackson was moving towards the couch, but he glanced in her direction as he slumped into its cushions. "Hey," he said as he looked away again. He grabbed a cigarette from the silver case on his table — or rather another one, based on his full ashtray and the smell that had hit Cara as soon as she walked in.

"Hey," she said as she joined him on the couch. Jackson grabbed a second cigarette from his case. He put both in his mouth, lit them, and handed one to her. Cara couldn't help but be warmed by the action, and the smallest of smiles crossed her lips.

He stared at her blankly. "What?" His voice wasn't cold, but Cara felt a chill in her veins all the same.

"I'm sorry," Cara said, dropping her mouth into as deliberate a frown as possible without looking fake. "I couldn't help it, it's just you reminded me of our first date when you did that."

"Hm." Jackson turned away and smoked in silence. Cara didn't know how she was going to do this. It seemed she'd been saying the wrong thing as soon as she asked to be let in.

She took his free hand in hers. He closed his fingers around her hand. "Thanks for coming over," he said.

Cara nodded. "Of course."

Jackson smoked some more and stared at his television, even though it was off.

"Do you want to talk about it?" Cara asked.

Jackson shrugged.

"Do you … want me to do something for you? Order some food, maybe?"

He shook his head.

"Do you want me to just sit here and stare at the wall with you?"

Jackson let out a small laugh, one that disappeared as quickly as it arrived. It was still enough to help Cara relax. She scooted closer to him. "What happened — how did it happen, I mean," she added before Jackson could restate what she already knew.

Jackson stubbed out his cigarette. "Chris told me she had cervical cancer. They found it too late to be able do much about it." Jackson sighed as he leaned back against the couch. Cara added her own cigarette to the ash tray, then leaned back with him and put her head on his shoulder. Cara curled her arm around him.

"I didn't think it could move that quickly," she said.

Jackson looked at her, and his expression almost made Cara wished he hadn't. "What do you mean?"

"Well, she found out about it and then died from it all after seeing you, right?"

"No. Chris said she found out around Thanksgiving last year. She was visiting for the holiday and her mom made her go to the doctor for a check-up." Jackson snorted. "Thirty years old, traveling all over the place and she can't work in a visit to the damn doctor."

"It sounds like there wasn't much they could do even when she went."

"We'll never know now, will we?"

Cara knew from his tone that he didn't want a debate. "No," she said, "I guess not."

"And we'll never know if there was something they could do." Jackson slumped over his knees and ran his fingers through his hair. Cara stroked his back.

"It sounds like there wasn't. She died from it."

"She didn't die from that."

Cara was glad Jackson couldn't see her furrow her brow or scramble for what she was supposed to say. Jackson gestured towards a letter on the table, one that Cara hadn't noticed when she sat down. Cara stared at it and thought, his mother. His fucking mother.

"It's not from my mom."

Cara gave Jackson a pointed glance even though he couldn't see it. "Reading my mind again?"

"Hard not to when you're digging your nails in my back." Cara loosened her grip, and Jackson looked at her with a small smile. "Talk about first date reminders," he said.

Cara laughed a little, and took the letter while she was feeling brave. She saw that it was from Moira.

"I got it today," Jackson explained. "But I didn't open it until after Chris called me."

Cara was already lost in its contents. She skimmed the parts where Moira wrote about their friendship and how much knowing Jackson had meant to her — she figured that was meant to be between Moira and Jackson — and focused more on Moira saying she had cancer. There was no hope of curing it, and it would eventually land her in hospice for her remaining months.

I didn't want to be tied down, Moira concluded. *Not like that, not sick and wilting and becoming a shell of the person you knew before my inevitable death. I decided to meet death on my own terms instead.*

"That's why she came here," Jackson said. Cara set down the letter and turned back to face him. His face was out of his hands, but he looked at the coffee table. "She wasn't just dropping in or coming to catch up. She was saying goodbye."

"Jesus. I can't believe she didn't tell you."

"I can't either." Jackson sat back up and leaned against the cushions too quickly for Cara to return her hand to his back. "I mean, what the fuck? Her own terms? Why didn't she get help?"

"It sounds like she couldn't get help —"

"She could have. She could've gotten medicine or something to keep her going a little longer."

"She didn't want to —"

"I fucking know that, Cara. I read the goddamn letter too, you don't have to tell me what she said."

"Then why are you asking a bunch of questions she already answered?"

"Are you serious? My best friend just killed herself and sent me a goddamn suicide note, one I read after my friend called me and told me she was dead *and* had cancer *and* was never coming back! You expect me to have all the answers and say the right things right now?"

Cara looked at her hands, her cheeks burning with a mixture of anger and shame. "No," she mumbled.

"Good, because I'm just ..." His voice trailed, and Cara made herself look up. Jackson stared at the ceiling and looked defeated. "I shouldn't have left," he said. "I never should've fucking left."

"You think that would've kept her from getting sick?" Cara knew that wouldn't have helped, nothing would have; but she knew better than to say so.

It still wasn't enough. Jackson sighed, and the sound of it was starting to wound Cara more than anything she'd ever thought she'd heard people say. "Of course not," he replied. "But I could've helped her, talked to her about some medicine and maybe made sure she got to the doctor more often …"

"She's not —" Cara stopped herself. Jackson looked at her.

"Not what?"

"Forget it."

"What were you going to say?"

"You don't want to hear it."

"I wouldn't ask you if I didn't."

Cara knew that every word he spoke was leading her to a trap, but still, she said, "She's not your responsibility."

Jackson didn't reply. Cara decided to keep going. "I know she was your friend and I know this hurts. I know you wish you could've stopped her from killing herself and could've stopped her from getting sick. But you couldn't."

"Not now —"

"Not before. Her own family couldn't get her to go to the doctor. Would she have listened to you?"

Jackson snorted sadly. It was enough for Cara to scoot closer to him and touch his knee. "No," he said. "She would've said I was just trying to pad my salary or something."

Cara chuckled quietly, and he smiled a little. "She made her choices," she said. "You're not responsible for them."

Jackson closed his eyes. "But I'm responsible for mine."

"You didn't do anything —"

"I left. I left Pinesboro, moved away from where she always ended up between her trips, moved away from *her* because I was afraid. I was afraid of death catching up with me like it always did — and I was afraid it would hurt her."

"What are you talking about?"

"I thought that maybe it was just Pinesboro, or maybe just me being in Pinesboro, and if I left then maybe me and the people I cared about would be okay. But it wasn't. It never goddamn is. I can never fucking run away from it."

"Of course you can't." Jackson spun his head to face her, but Cara sped along before he could stop her. "You don't cause people to die just by being near them. You're not re-sponsible — not for her, not for anyone. Jackson, she died. She did what thousands of people do every day. You had absolutely nothing to do with it, and thinking you did isn't going to change anything or do anything to make this better for you."

He stared at her. Cara felt herself falling into the pit that she'd suspected lay ahead, the trap she stupidly walked into. But it wasn't a trap Jackson laid for her. It was one she'd set for herself with her own mouth.

"What could possibly make any of this better for me?" he asked. His voice was steady, cool, and the most terrifying sound Cara had ever heard.

She tried to keep her own voice steady. "I don't know."

"Is there some trick to feeling better about my best friend dying, or about forgetting every fear I've felt my whole life because my mom won't let me forget it and everyone around me can't seem to stop dying?"

"I didn't mean —"

"Is there a way to be like you, just so fucking reasonable and practical when someone's died?"

Cara's eyes widened. "Me?"

"How can this not be a big deal to you? How can you be so cold right now?"

"I'm not —"

"How can you walk in here and hear that news and say things to me like lots of people die every day and that I shouldn't be afraid? How can —"

"How do you expect me to answer you when you keep cutting me off?" Cara snapped. Jackson stopped speaking, but the anger stayed in his eyes. Cara plowed on anyway. Trying to say the right thing had only gotten her in more trouble. She was in the pit, and the least she could do was shout from the bottom so she'd be heard.

"I'm not cold. I'm sorry, Jackson. Maybe I should've said that before, but I'm not perfect and don't always have the answers even when you want them so badly. I only know what I said, so that's what I gave you. I didn't know what else to say. I don't know. I don't know what it's like to go through this and I don't know what it's like to be with some-one going through this. I only know it's sad and I only know that you're afraid, and while it's okay to be sad and it's okay to be afraid, it's not okay to blame yourself for something that had absolutely nothing to do with you, not when you're already in pain. You don't need more pain. Don't put it on yourself."

"I don't want to —"

"I know you don't, and I know it's hard not to. I'm trying to help take some of that off of you. That's all I'm trying to do. It's all I want to do, all I've wanted to do since you called me — and honestly, all I've ever wanted to do whenever you've been upset about anything."

Jackson closed his eyes. "I know you want to help."

"But maybe this time, I was wrong. Maybe you needed that pain because it's what you know and how you cope. Maybe it's what you wanted —"

"It wasn't."

"Then what do you want?" Cara wished she'd sounded less exasperated, but it was too late to change that. All she could do was keep speaking and keep trying to help. "Tell me what you want, Jackson, so I can do it for you and help you."

He stayed quiet. Cara was about to ask if he wanted her to leave, but her words were halted when she saw a tear roll down his cheek.

Cara softened. Her anger and shame, his anger and grief, all of the words that he and she had spoken, all of it disappeared. She only heard him breathe as he wiped one tear away and two more appeared.

"I want to stop being afraid," he whispered.

Cara moved closer to him and circled her arm around his back.

"I want to be less afraid so I can stop hurting everyone I care about." His lips trembled as he spoke. "Especially you, Cara."

"Don't worry about me," she whispered as she took his hand.

"I'm sorry."

"Don't be. It's fine."

"I'm sorry I'm like this."

"I am too, but only because it's hurting you." Cara stroked his back and Jackson pressed his palm against his eyes. It did nothing to stop the growing stream of tears. His hand became as wet as his cheeks, and his voice only more choked.

"I want to stop hurting so much. I just want it to stop."

"I know."

"And I just … I just want her to be alive."

Jackson broke into sobs, unable to say anything more. He didn't need to. Cara enfolded him with both arms and he clutched her by the waist, sobbing into her shoulder as she stroked his back and his hair. She stayed quiet and he continued to cry, both of them doing all that they needed to do. It was all they could do, and in that moment, Cara trusted that it was enough.

CHAPTER 14

Cara woke up the next morning and saw Jackson packing. Moira's funeral was the next day. Jackson had barely gotten the question out of his mouth before Cara agreed to go with him the night before. Still, she hadn't expected to leave for the funeral so early. "How far away is Pinesboro?" she asked through a mouthful of sleep.

"Just a few hours," Jackson said as he threw a brush into his suitcase.

"You want to get there before lunch or something?"

"I figured we'd leave a little early so we could stop in Leslie first."

"Leslie? Why?"

Jackson looked at her as he added some clean underwear to his bag. "Well, you'll need some clothes, right?"

She did, but Cara still wanted to avoid the farm — and her mother — for as long as possible. "I can buy a dress and some underwear at Crabtree," she said. "The mall's closer than Leslie."

"It isn't any trouble. Leslie's just an hour away, right?"

"Right, but —"

"And don't you need to drop off the truck? Your mom doesn't have her own car, right?"

Cara hoped that Jackson didn't see her flinch at the mention of her mother. "No, but she doesn't drive it all that much."

"It really isn't a problem. Let's go. It'll be easier for you and your mom."

Jackson had no idea how far from the truth that was — but Cara didn't want him to know that. Even hearing about her mother and Leslie made her uncomfortable. She could only imagine how talking about it would feel, especially when the source of their strife was Jackson. Even if Cara felt like talking about her business with her mother, she didn't want to burden Jackson with knowing that, especially when he was dealing with so much already.

"Alright, yeah, let's stop there," she said as she got out of bed. "But just for a few minutes."

———

Cara stared ahead as she drove home, thinking of nothing while she had the chance to be alone. She only brought herself back to the road every few minutes to look in the rearview mirror and make sure Jackson's Camry was still behind her.

The familiar dirt driveway lay out to greet her. She and Jackson slowly rolled up to the farmhouse. "Nice house," Jackson said as he got out of the car.

"Wait here," Cara said before he could follow her.

He furrowed his brow. "Why?"

"I won't be long. I just need to pack a couple things."

"I can still come in and help you if you want."

"We can get on the road faster if I just go in alone."

Jackson shrugged and pulled out a cigarette as he leaned against his car. "Fine."

Cara sped towards the house before she could see whether or not he was hurt by being kept outside. Even if by some miracle Delores wasn't inside, she didn't want to spend time showing Jackson around and answering his questions — especially if he wandered around while she was packing and ended up in their basement. There'd be too many questions then, questions that Cara never wanted to answer.

Cara walked inside and moved towards the stairs. She glanced towards the kitchen and saw with relief that the table was empty. Maybe she'd get out of the house and on the road to Pinesboro faster than she thought.

"Cara?"

Cara closed her eyes. She should've known she wouldn't be so lucky. Her anger from their argument slowly began to bubble as she mounted the top step. She stayed quiet.

"Thought that was you," Delores said as she exited her room.

Cara didn't look at her. She just went to her own room and began to pack.

Delores followed, but stayed in the doorway. "Honey," she said, her voice so soft that Cara knew she spoke around reopened wounds. "Can we —"

"I have to get going," Cara said as she threw some clothes and underwear in a duffle bag.

"Where?"

"Pinesboro." Cara knew her mother would be calling her all weekend if she didn't tell her. Her mother hadn't called her last night, though, even though Cara hadn't said anything about where she'd be. Cara softened a little at that thought.

"Pinesboro? What the hell's out there?"

"It's where Jackson's from. His friend died."

"Oh. I'm … I'm sorry."

Cara neatly folded her one black dress in the bag, then zipped it up with a sharp flick. "I'll tell him," she said. She barely glanced at Delores as she passed by her. She didn't have time to get drawn into an argument or even a reconciliation with her mother. Jackson needed her.

"Can we at least talk for a few minutes?" Delores said as she followed Cara down the stairs.

"No."

"Just five minutes —"

"Not now. Jackson's waiting for me."

"He's here?"

Cara closed her eyes again. "Yes," she said as she continued towards the door.

"Can I at least meet him?"

Cara finally turned around. Her mother looked wounded, but determined.

"I think I should at least say hi to the boy you're always running off with. See who my daughter's boyfriend is and say hello."

Cara kept a blank stare as she considered it. On one hand, she never wanted them to meet. On the other, it might stop both from asking questions about the other.

Delores softened a little as she folded her arms. "Jackson's important to you. I want to meet the man who's making my daughter so happy."

Cara sighed as she turned towards the door. "Fine," she said with a quick nod. "But just real quick. We need —"

"To go, I know."

Cara opened the door and walked outside. Delores followed behind her. Jackson smoked and stared at the trees. He looked towards Cara when the screen door smacked shut. He smiled, then looked surprised at the sight of Delores behind her.

"Mom wanted to say hi," Cara said with the best smile she could muster. Delores moved towards Jackson, which saved Cara from any pretenses. She wondered if Delores knew that Cara needed that more than anything, and tried not to warm at the thought.

"You must be Jackson," Delores said as she held out her hand. "I don't think I need to say that I've heard so much about you."

Jackson smiled as he shook her hand. "Nice to meet you, Ms. Vineyard."

"Delores, please. Only little kids or the bill collectors call me Ms. Vineyard."

"Jackson, can you unlock the door for me?" Cara asked. She didn't mind them meeting — not much — but it didn't need to be long.

"Sure," he said as he did so. Cara threw her bag in the back.

"I'm sorry about your friend," Delores said.

Cara looked up. Jackson's smile was gone, but he didn't look as hurt as the night before. "Thanks," he said with a nod.

Delores looked at Cara. "When will you be back?"

"Late tomorrow night, though I won't be back at the farm until Monday." She moved towards the passenger side of the Camry. "We should probably —"

"Get going, I know. It was nice to meet you, Jackson."

"You too," Jackson said with a wave.

Delores looked at Cara before Cara could open the passenger door. She could see in Delores' expression that they weren't done, even if Cara was leaving. Their fight would finish, and not with the fade that Cara hoped for with time apart. She could also see a tenderness, though, that told Cara she and her mother would never be finished — not with each other, and not from anything that could ever happen between them. Cara saw this in her mother's look because, deep down, Cara knew it was how she herself felt.

Even so, it was something that would have to wait. "Bye Mom," Cara said with a curt wave. She opened the door and got in the car. Jackson followed her and started the engine. Delores turned and went back inside.

"She seems nice," Jackson said as they pulled out of the driveway.

"She is," Cara said. She was aggravating and always on her ass about something, but deep down, she was nice.

"Everything okay?"

Cara kept her gaze out the window. She knew that just one look in Jackson's direction would tell him that everything was not.

"It will be," she said.

———

Cara was struck first by the grey, then by the green. It was cloudy when they drove into Pinesboro, and didn't let up as they drove down empty streets dotted with businesses and worn homes. "I wish I could say the weather's normally better," Jackson said as they pulled into the parking lot of a Motel 6. "But I don't want to lie to you."

"It's not that bad," Cara said. She stood in awe of the forest lying beyond the road, and the mountains lying beyond the forest. Layer upon layer of green, offering a promise of what was to come beyond the grey and drizzle of town.

"It's even better when it's a memory." Jackson walked into the front lobby to get their keys. Cara shrugged, leaned against the car, and lit a cigarette while she sat with her luggage. She knew this weekend would be hard for Jackson, that it'd been hard the moment they got on the highway and started to see how many miles away they were from the place Jackson never wanted to be again. "It always pulls me back," he sighed as they'd driven by a faded sign that said "Welcome to Pinesboro!"

Cara touched his knee, and said, "But this time you're not alone."

He only replied by taking her hand and giving it a squeeze. But it was enough.

Cara could only hope she'd be enough for him, at least enough for him to get through the next two days without falling into despair. "We'll just go to the funeral, then leave," Cara reminded him as they walked into their motel room. The reek of cigarettes hit them as soon as they were inside. Cara found it comforting.

"Right." Jackson hoisted his bag on one bed, then sat on the other. Cara joined him.

"We don't have to do anything else, see anyone else, or go anywhere else."

"I mean, I can show you around, at least."

"You don't have to if you don't want to."

"There're some things I want to show you, though. My old street, parts of downtown we liked visiting, my old school." A flash of contentment crossed Jackson's face for the first time since they arrived in Pinesboro. "There's a window that doesn't lock in the back of the high school, and I'd go there with people to make out at night."

"Well, we can do that for sure. Maybe after dinner."

"Maybe so. Or maybe after the funeral tomorrow. I …" He looked at his hands. His anger from earlier didn't return, but it was replaced with a sadness that seeped from his face to his posture.

Cara took his hand. "We don't have to go anywhere today. We don't have to go until you're ready."

Jackson nodded, and Cara kissed his cheek.

They stayed there the rest of the day, their solitude interrupted only by a delivery woman who brought them Chinese food for dinner. They watched TV, smoked, and held each other in silence. He was here, and for Cara, that was enough.

————

The funeral was a chorus of choked sobs, sniffs muffled by Kleenex, and parting words. Cara felt sorry for Moira and everyone who mourned her, but tears were hard to come by, given how briefly she'd known her before she died. She hoped she didn't seem insensitive nestled between Moira's aunt, who dabbed away tears every two seconds, and Jackson, who closed his eyes and sighed as everyone spoke. Cara squeezed his hand and stroked his palm. Her main concern was being there for him.

After the service, and after Moira's coffin was lowered into the ground, everyone gathered in the reception hall. The lights inside were almost a glare. Cara squinted as she walked through the mourners and picked at the food. Their tears in the cemetery were left on the grass, and all of Moira's friends and family spoke with small smiles and grave pleasantries, making the best of being brought together by something so tragic. Cara felt out-of-place, having only met Moira once; but people seemed to take a special interest in talking to her, the one person there who knew Moira the least.

"It's nice to meet you," Mr. Thompson said as he shook her hand.

"It was nice of you to come with Jackson," Mrs. Thompson added as she gave her a hug.

"Of course she would," Chris added as he gave her a hug as well. "What kind of significant other wouldn't?"

"That's in no way, shape or form directed at Michael, right?" Jackson said with a small smile.

"Michael said he can't do funerals," Chris said with a huff. "Can you believe it?"

"I don't think he's right for you anyway," Mrs. Thompson said.

"Because he's a guy?" Chris said with a grin.

"No, because he doesn't support you." Mrs. Thompson lightly hit Chris' arm while Mr. Thompson laughed. They continued speaking with Jackson, and Cara excused herself to get some punch. Everyone spoke with one another as she got her glass. Before they could speak with her again, she made a quiet exit. Cara just needed a moment away, a moment in her rightful place on the periphery.

She walked past the church, past the picnic area, and back to the cemetery. Two workers slowly filled Moira's grave. She nodded at them, and walked in laps through the stones. She watched the grass as she walked, keeping her eyes away from the bodies of people she didn't know.

"Looking for someone?"

Cara stopped, and turned towards the voice. A woman with strawberry blonde hair stood a few feet away. Her hair was cut short, and Cara saw a silver chain around her neck glint beneath the small bit of sunlight that decided to appear. She was tall and seemed almost frail in her thinness, but she held her head high, as if she wanted to assure people that she was proud beneath her timid exterior.

She looked at the ground, but Cara knew she'd spoken to her, even before she added, "You've walked by this row five times. Are you lost?"

"No," Cara said. "Just walking."

"Ah. I suppose you couldn't get lost in here. So many graves, but such a small space."

Cara nodded, and was about to walk away, when the woman asked, "Who do you know here?"

"No one."

The woman smiled, and despite her discomfort at being spoken to so bluntly by a stranger, Cara felt warmed by it. "No one comes here unless they know someone — this graveyard or this town."

Cara tried not to laugh, given her surroundings. The woman chuckled, then stared at the small stones at her feet. Cara moved closer to her. It couldn't hurt to at least be cordial to another mourner. "I'm here with my boyfriend," she said, "but I don't know anyone buried here. Not well, anyway."

"Lucky you." The woman sighed. "Sometimes it seems like everyone I know is here. But these two keep bringing me back — the two I lost before they were even mine. I should've known I would lose them. I lose everyone else."

A chill settled on Cara's skin as the woman's words brought up memories of what Jackson said his mother always said to him. She looked at the two tiny gravestones, and saw that each person buried there only had one year, one day, and one name: Price.

"And the ones I don't lose —" The woman absently touched Cara's elbow, and Cara looked up — "are the ones who take everyone else away." She smiled, and Cara felt sick. "Funny how that works, huh?"

The sick feeling only heightened when Cara looked in the woman's brown and hazel eyes surrounded by an amber ring. She'd recognize them anywhere. They'd drawn her in so many times.

"Cara?"

Cara paled as she turned around. People were emptying out of the reception hall, but only one walked towards her instead of the cars. Jackson smiled as he approached her. She wanted to tell him to run, to get in the car and drive away before he could see who was with her.

"Why'd you come outside?" he asked.

He noticed the woman behind her, and stopped. A stoniness Cara had never seen before crept over his features. Cara moved towards him before her own fears froze her in place.

"Here with your boyfriend, huh?" The woman's voice became sickly sweet, like a liquor laced with poison. "You didn't tell me you were seeing someone, Jack."

"What are you doing here?"

"Visiting my children. I didn't think I'd be visiting all of them today." She motioned towards the stones. "Don't tell me you've forgotten your brother and sister."

"You made sure I didn't."

"You tried, though. You tried before you were even born, making sure you got through while they remained a memory —"

"Jackson had nothing to do with your babies dying," Cara spat. Mrs. Price looked at her with mild shock. Cara felt a flash of embarrassment, but mostly for Jackson's sake. He squeezed her hand, whether in warning or thanks, she didn't know. But he remained silent.

"And you had nothing to do with it either," Cara said. "People die. It happens to everyone."

Mrs. Price's smile returned, as did Cara's sickness. The nervous bile in her stomach pooled and began to boil. Cara took a breath and tried to keep calm.

"But it follows us," Mrs. Price said. "It followed me through my womb — where it took two — and came out for more."

"Goodbye," Jackson said. He turned around, and Cara joined him even without him holding her elbow as he did so.

"It hung like a spirit in our house, one that wouldn't leave as long as Jack was home. Always spending time with Grandma, until he couldn't anymore …"

"Don't listen to her," Cara said as they began to walk away.

"And always off to Moira Thompson's house."

Jackson halted, but didn't turn to face his mother. Cara stopped, trying not to look at her either; and touched Jackson's cheek.

"You were there so much I thought you'd be married. You were with her when you came back for awhile. You were always connected, like friends are." Mrs. Price sighed as she surveyed the cemetery, her eyes falling on the workers as they shoveled the last mounds of dirt on Moira's grave. "And look where she is now."

Cara felt Jackson shake a little beneath her touch. She pulled him closer to her, and tried not to dig her fingers into his skin as Mrs. Price's words coursed through her veins with familiar heat.

"I still remember what you told me," Mrs. Price continued. "When you'd known Moira for a week, and said she was like the sister you never had." Cara glanced at Mrs. Price. Her smile was gone, and she glared in their direction. "You had a sister. You knew you did, I showed her to you every week; but you abandoned her and threw your living *friend* in my face and said she was someone you never had. She wasn't your sister …"

"I know she wasn't," Jackson muttered.

"I never had your sister, or your brother. I had you, and the death that came with you, and now everyone around me's been lost."

Jackson spun around as he wiped a tear that had sprung. "That wasn't my fault. None of it was."

"Something that's part of you isn't your fault, but that doesn't mean it isn't part of you. Look at your brother and sister's graves —"

"No."

"Look at everyone we know who's here —"

"I've seen them all before."

"Look at Moira's grave."

Jackson looked at the ground. Mrs. Price smiled once again, and motioned towards Moira's tombstone.

"I guess I was wrong. I guess she *is* like the sister you never had."

Jackson clamped his eyes shut. Cara held him close. Comforting Jackson was the only thing that kept her from running to Mrs. Price, tackling her to the ground, and bashing her skull on a headstone.

"I'm only reminding him of the things he can't escape from," Mrs. Price said, as if Cara had asked. "It's a curse we both share, one I took on when I grew him in my womb. I'm as much a monster as he is."

"He isn't a monster," Cara replied, careful to leave it at that.

"He tries to run, to find solace in others; but death will always find him because it was with him before he was even born. It was the price I paid for being selfish, for asking for blessings instead of looking within my own soul and seeing what sins were keeping those blessings from me."

"So stop making him try to pay it for you."

Mrs. Price laughed, and it was an uglier sound than all the smirking hitchhikers she'd finished off combined. "You don't want to see him as he is, because you love who you think he is, right? An innocent man with a monster for a mother? Look around us. Who he is is all right here. Stay with him, and you'll see it for yourself — maybe even first-hand, when you fall asleep one night and never open your eyes —"

Mrs. Price stopped speaking as Jackson bolted towards her. He stopped an inch away from her. She kept her poise, but Cara saw a slight tremble in her lip.

"Don't you ever, *ever* threaten her," he said.

"I didn't threaten her," Mrs. Price replied. "I told her the truth."

"Don't speak to her, or —"

"Or what? You'll hurt me?" Mrs. Price laughed again, and Cara wished she could cut her throat. She looked at the ground, trying to quell her familiar thoughts that were only safe with strangers. "You can't hurt me more than you al-ready have for twenty-seven years."

Jackson turned around. Anger replaced the sadness in his eyes. He walked towards Cara. "Let's go," he said.

"I'm your mother," Mrs. Price called after them. "You'd never hurt me. You're part of me, a part of me that I didn't know was too dangerous to let out until it was too late."

"Let's go home," Jackson said as he unlocked the car.

"Do you know what it's like to know that?" Mrs. Price pointed at the stones. Jackson ignored her, and Cara looked down as she got in the car. "To know that you've sentenced everyone around you to your sins?"

CHAPTER 15

Cara felt nothing but anger, anger that started in the grave-yard and stayed at a steady, familiar hum in the car. She stayed quiet as Jackson sped into the Motel 6 parking lot, stayed in the car while he got their bags and returned their keys, and didn't say a word as they peeled off. Her eyes stayed out the window as he sped out of town, turning through the local streets as fast as he could before reaching the highway. He didn't speak. He didn't need to. He didn't even need to flip off the sign they sped by that said, "Now Leaving Pinesboro. We hope you'll come back!" Cara knew he'd never return.

"I can see why you left," she said once they'd made their way down the highway.

Jackson didn't reply. Cara glanced at him, and saw him staring straight ahead. She gave a small shrug to herself and looked back out the window. She'd talk to him later.

"I'm never going back again," he said. "Not as long as that fucking witch is there."

"Good."

Jackson stayed quiet. Cara stewed in all her thoughts. They rammed at her head, desperate to leave through either her mouth or her hands.

After awhile, she couldn't help herself. She had to share at least some of them. If Jackson would answer her, maybe they'd be less muddled. Maybe she could make sense of them, and make them disappear — or at the very least, make them into tangible anger that she could work with.

"The things she said … the things she said about me —" Jackson took a breath, but Cara continued anyway — "did she say that about Moira?"

"Yes."

Cara's blood began to simmer. She wanted it to. "And she said that about your grandmother?"

"After she died."

"Why would she talk to you when she didn't even want you to live with her?"

"To remind me of what I am —"

"You're not —"

"What I am to her."

Cara pressed her lips. Jackson added, "And because I'm her goddamn son. It's why she writes, it's why she'd see me at work after I moved back —"

"At work? Couldn't you just throw her out?"

"Not when she was picking up her prescriptions." He snorted. "Painkillers. All her bullshit about how what I do kills people, and she's on fucking painkillers. You know what she said to me on my first day? That I was counting pills for her just like I did for Grandma. Then she shook the

263

pill bottle and said, 'Hope it turns out better for me than it did for her.'"

If only it turned out that way for Mrs. Price. Cara kept that to herself, even as the thought trembled at her lips and coursed through her veins with the complete picture her anger craved.

"But she didn't want me to forget what I was to her," he continued. "She never did, and she never does. I know she was at the cemetery today because of Moira's funeral. I know she figured she'd see me, or that I'd see her and try to talk to her like a fucking idiot."

"You came over there because of me. You didn't even know she was there."

"Even if I saw her when everyone was leaving, I would've probably tried to talk to her. She's right, Cara — I'm her son, and even when I want to forget everything she's done to me, I can't forget that she's my mom. I can't throw out her mail, I can't stop trying to see her in the rare moments I think she'll be there for me, and I can't. Fucking. Stop!"

He pounded the steering wheel. A stray beep of the horn escaped into the nothing ahead of them. Jackson returned his clenched fist to this thigh. Cara enclosed it in her hand.

"It's not on you to stop it," she said.

Jackson sighed.

"It's not all on you. She hurts you, Jackson. She hurts you on purpose. She says you'd never hurt her because she's your mom, but she hurts you all the time even though you're her son. What kind of mom would do that?"

"I never said she was good."

"I never said you did."

"But good or bad, she's my mom."

"What does that matter? It doesn't matter to her. Any time you show a sign you don't believe her lies, she comes back to remind you of them so you'll depend on her. She wants to keep a connection with you, but she only wants one if that connection is you being afraid. Why do you think she always tells you what she thinks you are?"

"Because she believes it."

"Who gives a shit? It's not true, and even if she thinks it is, she only says it because she won't love you unless you're afraid. That's her condition, and she's supposed to love you without condition. She doesn't, and you don't have to love her just because she gave birth to you. You don't owe her anything she doesn't give you herself."

"It's not that easy."

"I'm not saying it's easy. I'm just saying that if anything you're holding onto with your mom is because you think she's right or because you think you'll be alone if you cut things off, that it's not true. You won't be alone —"

"I know —"

"And she's not right. She's not right about anything. Not about you, not about Pinesboro, and not about anyone you know, living or dead."

Jackson didn't speak. Cara knew he needed time.

Minutes passed. Cara wondered how much time he would need.

When they passed their third exit without a word, Cara began to speak. "Are you —"

"I don't want to talk about this anymore," Jackson said. He didn't look at her.

Cara removed her hand from his and folded both in her lap. She tried to stare ahead and not look at him. The threads of Jackson's silence slowly stitched into a blanket that spread across the car and draped over Cara with increasing weight. She thought of the last time she spoke to Moira, and how Moira said his silence was worse than any fear or anger. For the first time, she understood what she'd meant.

But Cara was used to silence, and used to draping it around her when she needed a moment — or several — to seethe. She closed her eyes and let Jackson spin an angry tapestry between them, one that Cara trusted would either be thrust aside to let them breathe each other in, or folded around them both to let them suffocate together. Cara didn't mind either way, so long as she was with him when it happened.

———

Jackson parked in his lot and got out of the car without a word. Cara followed behind with her bag. They walked into his apartment. Jackson slowed his pace, but still kept his eyes off of her. Cara found it easier to stay quiet in an apartment with multiple rooms and spaces to go to. She dropped off her bag in his bedroom. She decided to just go to bed. Sleep would help them both.

Cara wandered back out to the living room and saw Jackson standing near the kitchen table. He stood still, his hands in his pockets. He breathed deeply, but otherwise didn't make a sound.

She turned to go back in the bedroom. He'd figure out that she was going to bed.

"Cara?"

Jackson stayed facing away from her, eyes on the ground; but hearing her name was enough. "Yeah?" she asked, hoping she didn't sound too eager.

"It's … it's not true, right? What she says?"

"Absolutely not." Cara circled her arms around him and leaned her cheek against his back. Jackson placed his hand over hers.

"None of it?"

"Not a word." Cara saw the return of all her dreamed responses to Mrs. Price's words in the graveyard. She closed her eyes and allowed herself to relish them, as doing so helped keep her calm for him. How could Mrs. Price hurt him so easily? How could Cara have let her get away with it?

"Not even …. not about you, right?"

Cara brought her thoughts back to Jackson and made them stay there. He needed her, not her darkest fantasies. "Of course not."

"You're not afraid of what she said?"

"No. Well, only of what it does to you." She kissed the back of his neck and Jackson sighed.

"You're not afraid?"

"Not when I'm with you." Her kisses dotted his shoulders, the nape of his neck. Cara tried not to turn herself on, but kissing him helped her and seemed to help him, for he leaned back and relaxed a little more with each and every one.

"You're not afraid to die?"

"Not at all." If there was one thing in her life she had a grasp on, it was death. She smiled a little at the thought, and began interspersing her kisses with gentle bites. "I'm not going anywhere, Jackson."

"Good." He sighed as he spoke, sighed with such relief that Cara increased the intensity of her kisses and bites.

"No one's going to touch me — or you." She held him closer and ran her free palm up his chest as he leaned into her kisses and whispers. "If anyone did, I'd kill them."

Cara hoped Jackson couldn't feel the chill that coursed through her skin. She paused from kissing him, and scrambled to think of something to say that would explain away her lapse. She could say that — it was a lapse, a slip of the tongue, something that glided off of her in the heat of the moment.

Before she could say anything, though, Jackson gripped her hand tighter. He otherwise didn't move. He only asked, "You would?"

Cara paused for a moment. Maybe he hadn't heard her correctly. No — he had to. Maybe she was the one who hadn't heard right. Or maybe she had, and just hadn't heard him ask the question in quiet earnest as opposed to shock or disgust.

She decided the only way to test the waters was to answer him. "Yes," she whispered, hoping with all hope that Jackson wouldn't shove her away, wouldn't kick her out and tell her to never come back.

Jackson stroked her hand with his thumb. "Tell me how."

This wasn't happening. This couldn't possibly be happening to her. It wasn't possible that someone so perfect, someone who was so perfect for her, was actually perfect for her in every possible way. "Tell you how?" she asked, if only to buy time as she struggled with her disbelief.

"Yes. Tell me."

"I —"

"I'm tired of being afraid. I'm tired of thinking about death the way I'm supposed to, the way everyone wants me to. They all want me to fear it or look away from it or let it do what it will." He gripped her hand. "I want to confront it. I want to hear about it and not be afraid. And I'm not afraid when I'm with you."

Cara leaned into the nape of his neck as she warmed with his words. "You don't have to be," she whispered.

"I'm not —"

"The only people who need to be afraid are the ones who'd touch either of us." Her words coursed through her veins and ignited her like she hadn't been in days.

Jackson stoked the fire by stroking her hand, her palms, her fingers. He lifted her hand and kissed it. "Why do they have to be afraid?"

"Because of what I'd do to them."

He moved her hand down his chest. She wanted so badly for it to be bare. "What would you do to them?"

"I'd shove them away. I'd shove them to the ground and lift them up only to get a stronger push. One that would daze them."

"Hmm." Jackson didn't speak further. Cara wondered briefly if that was enough, maybe too much, but her questions ceased when he stopped moving her hand. He pressed it over his growing erection.

"Just daze them?" he asked.

"Right." Cara unzipped his fly and began to stroke him.

"What's …" He breathed in, his words harder to come by as he grew stiffer and she stroked harder. "What's next?"

"Some punches. Maybe a slap. Blows I can deal myself." She would never take this long to kill someone, but Jackson didn't need to know that. This was a game, one to enfold him in what he feared; and her swiftness in reality would serve neither of them well in his moment of fantasy.

"You got a strong punch?"

She gripped him harder and he groaned with deep, rippling pleasure. "You tell me."

"Tell me more. Tell me what you'd do next."

He was hard enough now that she knew she could cut to the chase. "I'd look at them bleeding on the ground," she said, moving closer to his ear. "I'd look at them lying helpless and broken, thinking they're going to get away …"

"Mmm …"

"Thinking they're going to get away with everything they've done, everything they've said …"

"What'd they say?"

They knew what they'd said. Cara knew. Cara knew and heard it every day. She heard them now, heard them whispering in her ear about how she was worthless, how she needed to go away, how she needed to bury herself on the farm and never emerge if she wanted to be safe. She heard them and she didn't care. She heard them and was ready to prove them wrong. She was ready to shut them all up.

"But they won't get away," she hissed. "Because I'm in control …"

"Yes …"

"I hold their death in my hands …"

"You do …"

"And all I need to do is take out my knife, slit her throat …"

"Her?"

"And she'll never speak to me again."

"Who're you — shit!" Jackson gripped his hand over hers as he came. Cara broke from her thoughts as he buckled over to keep his cum from getting on the floor.

"Shit," he repeated. "Shit, shit, shit." He rushed to the sink while Cara moved to his paper towel rack, both of them cleaning themselves in silence.

Cara stood still once she came back to Jackson and saw him looking at her. He didn't look terrified, but the sense of brave escape she'd heard in his voice was nowhere to be found in his eyes.

"Who were you talking about?" he asked.

"No one," Cara said with a small shrug. "Anyone."

"You said her."

"I said them."

"You said her and she."

"I didn't mean anyone." She'd thought of many people, both the hers who'd angered her and the hims she'd killed; but Jackson's expression told her he wouldn't understand that, even if she left out the actual killing she'd done.

"Of course you meant someone," he said.

"What does it matter?"

"Because it's real when it's someone."

"We were just talking —"

"*You* were just talking."

Cara felt stung even before she saw anger flash in Jackson's eyes. He continued, "You were talking about all this —"

"You asked me too."

"I didn't want this. You took it too far. You …" Jackson looked down. He turned towards the table and held the back of the chair. Despite the sting from his words still prickling on her skin, Cara moved towards him and touched his arm. He stayed still.

"I didn't mean anyone," Cara repeated. "It wasn't real."

"I think I need to be alone."

Cara dropped her hand from his elbow. "I swear, I didn't —"

"I believe you, but I … this has been a lot, and I need to be by myself."

"You don't need to be. You don't have to be alone —"

"But I want to." He stood up and turned to face her. "I want to be alone."

Cara stepped back. She wanted to feel angry, but all she felt was heartbreak.

She hated it.

"Just for tonight," Jackson said. It did nothing to soothe her. "I need to —"

"Be by yourself. I got that." He didn't want her there. He didn't want her.

"It's not you, it's —"

"It's just what I said, right?"

"I just need a moment —"

"So take it. I'll go." Cara went to the bedroom and grabbed her bag. She returned to the living room and walked towards the door. Jackson followed her and grabbed his keys. Cara cursed under her breath. She'd forgotten that he'd need to drive her. She was tempted to hitchhike, but felt that desire flee when he touched her back. All he needed to do to bring her back, to temper her anger and fears, was to touch her. She wished it wasn't so easy.

She wished more that it wasn't so easy for him to hurt her.

They drove to Leslie in silence, but this time, it was Cara who stayed quiet. Jackson occasionally touched her thigh or squeezed her hand, but otherwise, the only thing between them was the music on his radio. Cara didn't want to speak. She told herself it was because she was angry, because he'd upset her and cast her out. Deep down, though, she knew that she didn't want him to hear how hurt and embarrassed she was. She'd gone too far, just like she'd feared; and he wanted her gone, just like her mother predicted.

Cara closed her eyes. She would have to see her mother, and worse, she'd have to tell her that she'd been right. Cara thought of breaking her silence to tell Jackson to drop her off at a bar or somewhere away from the farm, but by the time she thought of it, it was too late. Jackson turned into the driveway and was already approaching the farmhouse.

Jackson parked and turned off the car. Cara felt a sense of anger and dread. He wasn't just going to drop her off. How else did he want to humiliate her? How much further did he want to push her away? Cara closed her eyes again, and tried with all her might to get the thoughts in her head — the thoughts that used to disappear when she was with him — to quiet themselves.

"Thanks for coming with me," Jackson said as he touched her shoulder.

Cara snorted quietly. "You're welcome."

"Really, it meant a lot."

"Until it became too much?"

Cara felt his fingers flinch. She kept her eyes off of him, if only so she wouldn't have to see him look wounded. Even with her own wounds, she'd never be able to ignore his.

She hated that more than she hated how easily she fell apart with the slightest break in his demeanor.

"It was a lot," he said.

"I know. And I made it worse. I'm sorry."

"You didn't —"

"I did, and please stop saying otherwise. I can fucking handle it, okay?"

"You made things better more than anything else."

"Good night."

His hand moved to her hand, which stopped her from leaving. "I just need a little time alone. That's all."

She snapped her hand away. "So fucking take it! I'm trying to give you that, but you keep talking to me and holding me and making it seem like you don't want to be alone. If you want to be alone, then let me goddamn leave."

Jackson didn't reply. Cara couldn't take it anymore. Every moment with him in the car made her wonder why she was being dropped off. She hated being kicked out, but she hated the uncertainty more. At least if she left, she'd know where she stood with him.

Cara unlocked the door. "Good night," she said again.

"Good night." She opened the door, and Jackson touched her elbow. "Cara?"

Cara stopped. She slowly turned towards him. She didn't ask what he wanted. She didn't want to. She wanted him to tell her himself. She also didn't want him to hear how much she wanted him to ask her to stay.

Jackson leaned forward and kissed her. Cara kept her hands away from him, but still kissed him back, still tilted her head as he leaned closer and held her cheek. She wanted so badly to stay with him, to kiss him in his bed and hold him all night.

But he didn't want that — not when he heard what she was capable of. She felt a small lump rise in her throat, and kissed him harder to keep it down.

Jackson pulled away, but kept his hand on her cheek. "I love you," he whispered.

Cara nodded curtly. "I love you too."

"I love *you*, Cara. I love all of you."

Cara didn't speak. She knew he was speaking to all of her fears that began to surface the minute he said he wanted to be alone, all of her fears that previously kept her from saying too much. They were fears she'd never shared with him, fears she'd never shared with anyone but herself. And yet, he knew them. He knew all of them — and that scared Cara most of all.

Cara got out of the car and kept her eyes forward. She heard silence behind her, and knew Jackson was watching her instead of driving away. She refused to look at him, to look in his eyes and surrender to the control her heart was all too willing to give him. She controlled her heart. She would decide when it would be given and when it would be broken — even if that meant breaking it herself.

She climbed her stairs in silence and walked to her room. She lay on her bed and stared out the window.

"You're home early."

Cara didn't reply. Delores walked into her room and sat behind Cara on her bed. She gently stroked her hair, like she'd done when Cara had a bad day at school and didn't want to talk about it. Her mother didn't pry. Her mother knew not to.

Her mother knew. Her mother knew, and still loved her. In that moment, it was all the comfort Cara needed.

CHAPTER 16

Sleep did little to help Cara. Jackson kept appearing in her dreams, flickers of the night she could've had if she'd kept her damn mouth shut. She'd see him looking at her, feel his chest moving against her as he breathed, hear the gentle snore he insisted he didn't do while he slept. Then she'd wake up in her own bed, and feel crushing disappointment each time she realized where she was.

Consciousness wasn't much better. She did her best to bury thoughts of Jackson as she got dressed. She needed to think of other things, especially with the almost certain possibility that other things would be all she had going forward.

Jackson told her it would just be one night, one night he needed alone. Cara wasn't so sure. Even if it was one night, and Jackson texted her later and told her his door was unlocked, she couldn't be sure that scaring him would only be a one-time thing. She couldn't be sure that she wouldn't slip up again, that she wouldn't fantasize with him and start sharing her realities — all of them, each and every piece of darkness that she'd previously left buried on Vineyard Farm.

One thing she was certain of, though, was that he wouldn't share those realities with her — not without fear and not without casting her away. Pushing her back to the farm was his response to spoken words and shared imaginings. What would he do if he ever discovered there was more to her than his dreams?

Cara didn't want to find out. Much like her words were all it took to scare him, his asking her to be alone, as well as his look of worry, was all it took to break her heart. What would she do if he ever looked at her with the cold anger she'd seen for his mother in Pinesboro? What would she do if he told her he never wanted to see her again, that he never wanted her to come back? What would she do when he no longer wanted her?

Cara feared that she would break entirely, that her pieces would scatter and wilt in the empty pumpkin patches across their farm. She sighed as she walked down the stairs. At least now, she wasn't entirely broken. She could stay that way so long as she stayed away from him.

———

Cara walked downstairs. As much as she wanted to spend the day wrapped in her loneliness, she had money to earn. She also knew she'd have to face her mother eventually.

Cara walked in the kitchen and saw Delores sipping coffee. A blueberry muffin waited for her on the table.

Delores gave her a small, hesitant smile. "You sleep okay?"

Cara gave a curt nod, then sat down. She peeled the paper off the muffin one ridge at a time.

"I'm … I'm sorry," Delores continued. "For whatever happened with Jackson."

Of course she wasn't sorry about their own fight. Cara's shoulders slumped as she bit into her muffin. Delores didn't have to be sorry — she'd been right.

Cara could feel Delores watching her, could almost feel all the questions she tried to keep down by drinking her coffee in tiny, frequent sips.

"You were right," Cara said. It took all her strength to speak.

Delores nodded, but Cara noticed that her hand shook a little as she did so.

"I didn't tell him," Cara clarified. "I just … I could tell."

"How?"

Cara swallowed around the lump forming in her throat, the one she couldn't wait to disappear for good. The one that only seemed to surface when she remembered Jackson. She wondered how long it would take for both the lump and the memories to disappear.

Delores took Cara's wrist and gave it a comforting squeeze. "You don't have to tell me," she said. "Not until you're ready. Not ever, if you don't want."

Cara nodded in thanks, for she still couldn't risk speaking without crying — especially when her breaking heart was being filled by her mother's tenderness. It was too much. It was all too much, and Cara needed all of it to disappear.

"I have to go to work," Cara said, leaving her muffin unfinished as she stood up.

"Okay. See you tonight."

Delores didn't even ask if she'd see her tonight. She just knew, just like she always knew. Cara blinked as she walked towards the door.

————

Cara did her best to smile or at least look okay when she was at work. Fortunately, Keith had an ample opportunity for her to be alone. "Got a short delivery list today," he said as Greg walked by with a keg. "But a long drive: Asheville. You okay with that?"

"Absolutely," Cara couldn't wait to get lost in the mountains.

"Just take off work once you're done. You can do the rest of the deliveries tomorrow."

"Sounds good."

"But before you go —" Keith smiled a little. "How was your weekend?"

Cara couldn't pretend to smile even if she wanted to. "I was at a funeral," she said. She figured that was enough to explain her mood.

Sure enough, Keith looked at her with surprise and pity. "Oh my God. I'm … I'm sorry. Who was it for?"

"Moira."

"The woman who was here before?"

"Yeah. She had cancer."

Keith looked down and let out a sigh, one that carried a small whisper: "Fuck." He looked back up with apologetic eyes. "Sorry, just —"

"Don't be. I think that's an appropriate response."

Keith patted Cara's arm. "Well, tell your boyfriend I'm sorry," he said. She tried to ignore the sting she felt at hearing "boyfriend." She nodded again, then waited as patiently as she could for Greg to finish loading the truck.

The drive to and from Asheville was almost ten hours round trip. It still wasn't enough. Cara drove into Leslie feeling as weighted as she had that morning. She wanted to stop feeling this way. She wanted to feel alive again, to feel the ignition in her skin that only two things ever seemed to bring her. One of those things was gone. The other didn't have to be.

Cara saw someone walking on the side of the road. She raised her eyebrows. She imagined picking them up, imagined taking them deeper into nowhere and then leaving them to rot in the water. She imagined their screams as they realized they were about to disappear.

It did absolutely nothing for her.

Cara blinked as she drove past the pedestrian. Jackson had taken over everything within her, everything that made her feel alive, to the point that nothing else could.

Her phone chimed. The single chime deepened the crack which had begun forming in her heart since yesterday. Cara swallowed as she pulled over and checked her phone.

Come over tonight?

It was all she'd wanted yesterday. She'd spent so much time wanting it yesterday that she'd been miserable today. Cara couldn't take the misery of wanting him, the agony of worrying that she'd say too much and repel him for more than a day. Most of all, Cara couldn't handle him knowing that about her. She didn't want him to have to comfort her. She wanted everything he did to her, everything he made her feel, to just fucking disappear.

Can't, she wrote back. She tossed her phone on the passenger seat, then continued towards the farm.

————

Cara moved through the farm and her work in silence for the rest of the week, the people around her finally knowing to leave her alone. Keith kept things to "Good morning," Sadie only talked about herself, and Greg kept his communication to where to put the kegs. Even Delores left Cara be, for the most part. She'd talk about her day at dinner, and let Cara nod or stare out the window in reply. Cara didn't want to speak, and didn't need to with her mother. Her mother would let her be, and her mother would let her disappear.

Jackson wouldn't disappear so easily. He called her the morning after she said she couldn't see him. Cara let it go to voicemail. She didn't want him to hear her voice tighten or her curt responses. She didn't want to hear his voice and lose all her resolve at the sound of it.

He texted her that afternoon: *Coming over tonight?*

Cara knew he'd only try to call again if she didn't answer. *Can't. Chores.*

There was no way Jackson believed her, but all he wrote back was, *Okay.* Cara hoped her blatant lie was enough to get him to stop.

On Wednesday, he called her again. She didn't answer.

He didn't text. But he called her once more that afternoon. Cara saw he left a voicemail. She deleted it without listening to it.

She heard the chime for one last time that week as she pulled into her driveway. All Jackson wrote was, *Please call.*

Cara didn't. She also didn't write back.

Jackson neither called nor texted her after that.

———————

Her silent phone was a comfort, but a cold one. Cara felt the weight of its silence as she moved through work and moved through the farm. She felt like a ghost floating through her former life, the one she'd had without Jackson. She trusted she'd eventually pass on into a life without him. She could only hope it would happen soon.

Cara spent Friday in complete silence. The weekend ahead would be spent entirely at home. Cara had nowhere to go and no one to see. It was like graduation again, look-ing ahead into all the possibilities and knowing she only had one: to fade into nothing with all the dead vines on Vineyard Farm.

This time though, she wasn't afraid to fade. She imag-ined sleeping in the dirt of the empty pumpkin patches, or walking into the woods and rolling into the water along with the bodies she'd dumped in the lake. She wouldn't do it, of course — not yet anyway — but imagining it gave her a peaceful sense of comfort. One less exciting than killing, but one that helped her in its own way. She looked out the window as she and Delores ate dinner on Friday night. She looked at the woods and imagined disappearing forever into their branches.

"Cara."

Cara turned to face her mother. Delores looked at her with the blend of kindness and sternness that Cara knew would come with a comforting lecture. She braced herself for what her mother had to say.

"Do you know why I keep everything you bring home?"

Cara furrowed her brow. Of all the things her mother could talk about, she wasn't expecting that. "Why you keep everything?" she asked.

"Yes. Why I take the hats, the belts, the ugly key rings —"

"I know what they are."

"And you know why I take them?"

"Because …" Cara swallowed. "Because you're proud of me?"

"Yes — but I would be even without them."

Cara looked down before she could be warmed by her mother's small smile. "You know why else?" Delores asked.

Cara snorted a little as the memory of their argument resurfaced. "To rat me out?" she said. It angered her to remember, but the anger pierced through the numbness she'd had since Monday morning. She couldn't deny that it felt pretty good.

"Never." Delores touched Cara's elbow, and Cara slowly looked back at her. "I'd never do that, and I … I'm sorry for making you think that I would."

Cara nodded. Believing her mother would help her get to whatever point she wanted to make all the faster, and then Cara could resume her evening of silence.

"But when you bring home your souvenirs, don't you notice that I touch them all?"

Cara sat in silence. She thought of the first time her mother had found her — and found evidence they spent all the next morning cleaning off the truck. She thought of how her mother had lifted the first victim's belt, and how many things she'd brought home and handed to her mother — all without wearing gloves.

"Fuck," she breathed as she put her head in her hands. "Fuck, fuck, fuck."

"No one's going to find them —"

"I'm so fucking stupid."

"And even if they did, your fingerprints wouldn't be the only ones on them."

Cara finally looked up. Delores gave her a gentle squeeze as she smiled at her. "All I want to do is protect you," she said. "It's all I ever want to do, and it's all I'll ever do — no matter what, and no matter where you are. I love you."

"I love you too."

"But I can't be the only one that does, and I can't be the only one you stay with, or else you're going to fade away."

Cara watched her mother in silence. Delores kept eye contact with her, daring Cara to look away or protest.

"You've been home all week," Delores continued. "It's just like when you were in school and here every day. It was just like old times."

"Don't you want that?" Cara asked.

"It's just like all the old times." Tears began to speckle Delores' eyes. "It's just like when you were sullen and sad, when you were fading away and a shell of the little girl I remembered. She didn't come back until you talked about taking care of that hitchhiker. She sparked and grew into the woman I knew you'd become, strong and no-nonsense and taking matters into her own hands. It was what you could do when you were away from the farm. And when you met Jackson —"

Cara flinched at his name, and said, "That all disappeared, right?" She hoped sarcasm would lessen the sting, but she only felt worse.

"No. It became something different, something which took you further away —"

"Which made me disappear —"

"Which made you happier than I've ever seen you. You spent less time here, but when you were here, you had more bite and more energy than I've ever seen. You were becoming more of your own person, and I felt like I was talking to a separate person instead of my daughter."

"I'll never stop being your daughter." Cara spoke matter-of-factly, but saw her mother smile as if she'd said something sweet and endearing.

"Of course you won't. But you can't only be my daughter. That was what I wanted, all I wanted; but I can't have that if you're going to stay alive. You need to be more than my daughter, and I need to let you do that — and you need to let yourself be more than that. You shouldn't hide from people who love you because of what you think you are."

Cara folded her arms and tried with all her might to not remember the last time she saw Jackson. "You mean what they know I am."

"You only said you could tell what Jackson thought. Could you? Did he tell you he didn't want to see you?"

"No."

"Did he tell you that he didn't love you?"

Cara closed her eyes. "No. He … he said he loved all of me. That he loved me no matter what."

"So why not believe him?"

"Because I know it's not true! He … I didn't tell him everything, but he saw a piece of it, a tiny piece, and he got scared. I scared him, Mom. I scared the last person I want to make afraid. He saw it and he wanted me to go away."

They were interrupted by a knock at the door. "Who the hell is that?" Delores asked as she glanced towards the hallway.

Cara looked out the window, then snapped her head back to the table the moment she saw the Camry in the driveway.

Delores saw the look on Cara's face, and it was all the answer she needed. "Do you want to see him?" she asked.

"I kind of have to, don't I?" Cara replied, not looking up.

"Not if you don't want to. But I kind of think you do."

Cara couldn't speak, just like she couldn't lie — not about him. She nodded.

"I'll let him in," Delores said as she stood up. "And I'll get out of your hair for a bit." She grabbed the truck keys from the peg on the wall.

"Mom?"

Delores stopped and looked at Cara. Cara did her best to smile.

"Thanks — for talking to me."

Delores nodded, then turned to leave.

"Mom?"

Delores turned again, but with a small smile. "You want me to answer the door or not?"

"Yeah, just … I love you."

Delores nodded. "I love you too, sweetheart."

She disappeared into the hall. Cara sat at the table, even as she heard the door open and heard mumbling between Jackson and her mother. She waited until she heard the door close. Jackson didn't appear. Cara knew he was waiting for her in the hall, waiting for her to appear when she wanted to — his one concession to her in exchange for coming by the farm himself.

Cara knew she needed to talk to him. Whether she told him goodbye or told him a sliver of the truth, she had to tell him something. She didn't know what she'd do if he left her for good afterwards, but whatever it was, she was glad she'd told her mother she loved her before she left.

———————

Jackson stood in front of the door. The hall light wasn't on, but she could still see every outline, every feature perfectly. She'd traced her fingers over every inch of him so many times that she had him memorized. Her fingertips crackled at the thought, and she closed them into her palm. It wasn't the time for that, something she knew even before she saw how sad he looked despite his best efforts to look neutral. She could see it most clearly in his eyes, his beautiful eyes that locked onto hers and, despite their sadness, were relieved to see her.

"Hey," he said.

"Hey," she replied.

They stood in silence. Cara shifted her feet, unsure if she should speak first. She had things to say to him, so many things; but all that came to mind were inanities. "How have you been?" she asked.

He shrugged. "Not great. You?"

She nodded as she looked down. "Okay," she replied. Jackson sighed a little, and though it didn't contain any malice, she still felt pained at the thought of hurting him further.

Her eyes fell on a paper bag next to his feet. She looked back up at him, and did her best to form a small smile. "You bring dinner?" she asked.

Jackson smiled a little. "No," he replied as he reached in the bag. "Just some stuff of yours I found around the apartment." He lifted out a white lacy bra. "Good thing your mom left."

Cara chuckled. "You figured I wouldn't come get these or something?"

Jackson's smile vanished, and Cara's skin grew cold. "Honestly? I don't know." He moved closer to her, and Cara made herself keep her eyes up. "What should I have thought, Cara?"

"I don't —"

"Because it's hard for me to know when you won't see me or talk to me or even send me a goddamn text."

"Jackson —"

"And I understand if you need time to yourself after what happened last week. But I can't understand that if you don't tell me, and if you keep not telling me when I try to find out."

"You wanted time alone last week too."

"Yeah, but I at least had the decency to say that to you. There's taking time, and then there's disappearing. I felt like you wanted to do the latter."

"I didn't want to." She had to — but Cara kept that to herself.

"I don't want you to either. And honestly? You can't. After all we've shared, after everything we've said and done with each other, what we have deserves better than unanswered phone calls and you avoiding me until I have to drive out here and hope you'll talk to me. Both of us are too old for this high school bullshit. If you don't want to see me anymore, say it to me. It'll hurt, but not as much as it would to leave me wondering where our future together went."

All week long, Cara had thought of disappearing from him forever. Hearing him say it, though, broke her heart into a chasm. It gaped inside her chest and begged to be filled with something, anything. Cara knew better than to fill it with Jackson. Instead, anger seeped into its maw. Cara's anger grew and bubbled. It was with herself, but it was easier to take out on him.

"Do you want me to say that?" Cara spat. "All you've talked about is me calling things off. Is that what you want?"

"Of course not! I'm a fucking mess without you. Look at me: this is what I'm like when I haven't seen you for a week."

"But you didn't want to see me."

"I wanted one night by myself, just one night to get my thoughts together without —"

"Without seeing me, because you saw who I was and you didn't want to see that anymore."

"I didn't —"

"And I can't take that, Jackson! I can't take knowing there are parts of me you'll see and all they'll do is make you push me away."

"*You're* pushing me away, Cara. That's all that's happening right now. Why? Why are you so convinced I'm on my way out the door? Why are you so convinced you scared me so much on Sunday that I'd never want to see you again, when I've been calling you all week and when I'm right fucking here?"

Cara had been convinced he'd want to disappear on his own volition — that by not answering him, and removing herself, she'd save him the trouble of realizing she didn't deserve him. But Jackson was right — he was there, and he'd come to her himself. The thought cooled her broken heart. It didn't mend it, but it cooled it enough for her to pause and sigh.

Jackson moved towards her and held her elbows. Cara shuddered with relief at his touch. "I'm right here," he said. "I'm not going anywhere."

"You will," she said, her voice shaking.

"Not without you."

"You'll want to. You'll want Sunday night again."

"Maybe, but not for forever. I love you so much, and absolutely nothing could change that."

Cara thought of his frightened face on Sunday. She had to. It was the only way she'd keep her resolve. "Nothing at all?" she asked.

"Nothing."

"Nothing I said on Sunday?"

"No."

"Even though …"

Jackson looked at her as he touched her cheek. "Even though what?" he asked.

Cara looked in his eyes, and convinced herself she saw it — the fact that despite all his words, all he said to her, he'd have conditions for whether or not he would love her. He told himself otherwise, but Cara knew the truth. She also knew that the truth was the only way he would leave, the only way he'd leave her behind and leave her to rot on Vineyard Farm.

It was the fate she deserved if she was to live a life without him.

She took a breath, and said, "Even though the things I said on Sunday weren't just pretend?"

———————

Jackson didn't believe her at first. Cara wasn't sure why she thought he'd be so easily convinced. "It was just a fantasy," he said. "We … we were just talking, just making something up."

"We were making up the situation," Cara said. "But I wasn't making up what I'd do."

"You weren't —"

"I wasn't making up what I've done."

"I know you've killed animals, vermin on the farm …"

"I haven't just killed animals."

Jackson looked at the floor, the wall, anything but her as he gathered his thoughts and tried every which way to explain away what he heard. "So, a criminal, right?" he asked. "Self-defense, or —"

"No."

"Or an accident. You did it by —"

"It wasn't an accident."

"You're telling me —"

"That I'm a killer."

Jackson finally froze. Cara did her best to keep her eyes up as the words sat between them in the hall.

"I'm a killer," Cara repeated. "I've killed people. It's something I've done, and while it's something I haven't done in months —"

"Months?"

"I can't promise that it's something I won't do again."

Jackson looked up at the ceiling and ran his fingers through his hair. "I just … I can't see it. This doesn't make sense."

"How?"

"I can't see you doing this."

"You saw it on Sunday."

"I saw a fantasy —"

"One that felt real, right?"

Jackson swallowed. He shook his head, and Cara imagined him trying to shake all thoughts of her out of his memory forever. She wished he'd do it in his Camry and let her move on to whatever fate she chose for herself once she was alone.

He looked back up at her. He didn't look scared, nor angry. Rather, he looked determined to bury whatever he'd heard.

"I can't believe it," Jackson said. "It just doesn't make sense."

Cara knew that he wouldn't believe it until he had no choice. She knew the only way he'd believe it would be seeing it himself.

"Then follow me," she said as she nodded towards the stairs. "I want to show you something."

———

Cara heard silence as she walked towards the basement, and wondered if Jackson decided against going with her and bolted out the door. When she turned to turn on the stairwell light, though, she saw him following behind her.

"I didn't make a run for it," Jackson said.

Cara looked ahead of her to keep her embarrassment out of sight. "I wouldn't blame you if you did," she replied.

"I figure if you were going to kill me, you would've done it by now."

Cara stopped and whipped her gaze back to him. He had a small smirk on his face, but it wasn't enough to lighten her expression.

"I would never hurt you," she said, her voice and gaze steadier than it'd been all night. "I've never thought of it, and I never will."

Jackson's smile disappeared. For the first time all night, he looked like he believed her.

He watched her in silence for a few moments, then nodded. "I know. I know you wouldn't."

Cara believed him. She nodded, and they continued the rest of the way down the stairs.

———

"Don't touch anything," Cara said as they looked at her mother's display.

Jackson processed everything in front of him. He saw the belt, the hats, the wallets and key rings. He saw them spread out and mingled in with all of Cara's accomplishments.

He pointed at a red ribbon hanging on a cork board. "You were in a spelling bee?" he asked.

Cara wrinkled her brow. "Yeah. Fifth grade. Second place."

"Huh." He continued looking at the cork board. "And first runner-up in a science fair —"

"Why are you looking at those? Don't you see —"

SONORA TAYLOR

"The bloody belt buckle? Of course I do." Jackson stepped back and gripped his pockets. Cara saw his hands trembling, and she forced herself to not take them in comfort. She couldn't comfort him, could never comfort him when she was the one causing him to shake.

"But this is a lot," he said. "This is a whole fucking lot."

"I know."

"Why did you do this? Who were they?"

"People I picked up on the side of the road."

"Why do you have all this stuff?"

"Mom keeps it."

"Your mom knows?"

"Yes."

"Jesus Christ." He turned towards the wall and shook his head again. "Does she help you or something?"

"No, she just … she just keeps this stuff because she's proud of me."

"Un-fucking-believable." He turned back to face her. "I can't fucking believe this."

"You should."

"So all this, everything you've told me and shown me, I should just believe it?"

"It's true."

"If it is, if all this is true and all this shit on here is from people you've killed, then you're basically confessing to me."

"I know," she said as she looked away from him. Cara glanced towards her mother's display, the table filled with everything she'd done that made her mother proud. She felt nothing.

"I know I'm confessing," she continued. "I want to. I want to tell you because you need to know. Because you deserve to know who you're falling in love with, deserve to know that you had every right to be scared before, and deserve to know what will constantly scare you the longer we stay together. If that means that when you leave here you go and tell the cops, so be it. I'd rather rot in jail than live with the fact that who I am made me lose someone like you."

Cara closed her eyes to quell the sudden burn of tears. She hoped she could keep her resolve long enough to give him a proper goodbye. It grew more difficult when she felt Jackson gently touch her arm.

"I won't tell the cops," he said.

Cara nodded. "I won't hurt you," she said. "I'll leave you alone, and I — just know that I loved you. I do love you. I love you more than I've ever loved anything or anyone, and that'll never change."

A single tear escaped down her cheek. Jackson brushed it away before she could do so herself.

"I love you too," he whispered.

It was Cara's turn to shake her head. "You won't stay —"

"Do you want me to stay?"

"How can you want to stay?"

He smiled at her. "I mean, death seems to follow me wherever I go. It'd kind of make sense for me to have a soulmate who's a murderer, right?"

Cara couldn't help but laugh a little. Jackson kissed her temple as he pulled her closer.

"But seriously, Cara? I want to stay with you. I want to be with you, and nothing you've said to me tonight, or said and done before, has scared me more than the thought of not being with you."

Cara took in a breath. It shook in her throat as she tried not to cry. She couldn't believe it. Jackson ran his fingers through her hair and kissed her cheek, her neck. "Last week was a nightmare," he said between kisses. "And my life was hell before I met you. You couldn't possibly make it worse."

"Not even with everything I've told you?"

"What did I tell you last week?"

Cara struggled to remember. So much had happened, and all of it swirled in her head in a maelstrom that even Jackson wasn't capable of quieting.

"After we went hiking and had dinner and went to bed," he continued. "What did I tell you?"

Cara remembered that evening. It had been the most peaceful moment in her life — and would likely be the last. "That you loved me," she said. "But —"

"After that."

Cara scrambled to remember what else, and then it settled on her memory — and began to quiet everything else. "That I could say anything I want to you."

"Anything except what?" Jackson kissed her between her eyes, and Cara smiled just a little.

"Anything except goodbye."

"And that's still the only thing you could tell me that would make me leave."

Cara wanted to tell him so much. She'd already told him so much, perhaps too much. But he was still here. He still held her and kissed her, still told her he loved her and that he wanted to stay. She wanted to tell him how much that meant to her, wanted to show him how much loving him had saved her from drowning so many times. The only thing she didn't want to tell him was goodbye.

She buried her face in his shoulder. "I don't want you to leave," she said. He kissed her hair, and she sighed as he held her tightly. "I don't want to say goodbye."

Jackson lifted her head and looked in her eyes. He looked at her with more kindness and love than she'd ever seen.

"So don't," he said.

———

Cara stared ahead as Jackson drove to Raleigh. The sun had set and all she saw were branches in the moonlight. The leaves were full and lush, not yet dead from summer's stifling humidity. They obscured the moon from her view; but she liked the way the leaves looked as shadows.

Jackson stroked her leg as he drove. Cara still found it hard to believe that she was in the Camry and going back to Jackson's apartment. She made herself look at the car, look out the window, look at him to remind herself that this was real. She'd told him everything — and here he was. Here she was with him.

Jackson glanced at her, and smiled when he saw her looking at him. Cara gave a small smile back, then looked back out the window.

"So," Jackson said. Cara kept her gaze forward. "You want me to bring you back tomorrow, or —"

"No," Cara replied. She couldn't go back. The only way she could leave for good was to leave without seeing her mother, to say goodbye through a note on the table and without giving her mother any chance to convince her that what was happening with Jackson wasn't real or wouldn't last in an effort to keep her on the farm. Cara believed Delores meant what she said about not being the only one who could love her. She also knew Delores spoke to someone she thought she was losing already. Cara wouldn't put it past her to change her tune when she saw that Cara wasn't disappearing, that she'd been revitalized by Jackson and his well of understanding, and risked disappearing on happier terms.

"I want to live with you," Cara continued. "Like we talked about last week."

Jackson's fingers paused their circling on her thigh. Cara wondered in a flash of panic if everything she'd told him changed his mind. "It'll be a wedge between you," she heard her mother say. She closed her eyes.

Jackson squeezed her leg and brought her out of her thoughts. "Sure," he said. "Of course. I'll have to talk to the landlord about getting you on the lease, but you can go ahead and start moving in."

"Haven't I already?" Cara said with a small smile.

Jackson laughed a little. "I'm sure there're some things of yours I missed that aren't in the grocery bag. You've got more stuff than that though, right?"

"I can go back to the farm during the workday and get things." It'd be the best way to avoid Delores and risk weakening her own resolve.

"Sure. You can borrow the Camry."

"Oh, I don't need to."

"You gonna walk to Leslie and carry your stuff back?" Jackson grinned as he nudged her. "I know the Camry isn't as big as the truck, but it'll get you around a lot quicker."

Cara didn't laugh. She'd forgotten that she didn't have the truck, and wouldn't have it anymore. She wouldn't be living on Vineyard Farm anymore.

Cara looked down at her knees, unable to speak. The thought of not living with Jackson pained her more than the thought of leaving the farm, but that didn't mean there wasn't pain with her departure — pain that her mother didn't need to inflict. Cara felt it on her own.

Jackson's fingers ran through her hair. "I know it's hard to move out," he said. "I know you'll miss her."

Cara nodded. "It's what I want, though," she said.

"I know. I also know it's still hard. You can talk to me about it whenever you want."

"Thanks. But I don't want to talk about it now." Cara had talked enough that night about things that were hard. There were pieces of her she could keep between her and her mother. There were pieces of her she could keep to herself.

————

Cara walked into Jackson's apartment. She kicked off her shoes and hung up her purse on his coat rack, just like she always did. Just like she always would.

Cara stood still for a moment as the thought sank in. She was home now, in a new home. She wasn't on the farm anymore. She wasn't alone. For the first time all night — for the first time in days — she felt a sense of peace. Her only fear came from the thought that she'd ever considered giving it up. That she ever considered letting Jackson go and staying back in Leslie because of things she believed, things her mother told her.

She felt a rising bit of anger at her mother, then pressed it down. She was away from her now. She'd proven her wrong. Cara needed to leave it at that.

Jackson's hand settled on her back. Her anger quieted completely, and Cara felt no need to bury anything. She turned around and looked at him. He looked at her with tenderness, one she could see clearly even though he hadn't turned the lights on yet.

Jackson moved his hand to her cheek. "I really missed you," he whispered.

Cara encircled her arms around his waist. "I really missed you too," she whispered back.

Before he could say anything else, Cara leaned up and kissed him. It started as one, then became a few. It started gentle, then became fervent. Every time she kissed him, Cara felt an urge to do it more and more. It felt different than all the times they'd kissed before, like there was nothing between them after everything was between them before. Now there was nothing, nothing except the reckless abandon that made Cara launch herself into Jackson as they moved towards his room.

Jackson responded in kind. He kissed her neck and shoulders, tore off her shirt and kissed her breasts through her bra, pulled down her bra and kissed her all over as he unzipped her jeans. Cara shoved him on his bed as she pulled off his t-shirt and kissed him all over his chest. They lost themselves in one another, having been too far gone before. As they kissed and touched one another, Cara vowed to herself that she would never disappear from him again. She was in the only place she wanted to be, and hearing only what she wanted to hear. She would keep it that way. She would keep him. They would keep each other.

CHAPTER 17

October 1988

Delores walked the grounds of Vineyard Farm. She wondered how much longer they could call it a farm. The mound of dirt that used to be their biggest pumpkin patch gaped up at her, its rotted vines pointing a finger at her for failing to keep up her uncle's livelihood.

Delores shook her head. The pumpkins had begun to wither long before Uncle Leo had died. Terry told her that letting the pumpkins go would be for the best. "You've got that desk job out in Garner. That pays more than these Jack-o-Lanterns ever will," he'd told her after the funeral as they both smoked outside on the porch, away from Cara as she slept upstairs. "Even Leo had it down to one patch by the time he got sick. He knew it was time to move on."

Terry always knew what to say, and was so good with Cara. Delores missed him terribly. She knew it was time for him to move on, that he'd been drawing up plans for his knife store before Uncle Leo showed the first signs of being sick. She didn't want to keep him tied to the farm just to keep her company and help with any vermin that still crawled through the fields looking for pumpkins or a spot under the porch when it rained. Terry was gone. Uncle Leo was gone. The pumpkins were gone.

It stung to think that Leo's pumpkin farm would end with her. Delores was the last Vineyard to till a pumpkin, and the Vineyard everyone in Leslie would associate with the end of a good thing. Delores frowned as she grabbed a cigarette from the pack in her back pocket. She already had a lousy reputation around Leslie. Why would ending the pumpkin farm make it any worse?

Delores smoked and walked towards the woods. The woods were always her favorite place to go when she visited Uncle Leo in the summer. She'd loved walking through the paths he had carved and would gape in delight at the large lake hidden beyond the trees. "It's Vineyard Farm's secret lake," Uncle Leo told her. "None of the people looking for pumpkins know about it. It's our secret, got it?"

It was their secret, and when she was old enough to walk there alone, it became hers. She'd dream of it when she was back home in Egret's Bay, the ocean a meager substitute for the lake's calm beauty. She walked there every day when she went to live with Uncle Leo, even as she grew bigger with pregnancy each month. And when Cara was born, she brought her to the lake as much as she could.

"It's our lake," Delores told her as they picnicked there on Cara's fourth birthday. "It's our secret, though, so don't tell anyone."

"I won't," Cara had said with a smile, one that only broke when she smacked an ant that crawled on their blanket.

Delores smiled as she thought of Cara. The moment she discovered she was pregnant, she knew she was giving birth to someone that would save her from herself. A family member to call her own, a piece of her that didn't bring her pain or doubt. There were moments with Cara that were hard, moments where she'd cry or be sullen or get sick or get into trouble, but they were worth every moment Cara smiled at her and told her she loved her.

Delores approached the clearing that led to the lake and stopped in her tracks. Cara stood stooped over the water. "Cara!" she said with a start. She hoped she didn't scare her.

If she was scared, Cara didn't show it. Delores admired that, how Cara always showed a brave face no matter what was happening around her. "Hi Mommy!" she said with a grin.

Delores stubbed out her cigarette and walked towards her. "What are you doing home from school?"

"School's over."

Delores checked her watch. It was indeed after 3 o'clock. "Why aren't you at daycare?" Delores asked. "You know you're supposed to stay there now, since Terry isn't here to watch you." She made a mental note to call the school and have them make sure Cara stayed at the after-school daycare program instead of getting on the bus.

"Why are you home?" Cara asked.

Delores had wanted a day to herself, a day without phone calls and Rhonda talking about her kids and people making demands. She wanted time alone with her thoughts, time to remember who she was before the end of the day came, and she went from being someone's secretary to someone's mother.

As Cara smiled at her from beneath her dusty Durham Bulls cap, Delores' frustration subsided. She could restart her routine a little earlier than planned. She could do that for her daughter. "Just took a day off," she said.

Cara nodded, and turned back towards the lake. Delores noticed a shoebox next to her on the grass.

"What have you got there?" Delores peered over at the box as she spoke, and jumped a little at the sight of two crawling mounds of fur.

"Mr. Fritz had babies," Cara said.

"Who's Mr. Fritz?"

"Our class bunny. One of them. Mr. Poplar's the other one. Mr. Murphy said he didn't know that Mr. Fritz was a Mrs. Fritz."

"Ah, I see." Delores chuckled to herself, despite her growing worry about having to take care of two new pets.

"I told Mr. Murphy I could take them." Cara turned to the box and picked out the smallest rabbit. It was white with brown spots — almost like freckles — and sniffed the air from Cara's palm. "I told him we had a farm."

"We do, but taking care of rabbits is a big responsibility. They can't just roam around the farm. They need to be fed, and taken to the vet, and …"

Delores stopped speaking as she watched Cara, who ignored her as she bent over the grass. She picked up a piece of orange yarn, one that matched the God's eye that Cara had brought home from art class the week before; and set the rabbit on her leg. The rabbit toddled, but didn't sprint, as it would when it became an adult. Delores tried not to imagine full-grown rabbits running through their yard.

"I'll take care of them," Cara said, her voice as quiet as it was when she was reading or concentrating on her homework. She gently tied the shoelace around the rabbit's waist. Delores snickered a little at the sight of it, like the world's smallest puppy was about to go for a walk.

"Mr. Murphy said that we couldn't keep them," Cara continued. She knotted the lace, and gave it a gentle tug to secure the knot in place. "He said they'd crowd the cage, and that Mr. Fritz would eat them. Do mommies eat their babies?"

"Animal mommies do. Sometimes."

"Would you eat me?"

"Never, sweetheart."

Cara grinned. "But what if I taste good?" She turned back to her rabbit, and Delores peered inside the shoebox at the remaining one, a brown rabbit with white paws. "Mr. Murphy kept the bunnies in another cage, but he said our classroom was too small for so many bunnies."

"Two hardly seems like a crowd," Delores observed. "Also seems small for a litter of rabbits."

"Mr. Fritz had five babies."

"Did the other kids take them?"

"No."

Delores looked curiously at Cara. The rabbit sniffed at her jeans, exploring the terrain of her legs while Cara held its leash. Her hands moved, and she focused intently on tying another knot. She tugged the string tight, and Delores saw a rock at the other end of the leash.

"They can't live in their cage, and they can't live on our farm." Cara held the rabbit in one hand and the rock in the other, and leaned towards the lake. "Bunnies eat plants, like the flowers we have around the porch. I remember Terry saying that about bunnies and possums and other critters we have to take care of." She dropped the rabbit in the lake, and Delores didn't even see it struggle. It sank too quickly, disappeared into the blue before it could try to stay afloat. "I didn't want those bunnies eating our flowers. I didn't want Mr. Fritz to eat the bunnies."

"Cara …"

"It'd scare the other kids. They all got scared before, when Mr. Murphy said they'd be eaten." Cara picked up the remaining bunny, and stood to face Delores. Her eyes were serious, nonchalant. Matter-of-fact. "Mr. Fritz didn't want them. No one wanted them. I took them."

Delores tried not to think of four rabbits sinking to the bottom of their lake at Cara's hands. She tried not to think of what she'd have to tell Mr. Murphy at their parent-teacher conference, when he'd likely ask how the rabbits were doing. She knew what Mr. Murphy would say, what teachers and principals and other parents always whispered to each other: that Cara needed help. Help that Delores couldn't give, because Delores was the bad mother and the bad woman that they all thought she was.

Cara pet the final rabbit. "Isn't he cute?" she asked. "He looks like my old stuffed bunny, the one that got too dirty for me to play with."

Delores smiled. Cara was a child. A resourceful one. One who saw a problem, and fixed it. Animal shelters killed dogs and cats every day. Mr. Fritz would've eaten the babies, or the babies would've gone home with children who'd grow bored with them and leave them to their parents to either take to shelters or abandon in lakes of their own.

"I remember," Delores said. "But that bunny isn't a toy. He's an animal."

"I know." Cara set the rabbit down. It sniffed at the grass, and Cara picked up the shoebox. Delores saw that the grass was bare — no more string or stones.

"He can live in the woods," Cara stated. "It would've been too crowded with five more bunnies. One more bunny is okay. He'll be okay."

Delores nodded, deciding to leave out that the fifth bunny would likely die from the cold if a hawk didn't eat it first. Cara didn't know these things. Cara didn't need to know these things. She was just a little girl.

She was her little girl — one who'd saved her from drowning the moment she was born.

————

May 2004

Cara was getting used to Raleigh. She kept her job at the brewery, even though her truck was gone. "I'm honestly surprised that death trap didn't croak sooner," Keith said with a chuckle when she first arrived to work in Jackson's Camry.

"It didn't die," Cara said. "It's just with Mom now." She hoped that Keith didn't notice her flinch at the mention of her mother.

"Well, let's get a truck that's just for brewery use. You can help me pick one out."

A truck for the brewery was one that Cara couldn't take home with her, one she couldn't take all over North Carolina after work. One she couldn't use for anything but delivering beer.

That was okay. The truck was for beer. The Camry was for getting to and from Jackson each day.

Cara dropped off Jackson every day on her way to work. He took the bus home when she had a late delivery, and often offered to even if she didn't, in case she wanted to go for a drive. She still liked driving at night, but she preferred to do so after they ate dinner together. She'd go out after he'd gone to bed, weaving past bright rows of stores and laughing college students. She'd get on I-40 and get further away, swapping the hubbub for the quiet of the trees. She'd often go to Lake Hollow and smoke a cigarette as she watched the stars twinkle on the water's surface.

Cara would sometimes drive past Leslie, but never to it. She'd go back eventually. She'd want to see her mother, after all. But not yet. She wasn't ready to return to her yet.

She was always ready to return to Jackson. Driving at night gave Cara a sense of calm, something that was hers and hers alone, a little time away to keep a balance between her and everyone else. But it was no longer a cave she wanted to hide in, away from everyone and buried beneath the ground. It was now a tunnel, one she visited and enjoyed the cool smell of earth beneath before emerging back out in the light.

"You don't have to leave the bedroom light on for me," Cara said as she walked into their room. She smiled at the thought. It was their room now. Theirs.

"It's fine," Jackson mumbled, his voice as thick and cottony as the pillow he lay on. Cara stripped to her t-shirt and crawled into bed with him. Jackson immediately curled into her and pulled her close. "Were you back at the lake?"

"For a little while, yes."

SONORA TAYLOR

"Where else did you go?"

Jackson always asked about her destinations. No matter how many times she told him she just liked to drive, he seemed convinced that she had specific places to go. "Just around," Cara said. "You know I just —"

"Drive, I know. But I like picturing where you go."

"And keeping a trail, right? Are you secretly an informant?"

"If I were, I'd be doing a terrible job." Cara chuckled, and Jackson smiled against her cheek. "But when you tell me where you were, I have a better chance of telling people you weren't there, if necessary."

Cara smiled, and began to drift to sleep as she leaned against his chest. She didn't leave any reasons behind that would require Jackson to lie for her. When she went out alone, she stayed alone. She felt sated by the quiet of the night and the music on the radio.

The thought of silencing people didn't go away, of course. She still heard a whisper every now and then, a word or a sentence that shot through her thoughts as she drove down the road. They sometimes became a hum, one that was quiet but one that persisted. She also sometimes saw someone walking alone, and thought of how she could silence the whispers of someone at least; and feel warmed by that thought.

It was a warmth that flickered and flamed, finding a little more kindling each time it caught in her brain. It hadn't engulfed her — not yet. But when it inevitably did, she wouldn't be afraid. Not when she had Jackson waiting for her.

———

311

June 14, 2004

"Do you want to go for a drive tonight?"

Jackson asked the question absently as he sorted through the mail. Cara kept her gaze on the television. "I hadn't thought of it," she said. "I figured we'd spend tonight together."

"That's what I meant. You want to go for a drive together?"

Cara looked away from the TV. Jackson still looked through his mail, but deliberated on each envelope more than she thought was necessary to see what each piece was.

"Sure," she said. "Where do you want to go?"

He shrugged. "Somewhere. Anywhere. A drive."

They'd never just driven together. Still, Cara couldn't deny that with each passing week, she missed him a little bit more when she was alone. "Yeah, we can do that. Maybe drive down the highway — that's what I like best."

"I know. That sounds good." He read the last piece of mail a little more carefully. "Maybe we can stop in Pinesboro."

Cara stopped before she reached the key tree on the wall. "Pinesboro? I thought you never wanted to go back."

"I thought that too."

Cara smiled as she moved towards him. "But it keeps pulling you back?"

Jackson didn't smile, but a quiet snort escaped his nose. "We can just drive if you want," he said. "But I kind of want to go now, when it's late and no one else'll be out. Scratch the itch when it's just the town and not the people in it."

"Right. I understand."

"I can show you around, give you the tour I never gave you last time."

"Only if we can make out at your old high school."

"You've got it." He finally smiled, but it vanished almost as soon as it appeared. "And … I kind of want to see Moira."

Cara didn't say anything. She just took his hand. Jackson squeezed it.

"Let's go," she said.

"Great." Jackson tossed the last envelope on the table. Cara glanced at the return address.

"It's not from my mom," Jackson said as he moved towards the key tree.

"I was just seeing who it was from," Cara lied, and she knew that Jackson knew it. "Has she —"

"Not since the funeral." Jackson pursed his lips as he grabbed his keys. "The last thing she sent me was Moira's obituary."

"Kind of redundant," Cara said as she rolled her eyes. "You already knew."

"But not without her commentary."

Cara looked up with the mixture of alarm and anger that she'd begun to associate with talking about Jackson's mother. "She wrote a note about —"

"It wasn't anything worse than what she said to me at the cemetery."

"I just can't believe —"

"I can. I would've been surprised if she didn't, honestly."

Cara had more questions, but she knew better than to press. Jackson wouldn't be cutting her off if he wanted to answer her.

"But it doesn't matter," he said. "She won't be at the cemetery tonight."

Cara wished she was, nestled right in between all the people Mrs. Price blamed Jackson for putting in the ground.

But even with everything Jackson knew, Cara knew that was something to keep to herself.

Jackson nodded towards the door. "You want to drive?" he asked as he tossed her his keys. Cara smiled as she caught them. Jackson walked out the door and Cara followed. She glanced down towards the shoebox as she exited, wanting to give it the evil eye in lieu of Mrs. Price.

Cara's glance became curious. The shoebox was gone.

June 15, 2004

Delores ate her muffin in silence. Early summer birds chirped outside the window. She wondered if Cara could apply her possum killing skills to animals that flew.

She remembered that Cara wasn't there. She set down her muffin and sighed a little as she sipped her coffee.

Delores missed Cara terribly. She knew that Cara needed to move out, that Cara needed to be with Jackson. She even knew why Cara needed to stay away for awhile. Cara would come back and visit eventually. She knew this in her heart.

It still hurt to see an empty chair next to her each morning.

Delores got up, leaving her muffin and coffee unfinished. She smirked a little as she reached for a pack of cigarettes on the top shelf of the cupboard. She'd kept them there to keep them out of sight and out of reach of Cara when she was beginning to walk and explore around the house. She kept them there even when Cara was tall enough to reach them and old enough to steal them. She wished she could've seen the look on Cara's face when she left an empty pack in its place with a note that said, *Buy your own cigarettes.*

Delores fought the wave of sadness that came with happy memories of their time together. They'd had plenty of time, and they'd have more. Cara would come back. Delores would be here when she did.

In the meantime, she could sit on the porch, smoke, and watch the sun poke through the trees before she had to go to work. She opened the door and felt it hit something.

Delores looked down with a furrowed brow. Her glance became curious. It was a shoebox.

———

The Night Before

The drive to Pinesboro was much better than it'd been two months before. Jackson smoked beside her as Cara drove along I-40. It was late, even for her drives; and she was almost taken aback by how empty the highway was. "I could have us there in thirty minutes," she teased as she pressed the gas.

"And get us arrested for reckless driving?" Cara saw Jackson's smile reflected in the windshield. "The irony of that would bother me more than anything else."

"Come on, who's going to arrest us? A deer?"

"Even if I felt like living out someone's NASCAR dreams, I don't think the Camry could break 100."

"My truck could — Mom's truck, I mean." Cara swallowed a little.

Jackson stroked Cara's leg, and she felt a wave of comfort at his touch. "I know you miss her," he said.

Cara nodded.

"I also know that truck couldn't break 80 unless it died and rolled down a hill."

Cara laughed. "You have no faith in that truck. It's stronger than you think." She cast a glance at Jackson, but kept her grin as she did so. "And don't you dare say, 'Oh, like its driver?' Because that's too fucking cheesy for me, even coming from you."

"Come on, give me some credit. I'd never say anything that bad. No one would."

"Key Ring did."

"Key Ring?"

"Oh, sorry. That's a hitchhiker whose key ring I kept afterward."

"Oh."

Cara wondered with a bit of tension if that was too open for him.

"Was that the blue monster key ring that was ugly as sin?"

Cara smirked a little as she relaxed. "Yes."

"And he actually said that?"

"Yes."

"You did the world a favor by cutting his throat."

They laughed as Cara interlaced her fingers with Jackson's. They drove on in silence.

———

The Morning After

Delores looked out at the driveway. There were tire tracks in the dirt, but no other signs that anyone had been there. She walked past the shoebox and to the edge of the porch, as if doing so would bring Cara back from the road. She knew it was from her, knew it even without lifting the lid. It had to be. No one just showed up at Vineyard Farm — no one except Cara.

Delores laughed a little to herself as she looked down at her stomach. She remembered standing on that porch twenty-two years ago, looking at her growing belly and wondering what her daughter would be like. She knew that her daughter would be all the things she couldn't. Someone who'd stick by her when no one else would.

Cara hadn't left her behind. She'd just left. She'd come back.

Delores glanced back at the shoebox. She did come back. Soon, she'd come back and stay a little longer.

————

The Night Before

Cara tried not to sigh as they drove past the "Welcome to Pinesboro" sign. Jackson needed this visit, and it was just a visit. They didn't have to come back — and even if they did, they didn't have to stay. She knew he'd never stay there longer than necessary.

Cara had to blink a few times to adjust to the darkness. Pinesboro's streets were peppered with street lamps and the glow of a few bars that were open late, but otherwise, the town appeared to close its eyes to everyone in it by the time it was night.

They went to see Moira first. The cemetery looked abandoned at night, the gravestones odd points of light under the moon. Jackson stopped in front of Moira's grave, then looked up at Cara, who'd hung back. She'd presumed he'd want to be alone with his friend.

One glance told her otherwise. Cara moved towards Jackson and stood next to him in silence. He took her hand.

They both stood still. Cara read Moira's name, birthday, death date. She read them over and over, as she only had two memories of Moira to think of. Jackson had years' worth.

"It's weird," Jackson said. "It's still weird to think that I can't say anything to her anymore." He spoke so faintly that Cara almost didn't realize he was talking to her.

"You can," Cara said. "You are right now."

"I can say things to her grave. Moira's gone."

Cara gave a half-smile, one she hoped Jackson could see or at least discern. "Not one for believing she's still with us somehow?"

Jackson smiled a little as well. "It's a nice thought, but it's a lie. Lying to myself won't make it any better. I'm sick of lies, especially from other people. I'm not gonna do their job for them and start lying to myself."

Cara furrowed her brow, but before she could ask what he meant, he pulled her close. He buried his face in her shoulder and sighed. Cara wrapped her arms around him. They stood still and held each other, both of them silent. Even the wind rustling through the trees sounded hushed inside the cemetery.

"I'm glad I have you," he whispered.

"Me too," she whispered back. She kissed his cheek. "I'll never lie to you."

"You'll never have to."

————

The Morning After

Delores picked up the shoebox and brought it inside. It was lighter than she expected. She wasn't sure what she expected, given she hadn't even expected the gift.

She suspected, though, that whatever it held was something Cara had to hide. Delores grew a little sad as she sat at the kitchen table. Cara deserved better than a life shrouded in mystery. She was who she was, and there were few people even Delores could expect to ever be proud of her for what she did. But that didn't mean Delores wanted her to be living in secret, dropping off shoeboxes in the early morning hours in the hopes that her boyfriend, someone who supposedly loved her no matter what, wouldn't see. Delores couldn't imagine that would last.

Yet she hoped it would — and not because she felt like she had to. She wanted Cara to be happy, and Cara was happy when she was with Jackson. Delores would take the souvenirs in secrecy in exchange for seeing her daughter happy. She could only hope that one day soon, she'd actually see her.

For now, she'd see what her daughter had left.

―――――

The Night Before

Jackson gave Cara his promised tour, telling her various places to turn and pointing them out. She saw his grandmother's and his favorite restaurant, different stores he spent his weekends in with Moira, and his old high school.

As promised, Jackson took her to the window that still didn't lock. They crawled into an old science classroom, tables and lab equipment sitting empty under the moonlight. Cara felt a small wave of memories crash against her, of the students and talking and whispering that had filled her own classrooms.

Her memories were broken by Jackson taking her by the waist and pulling her close. "The table back there was my favorite," he murmured as he kissed her cheek. "The one that the light from the window doesn't reach."

She smiled, but only a little, for his lips and then his tongue moved to her mouth as he walked her towards his former make out spot. They crumpled to the floor and lay beneath the table, kissing and touching each other in a fervent heap. Cara remembered her own sordid past, yet found this new memory much more enjoyable, since she was with someone she loved and with someone who actually knew what he was doing.

They returned to his car with smiles on their faces. "Well, I think I've gotten the full experience," Cara said as they got in.

"There's one more place," Jackson said. "If you want to go."

"Sure." Cara glanced at the clock on his stereo. "We'll only get three hours of sleep before work, but I'm not complaining. Where do you want to go?"

Jackson didn't respond. Cara glanced at him and saw his fingers curl and unravel over his knees. It was the only answer she needed.

"You don't have to take me there," she said.

"No, let's — let's go. I promised you a full tour, after all."

"This was fine, really."

"I need to go, Cara. I need to stop being afraid."

Jackson's fingers stopped moving. Cara watched him for a few moments. Jackson pursed his lips and kept his eyes locked on hers.

Cara didn't want to deny him his wishes. Still, in a final effort to assure him, she said, "Not going there doesn't mean you're afraid."

"It's just something I want to do before we leave. It doesn't feel complete if we don't at least go by. Everything I showed you is a part of my life here. I can't only show you the good parts." He smiled at her. "As good as a cemetery and a rundown school is, at least."

Cara laughed a little as she started up the car. "Let's go," she said. "Just tell me how to get there."

———

The Morning After

Delores lit her forgotten cigarette, then lifted the lid of the shoebox. She let the cigarette burn without smoking it as she stared at what was inside.

———

The Night Before

"It's up there on the right."

Cara slowed to a stop once she reached the house that Jackson pointed out. She jumped a little when she saw the illumined windows.

"Don't worry," Jackson said before Cara could ask anything. "Mom's asleep."

"Then why're the lights on?"

"She's afraid of the dark."

Cara snorted before she could stop herself. She laughed — she didn't have to stop herself. Sure enough, she turned and saw Jackson smiling as he lit a cigarette. "All that bile she spews left and right and she's afraid of the dark?" she asked.

"We all need something to be afraid of." Jackson smoked and stared out the window. Cara watched him. His hands didn't shake and his breathing was even. She looked at his reflection in the window and could almost see his memories rippling into his vision, like water lapping the shore.

"When we were together after the funeral," he said. "When we were fantasizing together ... who were you thinking about?"

Cara took a silent breath. She didn't want to remember that night. Even if Jackson knew the darkest parts of her, she didn't want to relive the embarrassment of slipping in front of him, or her shame at overreacting.

Jackson hadn't mentioned it since he went to the farm to talk to her. Cara figured if he was bringing it up now, almost a month later, then it was something he needed to talk about. She owed him that bit of comfort.

"I was thinking about a lot of people," she said. Jackson sighed as he stubbed out his cigarette, and Cara added, "People I'd killed, and how I'd killed them."

He glanced at her, but didn't speak. He didn't need to. Cara knew what he wanted to know.

"I thought of your mother when I said 'her,'" she said. "I was angry at her for scaring you. I'd been angry at her since the cemetery — hell, I'd been angry at her since you first told me about her."

Jackson didn't move.

"But it wasn't just her. I also thought of a bully of mine in school — a girl who used to make fun of me and whisper behind my back. She'd pretend to whisper about me to make me upset. She'd say things to my face and say them behind my back. A lot of other kids did, girls and boys alike, but she was the worst." Cara furrowed her brow as the whispers of her classmates began to buzz in her ears. "I still hear what they say about me. I remember and I hear it. I hear it until it's the loudest thing in my ears — and killing people helps it go away. It helps me know I can control something around me, stop someone from speaking even if I can't stop them."

"Why can't you stop them?"

Cara shrugged. "It was in the past."

"Sounds like it's still your present though."

"People will remember them. Random people walking on the side of the road are easier to hide. No one looks for them."

"But is it really enough?"

Cara sighed as her fingers tapped over a phantom cigarette. "It is for awhile," she said.

Jackson nodded, and looked back out the window. "I used to think going away was enough," he said. "I thought leaving the house would be enough to get away from what Mom would say to me. I thought that going to college, coming back and living somewhere else, then moving away for good would get me out of my head and help me forget it. Help me not believe it, and help me not be mad at her for saying those things to me." He laughed and sighed all at once. "It's so confusing sometimes. I've loved her and hated her at the same time."

"I know how you feel. I've felt the same away."

Jackson raised his eyebrows. "About your mother?"

"Yeah. I …" Cara swallowed, then made herself say the piece of her fantasy that was the hardest to reconcile. The pieces she heard in her ears that she really wished weren't from one particular person.

"I also thought of my mom when I spoke to you," Cara said. "We'd fought before you called me about Moira. We'd been fighting for awhile, but she was making it known she didn't like me dating and didn't like me leaving the farm so much."

"She didn't seem to mind meeting me."

"She came around." So Cara thought. "She said she'd rather see me happy and with you than sad and with her. She said me leaving was the best thing for me to stay alive."

Jackson smiled a little. "Sounds like it was the best way for her to stay alive too."

Cara laughed, but it shook on its way out of her mouth. "I've been so mad at her sometimes that the thought's crossed my mind, yeah. But I'd never actually do it." Cara didn't think she would, anyway. Perhaps Jackson was right. Perhaps Cara leaving was safer for the both of them.

Jackson was also right, though, about how going away wasn't always enough. Cara was flanked by whispers from her mother. She'd heard her mother when she made her first kill. She'd heard her mother after Jennifer's bachelorette party. She heard her mother when she was alone. Delores was silenced along with everyone else when she killed, but as with everyone else, it was only enough for awhile. She wondered what would ever be enough.

Jackson's voice, as it'd done so many times, brought her out of her thoughts. "Of course you wouldn't do it," he said. "She loves you."

Cara closed her eyes. She'd make herself believe it, if only to keep them both safe. "Yeah. She does."

———

The Morning After

Delores lifted a note from the shoebox. She recognized Cara's hurried scrawl: *I love you.*

"I love you too," she whispered. She hoped that wherever Cara was — at the brewery, or in Raleigh, or somewhere with Jackson — that Cara heard her in her heart.

———

The Night Before

"That's more than I can say for my mom," Jackson said.

Cara opened her eyes. She saw him looking out the window again. His narrow eyes were reflected in the glass.

"You don't think she loves you at all?" she asked.

"I know she doesn't. I wanted her to. I also wanted to love her, to give her the chances that Grandma and other people told me to give her because she was my mom. Moira was the only one here who told me I didn't have to understand her. She said Mom was cruel. I knew that, but it was nice to hear someone say it, you know?"

"Yeah, I do."

"But even Moira only went so far. I could only tell her so much about the times I didn't love Mom, when I didn't want to give her a chance. When I wanted what she said about me to be true, but not in the ways she thought. She spent all this time telling me I brought death wherever I went. If that were true, then how come she was still alive?"

"I don't think your mother was working with logic."

"Moira would tell me to just ignore Mom and spend time with her, with Chris, with her family. That it'd be better if I went away to school, if I had a girlfriend or a boyfriend, if I had something to distract me from Mom."

Cara thought of her and Moira's last conversation, how she'd almost begged Cara to not leave Jackson behind. She shuddered at the thought that she almost did. She tried not to think of where Jackson would be if she hadn't come back.

"But nothing can distract me from that," Jackson continued. "Nothing except her disappearing for good."

Cara snapped her attention to Jackson. He looked at her with a coolness that Cara knew wasn't for her.

"I talked about my mom almost all the time when Moira and I would go to the woods," he said. "I'd talk about how she scared me, how I was afraid she was right. Most of the time, though, I wasn't afraid — I was angry. I'd say I hated her, that I hated what she did to me. I used to tell Moira that I wished my mother was dead. But I never told her how I wanted her to die."

Cara knew that anger, and knew how much it needed to be contained. "It's something you can't tell anyone," she agreed. "Even though it's all you can think about."

"Yeah." Jackson smiled. "But I can tell you."

———

The Morning After

Delores read the next part of Cara's note: *Just because I'm not here doesn't mean I don't want to make you proud.*

She looked inside the box. She saw a folded pajama shirt and a locket on a silver chain. She lifted the locket first. It said "Alma" in looping cursive on a heart-shaped pendant. It was clean — no blood in sight.

Delores sighed as she set it back down in the box. Cara probably cleaned it so Jackson wouldn't ask questions in case he found it.

She glanced once more at the pajama shirt, then furrowed her brow. It was mostly clean, but there were remnants in the cloth that suggested only a quick blotting down before the shirt was placed in the box. Delores recognized the stain from all the times she'd cleaned Cara's pajamas when she'd gotten sick. It was vomit.

———

The Night Before

"Of course you can tell me," Cara said as she took Jackson's hand. "You can tell me anything."

"I know," he replied as he leaned his head against his seat. "And it feels so fucking good."

"Like your head just quiets down and everything makes sense?"

"Yeah, sort of. I ... when you said 'her' that night, I thought of her too."

"I've got to stop saying things during sex that make you think of your mom."

Jackson laughed. "It wasn't the first time I'd thought of it. It scared me, though, because I had that thought with you — when before, I wouldn't think things like that around you. I'd at least keep them buried and it wouldn't feel like an ache or a pain, just something stored away. But it came back — she came back, just like always. Just like I always let her. I don't want to do that anymore. I can't. I refuse to — especially after what she said to you. I won't let her make me think you're going to die."

"I'm not going to."

"And I'm not going to let her keep controlling my life. I'm not keeping the letters anymore. I burned all of them one night when you were out driving. I'm not going to keep hoping she'll be something she's not. I'm not going to let her do this to me anymore. And the only way I can do that, the only way I can quiet my mind forever, is —"

"To quiet her?"

Jackson paused, and looked at her with widened eyes. Cara wondered for a moment if she'd assumed too much, if she'd spoken too quickly.

Jackson smiled softly. It was one of relief, like he'd been under a pile of stones for his whole life, and Cara had removed the final rock.

"Yes," he said. "Exactly."

He'd barely spoken before Cara grabbed her purse. "Done," she said as she pulled out her knife.

Jackson grabbed her wrist. Cara looked up at him.

"I want you to help me," he said as he loosened his grip. "But it's something I need to do."

Cara flipped the handle towards him. "As long as I get to watch."

"No." Jackson pushed down her knife and Cara watched him with growing confusion. "People'll wonder about a slit throat."

"We can cut her wrists or something, make it look self-inflicted."

"We're getting on the same page." Jackson bent over his seat and picked something up from the floor. He placed it in his lap, and Cara saw that it was the missing shoebox. She looked inside as he lifted the lid. The letters were gone. In their place was one bottle of pills.

"But slit wrists are less inconspicuous than an overdose," he said. "And I know what she takes."

————

The Morning After

Delores placed the pajama shirt back in the box, folded it neatly so the sleeves covered the stain. She placed the necklace over the collar, as if it were still around a neck. Delores wondered if Alma's neck remained intact. She wondered who she'd been. Cara had never killed a woman before.

Delores wondered what made Alma different, what she'd done to incur Cara's wrath. Cara had her problems with women before, women who whispered about her. It was where her problems began. Whispers and sneers, glances in her direction as she tried to mind her business and do as she pleased. No one would leave her alone — something Delores and Cara shared.

Delores remembered the note in her hand and placed it on top of the shirt. In doing so, she noticed one last sentence: *I hope you'll be proud of him too.*

She stared at the note. Him. There was only one him that Cara would care about Delores caring about: Jackson. Jackson was what made Alma different. Jackson had done this. Jackson had done this with Cara.

Delores placed the lid on top of the box with trembling hands. When Cara left to live with Jackson, Delores figured her secrets would be left behind on Vineyard Farm, secrets that Delores would keep for her along with her old toys and a few clothes she left behind. She didn't think that Cara would have told Jackson everything. She never thought that Jackson would share everything with her.

Delores' thoughts were broken by a honk outside. Rhonda was there, ready to take her to work. Delores placed the shoebox under the table, even though Rhonda was outside and wouldn't see. She'd put it in the basement when she got home. She walked outside and did her best to smile as Rhonda waved.

"Ready for another work day?" Rhonda chirped as Delores got in the car.

"Ready as I'll ever be," Delores sighed. They pulled out of the driveway, the farmhouse and everything in it obscured by a cloud of dust.

"How's Cara doing? Has she come back to visit?"

Delores thought of the shoebox and the tire tracks in the driveway. "Not yet."

"I think it's so sweet she found herself a boyfriend."

Delores thought of the vomit-stained pajama shirt. "Yeah. Real sweet."

"I hope I can meet him sometime. What's he like?"

Delores thought of the way Jackson had looked at Cara when Delores had met him. She thought of how happy Cara was when she said his name. She thought of the items in the shoebox.

"He's perfect for her," Delores said.

Acknowledgments

Many will tell you the second novel is much harder to write than the first. I found this to be true. After completing *Please Give*, I had lots of trouble coming up with my next idea for a novel, or at least, one that would stick. I had several ideas sketched in my notes, and started writing out a few of them. I'd write some passages, run out of steam, then set them aside in favor of shorter projects that were also swimming around in my head.

During this time, I met with my editor and friend, Evelyn Duffy, to talk about revising *Please Give*. At the end of our meeting, she said that, while she enjoyed *Please Give*, she thought my talents were more pronounced in my horror. She encouraged me to keep up with the darker short stories, and to consider sticking with horror as I considered any future projects — including the long ones.

Until then, I hadn't thought much about writing a horror novel. Most of my horror ideas manifested into short stories, and I thought that my writing would come out as dark short stories and lighter novels.

Then I got the idea for *Without Condition* — and thanks to Evelyn's encouragement, I had the courage and motivation to see it through as a novel as opposed to a short story.

So first and foremost, I want to thank Evelyn, both for her work on my books and for her encouragement in our meetings, emails, and text messages. She'll often see first-hand my scattershot ways of thinking when it comes to writing — if you want an idea of how I talk about my works in progress, watch the unedited version of Patton Oswalt's filibuster in *Parks and Recreation*. But no matter how much

I veer off-course, she's always patient and helpful when talking to me.

Thanks also to Doug Puller, my frequent collaborator and friend, for formatting the book and for creating the amazing cover art. I'm consistently floored by his art, and am grateful that we get to work together.

Thanks to Gloria Bobrowicz, Lee Forman, and the editing team at Sirens Call Publications for publishing the first chapter in "The Sirens Call, Issue 42: The Bitter End." I hope to have more stories included in their great magazine in the future. You can read "The Sirens Call" for free at sirenscall-pub.com.

Thanks to Tiffany Michelle Brown and Rie Sheridan Rose for being my first readers. I'm not sure if I can blurb a tweet, so in lieu of a blurb, I'll include Tiffany's sweet initial review here: "Get ready to fall in love with a female serial killer coming-of-age romance with serious Mommy Dearest vibes. It's rad!!!!"

Thanks to the band Ghost, namely Tobias Forge, for inspiring the story. I got my first idea when I read about Forge saying his mother wouldn't stop bragging about him to her friends and neighbors, making his concealed identity a bit of an issue. They also record amazing music, and put on the best concert I went to in 2018.

Thanks, as always, to my parents, who've encouraged me to write since I was young. They loved reading my work, including a stick figure comic series I worked on regularly (and if any of you saw it, you'd see why I hire other people to do my artwork). They still love to read my work, and when you're an author, it's nice to know that there's always someone out there willing to read your stuff.

And, finally, I want to thank my husband Will. His love, kindness, and support get me through everything, be it writing my next piece or worrying about random unknowns (as worriers like myself tend to do). I know that whatever comes next, it will be with him; and because of that I'm not afraid.

Photo by Karen Papadales

About the Author

Sonora Taylor is the author of *The Crow's Gift and Other Tales*, *Please Give*, and *Wither and Other Stories*. Her short story, "Hearts are Just 'Likes,'" is included in Camden Park Press' *Quoth the Raven*, an anthology of stories and poems that put a contemporary twist on the works of Edgar Allan Poe. Her work has appeared in *The Sirens Call* and *Mercurial Stories*. She lives in Arlington, Virginia, with her husband.

Visit Sonora online at sonorawrites.com.